magnolia
the shooting script

magnolia
the shooting script

Paul Thomas Anderson

A Newmarket Shooting Script™ Series Book

NEWMARKET PRESS
NEW YORK

First Edition

10 9 8 7 6 5 4 3 2 1 (hc)
10 9 8 7 6 5 4   (pb)

Library of Congress Cataloging-in-Publication Data

Anderson, Paul Thomas.
Magnolia: the shooting script / Paul Thomas Anderson.
    p. cm.
    1. Magnolia (Motion picture)   I. Title.
PN1997.M147   A53   2000
791.43'72—dc21   99-059630

ISBN 1-55704-409-0 (hardcover)
ISBN 1-55704-406-6 (paperback)

QUANTITY PURCHASES
Companies, professional groups, clubs, and other organizations may qualify for special terms when ordering quantities of this title. For information, write Special Sales Department, Newmarket Press, 18 East 48th Street, New York, NY 10017; call (212) 832-3575; fax (212) 832-3629; or email newmktprs@aol.com.

www.newmarketpress.com

Project Editor: Jennifer Barrons

Designed by Timothy Shaner

Manufactured in the United States of America

OTHER NEWMARKET PICTORIAL MOVIEBOOKS INCLUDE:

Matrix: The Shooting Script and Complete Storyboards

Stuart Little: The Art, the Artists, and the Story Behind the Making of the Film *

Cradle Will Rock: The Movie and The Moment *

Saving Private Ryan: The Men, The Mission, The Movie

Amistad: A Celebration of the Film by Steven Spielberg

The Seven Years in Tibet Screenplay and Story Behind the Film *

Men in Black: The Script and the Story Behind the Film *

The Age of Innocence: A Portrait of the Film Based on the Novel by Edith Wharton *

The Sense and Sensibility Screenplay & Diaries *

Mary Shelley's Frankenstein: The Classic Tale of Terror Reborn on Film *

Bram Stoker's Dracula: The Film and the Legend *

Dances With Wolves: The Illustrated Story of the Epic Film *

Gandhi: A Pictorial Biography

The Inner Circle: An Inside View of Soviet Life Under Stalin

Neil Simon's Lost in Yonkers: The Illustrated Screenplay of the Film *

Wild Wild West: The Illustrated Story Behind the Film *

Wyatt Earp: The Film and the Filmmakers *

*Includes Screenplay

contents

introduction

I entered into writing this script with a massive dedication to writing something small and intimate and cheap. One hundred and ninety pages later, I feel pretty good about the result.

This is, I believe, an interesting study in a writer writing from his gut. Writing from the gut usually equals quite a many pages. Being a "new, hot young director" usually means that, for once, you can get away with not cutting anything. So for better or for worse, consider this screenplay completely written from the gut.

I am from the San Fernando Valley. For many years, I was ashamed of this fact, thinking if I was not from the big city of New York or the farm fields of Iowa that I had nothing to say. Once I got over who I was and where I was from, I found my love for Los Angeles. I hope that this is a true Los Angeles Movie. In particular, I have aimed to make the Mother Of All Movies About The San Fernando Valley.

I write to music so I better own up to stealing quite a many lines from Aimee Mann, who provides all the songs in the film. The first line of Aimee's song

"Deathly" goes something like this: "Now that I've met you, would you object to never seeing me again?" This may sound familiar. You can find it somewhere in the final thirty pages of this script. I heard that line and wrote backwards. This "original" screenplay could, for all intents and purposes, be called an adaptation of Aimee Mann songs. I owe her some cash, probably.

The connection of writing "from the gut" and "writing to music" cannot be found any clearer than in the "Wise Up" section of the screenplay. I had reached the end of Earl's monologue and was searching for a little vibe—I was lost a bit, and on the headphones came Aimee singing "Wise Up." I wrote as I listened—and the most natural course of action was that everyone should sing—sing how they feel. In the most good old-fashioned Hollywood Musical Way, each character, and the writer, began singing how they felt. This is one of those things that just happens, and I was either too stupid or not scared enough to hit "delete" once done. Next thing you know, you're filming it. And I'm Really Happy That It Happened.

I'll try and narrow down the blah-blah-blah here and get on with it, but being a writer, I can't stop, so let me thank a few people who made this possible:

I'd like to thank Fiona Apple. She is my girlfriend and we share a home. She is a songwriter. She is one of the great songwriters, and she taught me something that I'd never really known before: Honest and clear *is* possible and good and it makes for better storytelling. I think I knew this before I met her but I didn't exactly know *how* to do it.

While I was writing this script, she was writing songs. I was able to witness the translation of emotion into verbs, nouns, and letters that equaled "lines in a song." She taught me about clarity and about something I'd only sort-a-had, which is this thing I've talked about: "Trust the gut."

"Trust the gut" equals quite a many pages. So blame her. Thank you, love.

Thank you to My Actors. I like to call them "My Actors" because I'm incredibly possessive and protective of them, and all I do is in aid of watching them act. I think I've done best when I think of them. I aim to please them, I aim to watch them work and the result has meant quite a many pages. Blame them.

Thank you to my producer, JoAnne Sellar, for waiting patiently. Patience and constant support is what everyone needs, and adding some love and affection and parenting into the potion usually equals quite a many pages. So blame her.

Thank you to anyone who wanted to listen or read or see this picture. I've never been so happy, emotional, embarrassed, humble, egotistical, or surprised with myself as I am with *Magnolia*. I hope all that that implies is good for reading. I set out to write a great movie. In the most honest and unashamed way, I truly set myself up to write a great movie. I'm not ashamed. I've written from my gut and I will not be ashamed. Besides, it's far too late now.

And one thing I know is this: I'd do it again. So blame me.

Thank you, Dylan Tichenor, Jen Barrons, Daniel Lupi, Mike De Luca, "An Incomplete Education," by Judy Jones and William Wilson, Charles Fort, Michael Penn, Jon Brion, Bumble Ward, Peter Sorel, Brian Kehew, Esther Margolis, Linda Sunshine, and Timothy Shaner.

Extra Special Thanks to John Lesher. Someday I'll write the true thank-you page your way.

P. T. Anderson
Los Angeles, California
October 1999

<u>magnolia</u>

a P.T. Anderson picture   11/10/98

a Joanne Sellar/Ghoulardi Film Company production

OVER BLACK;

                         NARRATOR
                In the New York Herald, November 26,
                year 1911, there is an account of the
                hanging of three men --

                                              CUT TO:

1.   Black and White Lumiere Footage   1.
      Three men hung....bang...bang...bang.

                                              CUT TO:

2.   Newspaper Headline   2.
      comes into focus; "Three Men Hung."

                                         QUICK DISSOLVE:

3.   Sub Head   3.
      comes into focus; "...for murder of..."

                                              CUT TO:

4.   INT. APARTMENT/FOYER - EVENING   (Lumiere Footage Contd.)   4.

      A man in period dress (1911) walks in the door. CAMERA DOLLIES IN QUICK
      as he takes his hat off, shakes snow, looks off --

                         NARRATOR
                ...they died for the murder of
                Sir Edmund William Godfrey --

      Sir Edmond is greeted by his WIFE and two CHILDREN.

                         NARRATOR
                -- Husband, Father, Pharmacist and all
                around gentle-man resident of --

                                              CUT TO:

5.   EXT. STREET - NIGHT   5.

      CAMERA pushes in on the town sign, reads:

                "Greenberry Hill, London. Population 1276"

                         NARRATOR
                Greenberry Hill, London. Population as listed.

                                              CUT TO:

6.   EXT. PHARMACY - NIGHT   6.

HIGH ANGLE, looking down as Sir Edmond comes out the door,
locks up for the evening. CAMERA BOOMS DOWN and PUSHES IN
TOWARDS HIM, WHIPS RT TOWARDS:

                    NARRATOR
          He was murdered by three vagrants whose
          motive was simple robbery. They were
          identified as:

A COATED MAN standing in the shadows of the alley way nearby.

                    NARRATOR
          ...Joseph Green.....

CAMERA WHIPS RT. again, nearby ANOTHER MAN steps closer --

                    NARRATOR
          ...Stanley Berry....

CAMERA WHIPS RT. one more time and PUSH IN towards THE LAST MAN --

                    NARRATOR
          ...and Nigel Hill...

WIDE ANGLE, ABOVE SCENE.

The three men move in on Sir Edmund and start to knife him
to death, stealing his money and jewelry. CAMERA PULLS BACK
and up to include the sign of the pharmacy now;
"Greenberry Hill Pharmacy."

                                              CUT TO:

7.   LUMIERE FOOTAGE REPLAYED.   7.
      Three men hung. Bang...bang...bang...

                    NARRATOR
              Green, Berry and Hill.

FREEZE FRAME on the last hanging image.

                    NARRATOR
          ...And I Would Like To Think This
          Was Only A Matter Of Chance.

OPTICAL WIPE OF FLAMES FILL THE SCREEN, CAMERA PULLS BACK;

8.   <u>EXT. FORREST/NEAR LAKE TAHOE - NIGHT</u> (35mm/color/anamorphic now)   8.

CAMERA is in the midst of a large FORREST FIRE. CAMERA
WHIPS RT TO SEE:

THREE FIREMAN battling the flames. CAMERA PUSHES IN on
them as they scream and shout directions at each other;

                    NARRATOR
          As reported in the Reno Gazzette, June
          of 1983 there is the story of a fire ---

HIGH ANGLE, THE TREE TOPS.
The trees are on fire....moments later....

                    NARRATOR
          --- the water that it took to
          contain the fire --

WATER FALLS DOWN...
dropped from a FIRE DEPARTMENT AIR TANKER.

                                        CUT TO:

9.   <u>EXT. FORREST/NEAR LAKE TAHOE - MORNING</u>   9.

CAMERA pushes in towards FOUR FIREFIGHTERS as they survey the
area. The fire is out and they are walking through. The MAIN
FIREFIGHTER steps into a close up and looks;

                    NARRATOR
          -- and a scuba diver named Delmer Darion.

FIREFIGHTER'S POV, THAT MOMENT
CAMERA dollies in and TILTS up towards the top of the tree to reveal;

There is a MAN IN SCUBA GEAR hanging high in the tree.
He is wearing his goggles and his tanks and his wet suit.

                    FIRE FIGHTER (OC)
          What the fuck is that?

ANGLE, CU. DELMER DARION.
He still has his mask and mouthpiece

                                        CUT TO:

10. INT. PEPPERMILL CASINO - NIGHT - FLASHBACK   10.

CAMERA looks down on a blackjack game, BOOM DOWN and TILT UP
to reveal: DELMER DARION (40s)

                         NARRATOR
               Employee of the Peppermill Hotel and
               Casino, Reno, Nevada. Engaged as
               a blackjack dealer --

                                                        CUT TO:

11. INT. CASINO/LOBBY - EARLY MORNING - FLASHBACK   11.

CAMERA pushes in towards Delmer as he leaves for the night,
his uniform drapped on a hanger over his shoulder, he nods and
motions two fingers to his fellow WORKERS who say "so long."
(Note: He has a bandage over his forehead.)

                         NARRATOR
               -- well liked and well regarded as a
               physical, recreational and sporting sort --
               Delmer's true passion was for the lake --

                                                        CUT TO:

12. INT. LAKE TAHOE/UNDERWATER - DAY   12.

Delmer SPLASHES in and comes down towards the CAMERA. SOUND drops out,
becomes very quiet...

                                                        CUT TO:

13. EXT. LAKE TAHOE - THAT MOMENT   13.

The FIRE DEPARTMENT AIR TANKER comes flying in, heading towards
the lake, coming directly at CAMERA...

                                                        CUT TO:

14. INT. LAKE TAHOE/UNDERWATER - THAT MOMENT   14.

Delmer dives. Silent and peaceful.

                                                        CUT TO:

15.   EXT. LAKE TAHOE - THAT MOMENT

OVERHEAD ANGLE looks down on the calm lake....beat, then:

THE MASSIVE AIR TANKER FILLS THE FRAME, TOUCHING DOWN ON THE WATER,
FILLING IT'S BODY FULL OF WATER FROM THE LAKE. It enters CAMERA RT.
and exits CAMERA LFT.

ANGLE, THE AIR TANKER. It heads off full of water towards the raging
forrest fire in the distance.

                         NARRATOR
                    -- as reported by the coroner, Delmer
                    died of a heart attack somewhere between
                    the lake and the tree. But most curious
                    side note is the suicide the next day
                    of Craig Hansen --

                                                        CUT TO:

16.   EXT. RENO MOTEL - DAY - FLASHBACK

Establishing shot. (x3)

                                                        CUT TO:

17.   INT. MOTEL - THAT MOMENT

CAMERA PUSHES IN SUPER QUICK towards a MAN named CRAIG HANSEN (30s)
He shoves a RIFLE under his chin and pulls the trigger, blood and brains
splatter the cieling.

                                                        CUT TO:

18.   INT. AIR TANKER COCKPIT - FLASHBACK - DAY

HANSEN flying the plane. HOLD CU. as he moves towards the lake.

                         NARRATOR
                    ...volunteer firefighter, estranged
                    father of four and a poor tendency
                    to drink -- Mr. Hansen was the pilot
                    of the plane that quite accidentally
                    lifted Delmer Darion out of the water --

                                                        CUT TO:

19.   EXT. LAKE TAHOE - SHOT REPLAYED.

Quick flashback to the footage of the PLANE lifting the water
from the lake, SOUND CARRIES OVER....

                                                        CUT TO:

20.   INT. CASINO - NIGHT - FLASHBACK   20.

The Blackjack table where DELMER is dealing. DOLLY AROUND to reveal
a drunk and obnoxious CRAIG HANSEN, screaming about the cards he's
been dealt and taunting Delmer

                              NARRATOR
                    -- added to this, Mr. Hansen's
                    tortured life met before with
                    Delmer Darion just two nights previous --

Hansen SPITS and PUNCHES at Delmer Darion's FACE for dealing the
cards he's dealt. SECUIRTY GUARDS attack and pull him to the ground.

                                                      CUT TO:

21.   INT. MOTEL ROOM - DAY - BACK TO SCENE   21.

CRAIG HANSEN reading the paper, looking at the cover story,
that has a photo of DELMER DARION. He's crying and
mumbling to himself;

                              CRAIG HANSEN
                    ...oh God...fuck...I'm sorry...I'm sorry...

                              NARRATOR
                    The weight of the guilt and the
                    measure of coincidence so large,
                    Craig Hansen took his life.

Replay of Craig Hansen's suicide, except this time, right before he
blows his head off we hear him say, through tears;

                              CRAIG HANSEN
                    ...forgive me...

                                                      CUT TO:

22.   INT. CASINO - NIGHT - BACK TO SCENE   22.

Back to the fight DELMER and CRAIG HANSEN are having; CAMERA DOLLIES
IN QUICK TOWARDS Delmer on the ground with blood coming from his nose.
FREEZE FRAME.

                              NARRATOR
                    And I Am Trying To Think This Was All
                    Only A Matter of Chance.

                                                QUICK DISSOLVE TO:

23.   INSERT, CLOSE UP - HOTEL EVENTS BOARD.   23.

     It reads: Welcome! AAFS Awards Dinner and Reception
                                    Walnut Room
                                      8pm

24.   INT. HOTEL BANQUET ROOM - NIGHT (1961)   24.

CAMERA pushes in following two GUESTS through some double
doors and reveals the DINNER RECEPTION.

ANGLE, MAN BEHIND PODIUM.
CAMERA pushes in quick then blends to 60fps on a man in glasses:
DONALD HARPER, forensic scientist as he speaks into the microphone.

                         NARRATOR
                    The tale told at a 1961 awards dinner
                    for the American Association Of Forensic
                    Science by Dr. Donald Harper, president
                    of the association, began with a simple
                    suicide attempt --

                                                        CUT TO:

25.   EXT. ROOFTOP - MORNING - FLASHBACK (1958).   25.

A seventeen year old kid SYDNEY BARRINGER steps up on to the
ledge of a nine story building and looks down.

                         NARRATOR
                    Seventeen year old Sydney Barringer.
                    In the city of Los Angeles on March 23, 1958.

CAMERA DOLLIES towards Sydney landing in a CLOSE UP of his feet
on the ledge, they wobble a bit -- he jumps, dissapears from FRAME.

BEAT. The following happens very quickly:

ANGLE, looking up towards the sky...Sydney falls past CAMERA....

ANGLE, looking down towards the street...Sydney continues to fall...

ANGLE, a random window on the sixth floor of the building SMASHES....

ANGLE, Sydney's stomach...a BULLET rips into it as he falls...blood
splatters and his body flinches....

ANGLE, looking up towards the sky...Sydney's body and some shattered
glass FALL directly at the CAMERA...which pulls back a little to reveal;
a SAFETY NET in the foreground....Sydney's body falls LIMP into the
net...FREEZE FRAME.

                         NARRATOR
                    The coroner ruled that the unsuccessful
                    suicide had suddenly become a succesful
                    homicide. To explain:

                                                        CUT TO:

26.   <u>EXT. ROOFTOP - FLASHBACK.</u>   26.

    Replay of shot. Sydney steps up on the rooftop. CAMERA pushes
    in towards him quickly, this time moving into his COAT POCKET --

                NARRATOR
           The suicide was confirmed by a note
           left in the breast pocket
           of Sydney Barringer --

                        DISSOLVE INTO:

27.   <u>INT. COAT POCKET - THAT MOMENT</u>   27.

    CAMERA catches glimpses of the note, "....I'm sorry..."
    "...and in this time..." "...so I will go...." "...and be with God..."

                NARRATOR
           At the same time young Sydney stood
           on the ledge of this nine story building,
           an argument swelled three stories below --

                        QUICK DISSOLVE TO:

28.   <u>INT. BUILDING/HALLWAY - THAT MOMENT</u>   28.

    CAMERA pushes in towards the door of ROOM 638. We hear some screaming
    and yelling coming from behind the door;

                NARRATOR
           The neighbors heard, as they usually
           did, the arguing of the tenants --

                        QUICK DISSOLVE TO:

29.   <u>INT. APARTMENT #638 - THAT MOMENT</u>   29.

    An ELDERLY COUPLE (early 60s) are savagely fighting and
    throwing things. The OLDER MAN is backing away from the OLDER WOMAN
    who is coming at him with a SHOTGUN.

                NARRATOR
           -- and it was not uncommon for them
           to threaten each other with a shotgun
           or one of the many handguns kept in the
           house --

                OLDER MAN
           Put it down, put that fuckin' thing
           down Fay --

                OLDER WOMAN
           -- I'll fucking tell YOU. I'll shoot you
           in the face and end this argument and
           we see who's right --

> NARRATOR
> And when the shotgun accidentaly went off,
> Sydney just happend to pass --

The OLDER WOMAN stumbles a bit on some furniture and the SHOTGUN goes off -- FIRES past the OLDER MAN's head -- and SMASHES the window behind him -- SYDNEY falls past and gets shot in the stomach, then falls out of FRAME -- (They're oblivious to this)

> OLDER MAN
> You CRAZY FUCKIN' BITCH WHAT ARE YOU DOING?

> OLDER WOMAN
> SHUT THE FUCK UP.

FREEZE FRAME on the two of them yelling and screaming:

> NARRATOR
> Added to this, the two tenants turned
> out to be: Fay and Arthur Barringer.
> Sydney's mother and Sydney's father.

                                                        CUT TO:

30.   INT. APARTMENT - DAY - LATER   30.

CAMERA moves through the scene as POLICEMAN and DETECTIVES question the OLDER COUPLE. Neighbors and lookie-loos around.

> NARRATOR
> When confronted with the charge, which took
> some figuring out for the officers on
> the scene of the crime, Fay Barringer
> swore that she did not know that the gun
> was loaded.

> FAY BARRINGER
> I didn't know -- I didn't know --

> ARTHUR BARRINGER
> She always threatens me with the gun,
> but I don't keep it loaded --

> DETECTIVE
> -- and you didn't load the gun?

> ARTHUR BARRINGER
> Why would I load the gun?

                                                        CUT TO:

31.   <u>INT. APARTMENT/HALLWAY - THAT MOMENT</u>   31.

CAMERA moves through as OFFICERS are talking to and getting
statements from VARIOUS NEIGHBORS...CAMERA closes in on
an EIGHT YEAR OLD BOY, speaking with a DETECTIVE.

                NARRATOR
    A young boy who lived in the building,
    sometimes a vistor and friend to Sydney
    Barringer said that he had seen,
    six days prior the loading of the shotgun --

The DETECTIVE turns his head and calls to another --

                DETECTIVE
    Ricky -- c'mere a minute --

                              CUT TO:

32.   <u>INT. APARTMENT - DAY - FLASHBACK</u>.   32.

CAMERA moves into a bedroom area where we see a FIGURE from
the back sitting on the bed --

                NARRATOR
    It seems that the arguing and the
    fighting and all of the violence was far
    too much for Sydney Barringer and knowing
    his mother and father's tendency to fight,
    he decided to do something --

CAMERA reveals that it is <u>Sydney Barringer who is loading
the shotgun</u>. The YOUNG BOY is sitting nearby, watching Sydney
mumble to himself as he loads shells into the shotgun.

                              CUT TO:

33.   <u>INT. APARTMENT/HALLWAY - PRESENT</u>   33.

CAMERA moves in on the YOUNG BOY, who looks INTO CAMERA.

                YOUNG BOY
    He said he wanted them to kill
    each other, that all they wanted to
    do was kill each other and he would
    help them if that's what they wanted to do --

                              CUT TO:

34.   EXT. BUILDING/ROOFTOP - DAY - FLASHBACK   34.

This is a WIDE ANGLE REPLAY of the whole event. We see the whole
building...Sydney starts to jump and the film suddenly slows down...

A diagram is made to reflect the narration...this is done like NFL
coverage where the x's and o's and arrows and lines are drawn to
indicate placement and moves, etc.)

An X appears on the top of the building over Sydney.

                    NARRATOR
          Sydney Barringer jumps from the ninth floor rooftop --
          His parents argue three stories below --

An o is marked to indicate their position. Image goes into MOTION
with Sydney jumping...an ARROW is drawn that displays the PATH of
his fall --

                    NARRATOR
          Her accidental shotgun blast hits Sydney
          in the stomach as he passes the arguing
          sixth floor window --

Freeze Frame shows Sydney, hanging mid-air -- the glass shattering and
starting to fall to the ground -- an X marks the spot where he is hit.

                    NARRATOR
          He is killed instantly but continues
          to fall -- only to find, three stories
          below -- a safety net installed
          three days prior for a set of window washers
          that would have broken his fall and saved
          his life if not for the hole in his stomach.

A squiggly line with an arrow is drawn from Sydney to the net to
indicate the path -- UNFREEZE frame and watch Sydney fall into the net.

                                        CUT TO:

35.   INT. APARTMENT - DAY   35.

CAMERA moves in on the PARENTS then over to some DETECTIVES and OFFICERS
who are making sense of this, they nod to each other as if to say,
"well we know what we have to do..."

                    NARRATOR
          So Fay Barringer was charged with the
          murder of her son and Sydney Barringer
          noted as an accomplice in his own death...

CAMERA moves towards the little EIGHT YEAR OLD BOY as he watches
the older couple CRY and SCREAM as detectives begin to cuff them --

> NARRATOR
> ...and it is in the humble opinion of this
> narrator that this is not just "Something
> That Happened." This cannot be "One of those
> things..." This, please, cannot be that.
> And for what I would like to say, I can't.
> This Was Not Just A Matter Of Chance.

CAMERA pushes in towards the MOTHER as she screams and screams and the
officer's fight to regain control of her -- in the scuffle, the
apartment door is shut directly in the face of the CAMERA.

CUT TO BLACK.

> NARRATOR
> Ohhhh. These strange things happen all the time.

Main title que begins, then carries over following until noted:

Title Card: New Line Cinema presents

Title Card: a Joanne Sellar/Ghoulardi Film Company Production

Title Card: a P.T. Anderson picture

                                                    CUT TO:

36.   CAMERA DOLLIES IN Super Quick on a flower.(time lapse,bud blooms)   36.
Freeze Frame, continue w/optical Zoom and roate 360 degrees;total blur.
Flash title card:

                    M a g n o l i a

CAMERA keeps moving in further and farther until the image
gets incredibly blurry, then:

                                                    CUT TO:

37.   <u>INT. SUBURBAN HOME - DAY</u>   (Present Day, 1998)   <u>Sequence A</u>   37.

CAMERA DOLLIES IN QUICK towards a TELEVISION in a living
room. It is playing an infomercial, shot on video with a
hot shot guy FRANK T.J. MACKEY (30s) looking into the LENS.

> FRANK
> In this big game that we play it is
> not what you <u>find</u> and it's not what
> you <u>deserve</u> - It's What You Take.
> I'm Frank T.J. Mackey, Master of the Muffin
> and author of the Seduce and Destroy System
> of audio and videocassettes that will
> teach you the techniques to have any
> hard-body blonde dripping to wet your dock!

CAMERA moves INTO THE TELEVISION, QUICK DISSOLVE TO:

38.   <u>INT. BAR SET/LOCATION - THAT MOMENT</u>   38.

We are in the video (paneled 1.33) sales pitch/infomercial.
Various settings: The bar, a supermarket, a bedroom, a parked car.
Each has a few semi-geeks talking to a bunch of sexy young girls.

> FRANK (contd.)
> Bottom line? Language. The magical key
> to unlocking any woman's analytical ability
> and tap directly into her hopes, wants,
> fears, desires and panties.
> "Seduce and Destroy," creates an immediate
> sexual attraction in any muffin you meet.
> Learn how to make that lady - "friend" your
> sex-starving-servant. Create an instant,
> money-back guaranteed trance-like state
> that'll have any little so and so just
> begging for it.
> I don't care about how you look, what car
> you drive or what your last bank statement
> says: "Seduce and Destroy," is gonna teach
> you how to get that naughty sauce you want - fast!
>   (dramatic stop, then:)
> Hey -- how many more times do you need
> to here the all too famous line of:
> "I just don't feel that way about you."

                                          CUT TO:

39.   INT. SMILING PEANUT BAR - NIGHT   39.

CAMERA moves in on a young woman CLAUDIA (20s) sitting alone, bit drunk.
A vaguely creepy looking MIDDLE AGED GUY (40s) takes a seat next to her;

                        MIDDLE AGED GUY
        Hey.

                        CLAUDIA
        Hi.

                                            CUT TO:

40.   INT. CLAUDIA'S APARTMENT - LATER   40.

A series of quick shots where the following happens; CLAUDIA and the
MIDDLE AGED GUY stumble into her apartment. CAMERA DOLLIES in quick as
she snorts a line of coke from her coffee table....TILT up and PAN over
to him....

                        MIDDLE AGED GUY
        So?

                                            CUT TO:

41.   INT. CLAUDIA'S BEDROOM - MOMENTS LATER   41.

CAMERA DOLLIES in quick as they're having sex. He's on top of her,
she's below, CAMERA lands in a CLOSE UP of her face as she gets through
the experience...CAMERA moves up and past her, finds the reflection of
the TELEVISON in a picture frame on her wall....

                                            DISSOLVE TO:

42.   INT. TELEVISION IMAGE - CLIP - THAT MOMENT   42.

This is a promo for a game show called, "WHAT DO KIDS KNOW?" featuring
the host JIMMY GATOR (60s) We see various clips of him over the years,
hosting the show, at various clebrity events, etc. (Director's Note)

                        PROMO ANNOUNCER
                For over thirty years, America has hung
                out and answered questions with Jimmy Gator.
                An American Legend and a true television icon,
                Jimmy celebrates his 200,000th hour of
                broadcast this week --

CLIP OF JIMMY speaking to an INTERVIEWER.

                        JIMMY
                God, have I been around that long?

                                            CUT TO:

43.   <u>INT. JIMMY GATOR'S OFFICE - DAY</u>   43.

Blind's closed, door locked. Jimmy and a YOUNG SHOWGIRL from some other show are having sex on his couch. CAMERA DOLLIES IN FAST.

                             PROMO ANNOUNCER
                He's a family man who's been married
                for over forty years -- with two children
                and one grandchild on the way --

44.   <u>CU, PHOTOGRAPH.</u>   44.
A family photo of JIMMY, his wife ROSE, his son JIM, JR. and CLAUDIA. This photo is circa 1987. OPTICAL ZOOM INTO photo that isolates Jimmy and Claudia in the picture.

                                                  CUT TO:

45.   <u>INT. CEDARS SINAI MEDICAL CENTER - HALLWAY - PRESENT DAY</u>   45.

JIMMY and ROSE (50s) walk down a hallway towards a door.

                        PROMO ANNOUNCER (contd.)
                We've tuned in each day to see the
                human interaction between Jimmy and
                some very special kids over the years --

                                                  CUT TO:

46.   <u>INT. DOCTOR'S OFFICE - MOMENTS LATER</u>   46.

CAMERA pushes in on JIMMY and ROSE as they enter, WHIPS over to a NURSE who looks up, smiles says "hello."

                        PROMO ANNOUNCER (contd.)
                -- and we hope there's thirty more years
                of watching that happen.

                           JIMMY (to Nurse)
              ...Jimmy Gator...

                                                  CUT TO:

47.   <u>INT. SUBURBAN HOME - DAY</u>   47.

CAMERA DOLLIES in towards the televison again. A quick highlight clip shows a ten year old kid named STANLEY SPECTOR answering question after question on the show, "What Do Kids Know?" in a series of dissolves;

                                STANLEY
              ...Donald W. Winnicott....1911...North America....
              ...South America....the answer is four....
               ...the answer is 22...the answer is gravity....
              the answer is "The Life of Samuel Johnson."

                                                  CUT TO:

48.   INT. SPECTOR HOUSE - DAY   48.

CAMERA is HAND HELD and moving around a small apartment, watching a
ten year old kid STANLEY SPECTOR (dressed in a suit) as he dumps dog
food into two bowls for two dogs yapping around his legs while
he simultaneously tries to gather his backpacks -- His father enters:
RICK SPECTOR (late 30s) starts barking directions;

                         RICK
              Let's go,let's go, let's go, you shoulda
              done that ten minutes ago --

                         STANLEY
              We need more dog food --

                         RICK
              -- talk in the car, talk in the car,
              moves your ass, c'mon --

Stanley grabs two BACKPACKS and puts them over each arm. Rick grabs
another bag....heads for the door....Stanley is about to fall over with
these two full packs, but reaches for another bag on the floor...

                         RICK
              Cmon,cmon,cmon, that one to?

                         STANLEY
              I need this one.

                         RICK
              Why the hell do you need all four
              bags of books to go to school each day?

                         STANLEY
              I can't carry all of them.
              I need them. I need my books.
              I need them to go to school.

                                                        CUT TO:

49.   EXT. SPECTOR HOUSE - MOMENTS LATER   49.

CAMERA pushes in quick as Rick sits in the car, engine running, watching
Stanley struggle to get himself and the backpacks in;

                         RICK
              There's no reason for this many backpacks.

CAMERA LANDS IN CLOSE UP of STANLEY as he slams the car door.

                                                        CUT TO:

50.   EXT. SCHOOL - MOMENTS LATER   50.

CAMERA PULLS BACK from the parked car in a new location as Stanley gets
out of the car with his backpacks, Rick watches from the driver's seat;

                              RICK
                    Be ready at two --

                              STANLEY
                    Should be one-thirty.

                              RICK
                    I got an audition, I won't make it
                    here 'till two, c'mon, I'll see you
                    later. Love you.

                              STANLEY
                    Love you too.

Rick drives off real quick. Stanley looks around at his backpacks.

                                                              CUT TO:

51.   INT. 1960's SUBURBAN HOME - DAY   51.

CAMERA pushes in on an old television set playing a clip
from "What Do Kids Know?" (1968) The clip shows a younger JIMMY GATOR
asking questions to a ten year old kid named DONNIE SMITH.

                              JIMMY
                    Donnie, you have an answer?

                              DONNIE
                    Promethius.

                              JIMMY
                    It is!

TELEVISION CLIP continues and we see DONNIE and two other KIDS receive
a check from the younger JIMMY GATOR in the amount of 100,000 dollars
each. CU - Young Donnie Smith as he smiles, accepts check, shakes hands
with Jimmy.

TITLE CARD reads: Quiz Kid Donnie Smith - 1968

                                                              CUT TO:

52. <u>INT. DENTIST OFFICE/EXAMINING ROOM - MOMENTS LATER</u>   52.

DONNIE SMITH, aged 40, is reclined back in a dentist chair.
He has spiky hair, a small stud earing and a bad grey suit.

TITLE CARD reads: Quiz Kid Donnie Smith - Today

                              DONNIE
                    This is really exiting....bet you don't
                    get many people my age getting braces --

CU - Donnie opens wide and the pink gook-imprint is placed in his mouth.
CU - A Nurse holds it in there and smiles, says:

                              NURSE #1
                    You were really cute when you were
                    on that show --

                              NURSE #2
                    -- you can't answer any questions right
                    now though, huh? He-he-he.

CU - Teeth. The gook imprint is taken out of his mouth.

                                                        CUT TO:

53. <u>INT. DENTIST OFFICE/HALLWAY - LATER</u>   53.

CAMERA pulls back as DONNIE and his dentist, DR. LEE (Asian, 40s)
exit an examining room, smiling, through with their appointment...

                              DR. LEE
                    So we're all set to go, Donnie.

                              DONNIE
                    Great, great, great, so I'll see you
                    tommorrow morning.

                              DR. LEE
                    You're running around like crazy, huh?

                              DONNIE
                    I'm gonna be late for work.

                                                        CUT TO:

54. <u>EXT. 7-11/PARKING LOT - NORTH HOLLYWOOD - DAY</u>   54.

CAMERA pushes in towards Donnie as he pulls into the parking lot
in his little HONDA ACCORD. He's smiling and singing along to
a song* as he pulls into a parking space....

...but he's going just a bit too fast...and in a flash, he's
over the parking stopper and up on the curb....and taps the glass
store front just enough to have GLASS FALL AND SHATTER and DISPLAYS
FALL OVER ONTO THE HOOD OF THE CAR....

CAMERA pushes in on Donnie and some people running over to see
what's happend....

> DONNIE
> What the hell? What the hell?

> PEDESTRIAN
> Hey! It's Quiz Kid Donnie Smith.

> PEDESTRIAN #2
> Quiz Kid Donnie, why'd you drive
> into the seven eleven?

                                              CUT TO:

55.   INT. EARL'S HOUSE - DAY   55.

CAMERA pushes in real fast on the front door as PHIL PARMA (20s) enters.
He has a flat top, flip shade sunglasses that he flips up and he's
carrying 7-11 coffee and a donut....CAMERA WHIPS LFT to reveal;

In this nice house in Encino, a medical bed has been planted in the
middle of the living room. In the bed is EARL PARTRIDGE (70s) He is
very thin and bald and he is on his last legs, dying from cancer.

There are four or five MUTT DOGS that sleep on his lap and around
the bed and at the sound of the door they are up and BARKING.

A young MEXICAN NURSE sits next to Earl, motions to Phil and his post
is relieved. Phil moves in next to the bed, pets Earl's head;

> PHIL
> How's today then?

> EARL
> Fuckin' bullshit is what this is.

> PHIL
> Fuckin' bullshit is right, in'it?

CAMERA MOVES INTO A CLOSE UP ON EARL, MOVES INTO HIS THROAT, QUICK
DISSOLVE INTO:

56.   INT. EARL'S THROAT - THAT MOMENT   56.

CAMERA moves around his throat and through his body, looking at
his BLOOD STREAM and watching, like a MEDICAL FILM, the cancer as
it eats away at his body...as we see it at work we hear a WHISPER
that is EARL'S VOICE:

> EARL'S WHISPER VOICE
> ...fuckin regret, move through this life....
> ..and we do these things...get that back...
> ...forget, forget....fuck....fuck......
> ...make it right....and we do these things....

                                         QUICK DISSOLVE TO:

57.   <u>INT. EARL'S LIVING ROOM - THAT MOMENT</u>   57.

CAMERA PULLS BACK from Earl's throat to his MOUTH and his EYES and
he looks to Phil says;

                          EARL
              I'm onna need your help, Phil.
              ...you gotta help me something today...

CAMERA PANS over quick to PHIL.

                          PHIL
              I'll take care of anything, Earl.

CAMERA PANS/DOLLIES away and TILTS up to the cieling;

                                        QUICK DISSOLVE TO:

58.   <u>INT. EARL'S HOUSE/UPSTAIRS BEDROOM - THAT MOMENT</u>   58.

CAMERA dollies in on LINDA PARTRIDGE (30s) as she paces around in her
nightgown, pops a pill, talks on the phone;

                          LINDA
              Well, you're his doctor and that's
              why -- well tell me something -- tell
              me something --

XCU, She sees the the bottle of pills she is popping from is empty.

                          LINDA (contd.)
              And he needs more pills, then.
                    (beat)
              Fuck it, I'm coming to see you,
              I need to come see you to get him more
              pills and I need some answers so you
              better just talk to me, I'm coming
              to see you, I'm coming to see you --

She SLAMS down the phone.

                                        CUT TO:

59.   <u>INT. EARL'S HOUSE - LIVING ROOM - MOMENTS LATER</u>   59.

CAMERA moves with Linda as she comes down the stairs, walks
over towards Earl's bed, trying to hide her state. Phil stands
up and looks to her.

                          PHIL
              Hi, Linda.

EXTREME CLOSE UP 2-SHOT. Linda and Earl. He opens his eyes just a bit. She bends in and gives him a kiss on the forehead.

>   LINDA
>   I love you, my darling.

She turns quickly, speaks as she walks out;

>   LINDA
>   I'll be back in a while, Phil.
>   I have to go get some things and
>   I have to see something and I'll be back....

She continues to talk as she walks out the door.

>   CUT TO:

60. INT. GARAGE/LINDA'S MERCEDES - PARKED - MOMENTS LATER   60.

CAMERA DOLLIES IN real quick as she gets behind the wheel. She SMASHES her fists on the steering wheel and cries and cries and cries.

>   CUT TO:

61. INT. JIM KURRING'S APARTMENT - DAY   61.

A very straight ahead apartment in Reseda where JIM KURRING (30s) lives. SOUND of a 1-900 PERSONAL DATING SERVICE plays over following quick shots of Kurring getting ready for his day;

-Jim is sipping his morning coffee, reading the paper.
-Jim in the shower.
-Jim doing push ups.
-Jim watching and laughing a bit with the Today Show.
-Jim kneeling down by his bed, praying.

>   PHONE SERVICE VOICE
>   ...Press One to hear this person's personal
>   description of themself and Two to leave a
>   a personal message of your own --

The SOUND of touch-tone phone pressing "1."

>   JIM KURRING'S VOICE
>   Well, hello. This is Jim. I work in
>   Law Enforcement. I am an officer for
>   the L.A.P.D. and I work out of the Van Nuys
>   district. I love my job, and I love to go to
>   the movies. I try to stay pyhsically fit,
>   my job demands it, so I'm in pretty good shape.
>   I'm gettin' up there, though: I'm 32 years old
>   and I'm six feet two inches tall and I weigh about 160.
>   I'm really interested in meeting someone special
>   who likes quiet things....my life is very
>   stressful and I'd hope to have a realtionship
>   that is very calm and undemanding and loving --

The SOUND again of the touch-tone phone cancels Jim's description.

                         -   PHONE SERVICE VOICE
                    If you would like to hear more personal
                    descriptions from other men in your area,
                    press two now --

                                                        CUT TO:

62.   INT. VAN NUYS POLICE STATION - DAY   62.

      CAMERA observing the officers at a morning role call, DOLLIES and BOOMS
      DOWN towards JIM KURRING, sitting off to the side a bit by himself.

                         POLICE CAPTAIN (OC)
                    ...so much violence...but that's the way of the
                    world...good luck, as always...Serve and Protect
                    and all that other blah-blah-blah on the
                    side of the car it says --

                                                        CUT TO:

63.   INT. POLICE GARAGE - MOMENTS LATER   63.

      CAMERA DOLLIES w/Jim Kurring as he walks to his squad car.
      All the cops walk with partners, except him. Kurring throws on
      a pair of Oakley sunglasses and gets in the car --

                                                        CUT TO:

64.   INT. POLICE CAR - MOVING - LATER   64.

      CAMERA holds a CU. of Jim as he drives. He speaks to someone unseen;

                         JIM KURRING
                    This is not an easy job. I get a call
                    from Shirley on the radio: Bad News.
                    It's never good news. She tries to
                    be cheerful, tries to say something
                    nice, but uh-huh, it's just Bad News.
                    And It Stinks. But this is my job.
                    And I Love It. Because I want to do well.
                    In this life and in this world I want
                    to do well. And I want to help people.
                    And I may get twenty bad calls a day.
                    But one time I help someone, I Make A Save?
                    I correct a wrong or right a situation;
                    Then I'm a happy cop. And We Move Through
                    This Life We Should Try And Do Good.

      WIDER ANGLE reveals that he is talking to himself. BEAT. HOLD.

                         JIM KURRING (sotto, to himself)
                    ...Do Good. And If We Can Do That...And
                    Not Hurt Anyone Else....Well, Then....

                                                        CUT TO:

65.   <u>EXT. MAGNOLIA BOULEVARD - DAY</u>   65.

CAMERA looks straight down on an intersection. Jim Kurring's POLICE
CAR drives past....a little SUNLIGHT that hits the intersection goes
away as if covered very quickly by a grey cloud....<u>End Title Que and
Sequence A</u>.

                                              CUT TO BLACK.

TITLE CARD reads: <u>Partly Cloudy, 75% chance of rain</u>

                                              FADE IN:

66.   <u>INT. APARTMENT COMPLEX/NORTH HOLLYWOOD - DAY</u>   Sequence B   66.

CAMERA (STEADICAM) follows behind JIM KURRING. He walks through
a courtyard, past some young mexican and black kids playing,
up a staircase and arrives at a door that is half open;

                         JIM KURRING
              Hello?

He knocks, pushes the door open a bit, steps in: A very, very large
black woman, MARCIE (40s) appears, coming at him, ranting and raving;

                         MARCIE
              What? What? What now?

                         JIM KURRING
              Quietly, slow down, whoa --

                         MARCIE
              You can't just come in here.

                         JIM KURRING
              The door was open, I got a call --

                         MARCIE
              You're not allowed to just come in --

                         JIM KURRING
              Calm down.

                         MARCIE
              I am calm.

                         JIM KURRING
              I got a call to this apartment,
              report of a disturbance --

                         MARCIE
              There's no disturbance.

                    JIM KURRING
I got a call of a disturbance, you're
door was open, I just wanna see
what's goin' on --

                    MARCIE
There's no disturbance.

                    JIM KURRING
Then you've got nothin' to worry about.

                    MARCIE
You don't tell me, I know my rights,
just come right in, you can't --

                    JIM KURRING
Don't test me, you wanna talk about
what the law book says, we can do that,
push me far enough and I'll take you
to jail -- now calm down.

                    MARCIE
I AM CALM.

                    JIM KURRING
You're not calm. You're screamin'
and yellin' and I'm here to check
on a disturbance that was reported
and that's what I'm gonna do - now
are you alone in here?

                    MARCIE
I don't have to answer your questions.

                    JIM KURRING
No you don't: But I'm gonna ask
you one more time: Are you alone in here?

                    MARCIE
What does it look like?

                    JIM KURRING
No one else in here?

                    MARCIE
You're here.

                    JIM KURRING
OK. That's true. Is anyone else,
besides me and besides you in this house?

                    MARCIE
No. I said that.

                    JIM KURRING
Are you lyin' to me?

                    MARCIE
          I live alone.

                    JIM KURRING
          Maybe so, but I'm gonna ask you one
          more time: Is Anyone Else In This House
          Right Now?

                    MARCIE
          No I Said.

                    JIM KURRING
          Ok. What's your name?

                    MARCIE
          Marcie.

                    JIM KURRING
          Ok. Marice why don't you take
          a seat for me?

                    MARCIE
          I preffer to stand.

                    JIM KURRING
          I'm not askin', Marcie.

Marcie sits down.

                    MARCIE
          I didn't do anything.

                    JIM KURRING
          Maybe you didn't, but I'm here
          to find out about a disturbance.
          Some neighbors called said they
          heard screaming and a loud crash.

                    MARCIE
          I don't know a loud crash.

                    JIM KURRING
          And what about screaming?

                    MARCIE
          I said: I DON'T KNOW. You can't just
          come in here and start pokin' around --

                    JIM KURRING
          What's this, how did this happen?

INSERT, ECU. THE FLOOR.
An ashtray has fallen on the floor, cigarette butts all around.

> MARCIE
> An ashtray fell, I don't know, maybe
> last night, I just woke up.

> JIM KURRING
> You just woke up. And what'd you have
> a party last night, the way this place
> looks?

> MARCIE
> I went out last night.

> JIM KURRING
> Ok. Marcie. Starting now I want you
> to have a new attitude with me. The more
> you play games, the more suspicious I'm gonna
> become that you've been up to something.

> MARCIE
> It's a free country, you can
> think anything you want.

> JIM KURRING
> Yes I can, Marcie. And until you
> start givin' me some straight
> answers: I'm gonna assume that some
> mishchief has been goin' on here.

> MARCIE
> Mischief? What the fuck you talkin'
> about, mischief?

> JIM KURRING
> Bad and illegal behavior. That's what I mean.
> Ok? Mischief. Now have you been
> doin' some drugs today?

> MARCIE
> No.

> JIM KURRING
> You on any medication?

> MARCIE
> No.

> JIM KURRING
> Been drinkin' today?

> MARCIE
> It's ten o'clock in the morning --

There's a small THUMP noise OC. Jim turns his head quick and looks and Marcie freezes.

> JIM KURRING
> --- what was that?

> MARCIE
> I didn't hear anything.

Marcie stands up.

> JIM KURRING
> No. No. Stay down, Marcie, sit
> back down on that couch --

> MARCIE
> I don't have to do a god damn thing.

Kurring gets his handcuffs out and handcuffs her wrist to the couch, she goes crazy, screaming and yelling the whole time;

> MARCIE
> WHAT'S THIS? WHAT'S THIS? GOD DAMN
> BULLSHIT. BULLSHIT. DON'T PUT THOSE --

> JIM KURRING
> Marcie - CALM DOWN. CALM DOWN
> and don't do this. I want you to stay --

Continue with that until he's got her cuffed to the couch. He removes his REVOLVER from his holster and starts to move slowly down the hall to the back bedroom --

> MARCIE
> WHAT THE FUCK IS THIS BULLSHIT?
> WHAT THE FUCK ARE YOU DOING, MOTHERFUCKER?
> MOTHER-GOD-DAMN FUCKER. WHERE ARE YOU GOIN'?
> DON'T GO IN MY GOD DAMN BEDROOM.

Kurring keeps moving slowly, gun drawn, CAMERA behind him;

> JIM KURRING
> This is the LAPD. If anyone is
> back here I want you to come out
> and I want you to show yourself
> to me with your hands in the air --

> MARCIE
> THERE'S NO ONE IN THERE. STAY OUT
> OF MY MOTHERFUCKIN BEDROOM.

Kurring moves into the BEDROOM now and sees that the CLOSET is closed and probably the only place for someone to be hiding;

>   JIM KURRING
>   This is the LAPD, if anyone is in
>   the closet I want you to come out
>   and show yourself to me, slowly and
>   with your hands up --

>   MARCIE (OC)
>   THERE'S NO ONE IN THERE!

>   JIM KURRING
>   Marcie - quiet down! Now if anyone
>   is in the closet, come out now --

>   MARCIE (OC)
>   THERE'S NO ONE IN MY MOTHERFUCKIN
>   CLOSET AND STAY OUT OF MY BEDROOM,
>   STAY OUT OF MY GOD DAMN BEDROOM.

>   JIM KURRING
>   -- do not do this -- my gun is drawn
>   and If I Have To Open That Closet
>   you will get shot -- Step Out Now.

Jim inches towards the closet, flips it open real quick and
stands back, ready for something to jump out -- nothing.

>   MARCIE
>   I told you there was no one in there!

Jim looks down the hall at <u>Marcie who has physically dragged
the large couch handcuffed behind her</u>;

>   JIM KURRING
>   Marcie - Do not drag that couch any further!

JIM'S POV, CAMERA DOLLIES IN SLOWLY TOWARDS THE CLOSET.
He pushes some sheets aside and burries around to reveal:

A DEAD SKINNY WHITE MAN (50s) curled up in a ball on the
floor of the closet. He'd dead and he's been covered in dirty
laundry. He has a gag around his mouth.

HOLD on Jim for a moment, he panics a little and swings his REVOLVER
towards Marcie:

>   JIM KURRING
>   What the hell is this Marcie?

>   MARCIE
>   THAT'S NOT MINE.

Jim swings the aim of his gun back at the dead body.

>   CUT TO:

67.   <u>INT. EARL'S HOUSE – LIVING ROOM – DAY</u>   67.

Earl in bed, pretty out of it, but once in a while a couple clear
moments. Phil sits next to the bed, paper and coffee nearby.

                         EARL
              ...n'I dowanna do this...sit here,
              I can see the things, y'know...it's gettin'
              there that's the cocksucker...like...I see
              that pen...I see it, I know it's there,
              I reach out for it -- no --

He mimes the action, gets nowhere near the pen.

                         EARL
              ...no...no goddamn use.
                   (beat)
              I have a son, y'know?

                         PHIL
              You do?

                         EARL
              ...ah...

                         PHIL
              Where is he?

                         EARL
              I don't know...I mean, he's around,
              he's here, in town, y'know, but I
              don't know...he's a tough one...very....
              Do you have a girlfriend, Phil?

                         PHIL
              No.

                         EARL
              Get a girlfriend.

                         PHIL
              I'm trying.

                         EARL
              And do good things with her...share
              the thing...all that bullshit is true,
              y'know...find someone and hold on all
              that...Where's Linda?

                         PHIL
              She went out. She said she went
              out to run some errands. She'll be back.

                         EARL
              She's a good girl. She's a little
              nuts, but she's a good girl I think.
              She's a little daffy.

                    PHIL
          She loves you.

                    EARL
          ...ah...maybe...yeah...she's a good one...

                    PHIL
          When was the last time you talked
          to your son?

                    EARL
          ....I dunn...o....maybe ten...five,
          fuck, fuck....that's another thing
          that goes --

                    PHIL
          -- memory?

                    EARL
          Time lines, y'know? I remember things
          but not so -- right there -- y'know?

                    PHIL
          Yeah.

                    EARL
          "yeah." the fuck do you know?

                    PHIL
          I've seen it before.

                    EARL
          Other fuckin' assholes like me.

                    PHIL
          There's no asshole like you.

                    EARL
          ...cocksucker....

                    PHIL
          How come every word you say is either
          "cocksucker," or "shitballs," or "fuck?"

                    EARL
          Do me a personal favor --

                    PHIL
          Go fuck myself?

                    EARL
          You got it.

EARL gets hit with something and starts to MOAN a bit. Sharp
pain hitting him and he touches his hand to his face....

                    EARL
          ...I can't hold onto this anymore...

                    PHIL
          I'll get you another pain pill.
          Another morphine pill --

                    EARL
          ...gimme that fuckin' phone...

                    PHIL
          Who are you gonna call?

                    EARL
          I wanna see this...where is he,
          do you know?

                    PHIL
          Who?

                    EARL
          Jack.

                    PHIL
          Is Jack your son?

Earl doesn't answer. He's drifting a bit more now.

                    PHIL
          You wanna call him on the phone?
          We can call him, I can dial the
          phone if you can remember the number --

                    EARL
          -- it's not him. it's not him.
          He's the fuckin' asshole...Phil..c'mere...

Phil leans in closer to Earl.

                    EARL
          This is so boring...so goddman...
          and dying wish and all that, old
          man on a bed...fuck...wants one thing:

                    PHIL
          It's ok.

Earl hallucinates a bit, cries a little, tries to form the sentences;

                    EARL
          ...find him on the...Frank. His name's
          Frank Mackey --

                    PHIL
          Frank Mackey. That's your son?

                        EARL
            that'snotmy name...find Lily, gimmme that,
            give it --

Earl tries to grab something near Phil's head that is not there.
He's hallucinating more now, falls asleep a bit, mumbling;

                        EARL
            ifyougimmethat....overonthe....fuck....
            I can't hold ontothis anymore...

He gives Phil make an imaginary object and falls asleep. BEAT.
Stay with Phil a moment as he turns his head, looking around the
house a moment, looks back to Earl.

                                            CUT TO:

68.   INT. BURBANK HOLIDAY INN/BANQUET ROOM - THAT MOMENT   68.

FRANK steps into a CLOSE UP and holding a mic, says:

                        FRANK
            Respect the cock and tame the cunt, boys.

REVERSE, THAT MOMENT. The crowd of fifty GUYS who are taking the
"Seduce and Destroy Seminar" that Frank is teaching today laugh and
play along;

Frank is on a slightly elevated stage. Behind him a huge banner for,
"Seduce and Destroy," whose logo is a scared pussycat and a large wolf
with a big buldge in his fur. It reads: "No Pussy Has Nine Lives"

                        FRANK
            And you did hear me right. Tame it.
            Take it on, head first -- with your
            skills at work and say, "No. You will
            not control me. You will not take my
            soul and you will not win this game."
            'cause it is a game, guys, you wanna
            think it's not -- go back to the schoolyard
            and have a crush on Mary Jane -- respect
            the cock -- you are embedding this thought:
            I'm in charge. I'm the one who says yes,
            no, now or here. Shit, man. Sad but true.
            Sad But True. And you wanna know what?
            It must be the way.
            The thing about chicks and the thing
            about this course that we're going
            through today is how universal the whole
            thing is. I mean: I wish I could sit here
            and say that it's not -- because the reality?
            If each chick had something new, something
            really new that I'd never seen before?
            Fuckin' hell: I'd be in the money! Because
            I'd have to create a hundred new cassettes,
            a hundred new books, a hundred new seminars
                        (MORE)

                    FRANK (contd.)
and hundred new videos just to deal with each
and every situation a chick could create -
but that is just not the case. They are universal.
They are sheep. They are to be studied and
watched -- they have patterns that must be stopped,
interupted and resisted. I'd be makin' a fuckin'
butt load if they were actually as much of
a challenge as they want you to think they are!
Reality: They Are All The Same.
Each and every one of them. And once you learn
these methods: You're Set. You Don't Have To Come Back.
That's it. In solid. Boom. Done. Over. Why?
Because all women are the same. Period.
End of discussion. Sorry. It's true. Sad But True.
And anyone who wants to say that these methods
we work by are "unfair?" Yes, they are.
Guilty as charged. And so's the world.
It's a harsh, hard unfair place, but it's not
gonna stop me from getting my fair shair of hair pie --
Period. Sorry. End of discussion.

                                        CUT TO:

69. INT. HOLIDAY INN/LOBBY - THAT MOMENT   69.

Sliding doors open in the lobby and a young woman GWENOVIER (30s)
enters, takes off her sunglasses and looks around.

There's a bunch of Posters and Signs for the "Seduce and Destroy
Seminar with Frank TJ Mackey," etc. Frank's two sidekicks: DOC (20s)
and CAPTAIN MUFFY (40s) approach;

                    CAPTAIN MUFFY
You're Gwenovier?

                    GWENOVIER
Yeah.

                    CAPTIAN MUFFY
I'm Captain Muffy, I'm Frank's personal
assistant. This is Doc --

                    DOC
Hello.

                    GWENOVIER
Hello.

                    CAPTAIN MUFFY
We can go right in here. He started
about thirty five minutes ago, but
it's all getting pumped up now --

                                        CUT TO:

70. <u>INT. HOLIDAY INN/BANQUET ROOM - THAT MOMENT</u>   70.

Captain Muffy, Doc and Gwenovier enter and head for some seats,
CAMERA swings a 180 and moves down the aisle, towards the stage
as Frank speaks --

                         FRANK
              Number One: Get a calendar. I cannot
              stress this enough. This is a simple
              item guys. It's 99 cents at your corner
              store: Go And Get One. Fuck it, if you   *
              reach into your packet, you'll see I've   *
              been nice enough to include one, 'cause   *
              that's the kind of prick I am --   *
              You're gonna need this calendar and I know   *
              it sounds like a small thing, but having it   *
              makes all the difference in the world: *
              If you meet a girl and you're   *
              gonna work an A-3 Interuption --   *
              let's say an eight day waiting period before
              the next call -- how you gonna know when those
              eight days are up? Buy a calendar.
              Next move? Mark the calendar.
              Yeah, yeah, yeah. What did I pay my eight
              hundred dollars for? To hear Frank tell me
              to buy a calendar and mark it? Just stick
              with me and stick by the calendar. Mark it
              up -- use it to set goals -- If you wanna
              make that "friend" something else -- you gotta
              be hard on yourself, set goals:
                         (beat, to audience)
              You, there: And What's Your Name?   *

                                                           CUT TO:

71. <u>INT. EARL'S HOUSE/OFFICE - THAT MOMENT</u>   71.*

Phil flips through a little adress book, finds a number. XCU - It reads,
"Frank 8/509-9027" He picks up a phone and dials;

                         FEMALE VOICE
              Hello?

                         PHIL
              Hi. Is Frank there?

                         FEMALE VOICE
              I think you have the wrong number.

                         PHIL
              I'm looking for Frank Mackey.

                         FEMALE VOICE
              No.

                         PHIL
              Is this 509-9027?

> FEMALE VOICE
> Yeah. You have the wrong number.
> There's no one named Frank here.

> PHIL
> Alright. Thank you.

> FEMALE VOICE
> Yep.

Phil hangs up the phone.

CUT TO:

72. <u>INT. HOLIDAY INN/BANQUET ROOM - THAT MOMENT.</u>   72.

CAMERA with Gwenovier as she walks quietly over to the side
of the crowd to a VIDEO CREW that's been set up and is recording
Frank's seminar. She speaks sotto to a CAMERAMAN;

> GWENOVIER
> Sorry I'm late --

> CAMERAMAN
> -- we're all set upstairs.

> GWENOVIER
> Thanks.

She moves towards a row and takes a seat next to Captain Muffy
and Doc, speaks sotto again;

> DOC
> You have everything you need?

> GWENOVIER
> I'm set, thanks.

CAMERA moves away, Frank is kneeling down to a GUY in the   *
audience, interacting, speaking compassionately;   *

> FRANK   *
> Denise?   *

> GUY   *
> That's right --   *

> FRANK   *
> -- and she hurt you didn't she?   *
> I know, I know. I know how that   *
> can be brother, but let me tell you loud   *
> and clear what we will be teaching   *
> Denise when we put our calendars to work and   *
> set goals: *

Frank hops back up on the stage;

                    FRANK
          Little Denise, I say this: I mark it
          up and I write it down and you've been warned:
          "By the end of May, you will know I'm not gay."
          "On the fourth of June, Denise, you're
          gonna be lickin' my spoon."
          "And Come August, You Suck My Big Fat
          Sausage." I've SET GOALS FOR MYSELF.
          And what? I've said "enough is enough."
          Because why? She's not gonna be your pal.
          She's not gonna be your friend. You think
          she's gonna be there for you the second
          you need something? Think again - this fuckin'
          bitch Denise!
                    (audience cheers)
          But: Listen up: That is not to say that we don't
          all need women as friends, 'cause we're gonna
          learn later on in Chapter 23 that having a couple
          of chick-friends laying around can come in
          real handy in setting Jealousy Traps.
          But we'll get to that. Number One (this is page 18
          in your booklets, blue cover - go to it and
          follow along with me.)

The guys flip open their little blue booklets and follow along.

                    FRANK
          Create a crisis -- simple and clean,
          and if done properly can be quite
          effective in getting some bush.
          Here we go: Set a date with your so-called
          "friend." Let's say you make it 7:30.
          You call her on the phone --

                                        FLASH ON:

73. INT. GIRL'S APARTMENT - NIGHT   73.

CAMERA DOLLIES AROUND a young GIRL (20s) on the phone.

                    GIRL
          That sounds like fun, Frank.
          I love seafood.

                                        CUT TO:

74. INT. FRANK'S APARTMENT - NIGHT   74.

Frank on the phone.

                    FRANK
          So I'll see you about 7:30?
          Great, then. Bye-bye, Cindy.

He hangs up.

                                        CUT TO:

75.   <u>INT. GIRL'S HOUSE - ANOTHER NIGHT</u>   75.

CAMERA (HAND HELD) follows behind the GIRL as she walks from the kitchen
to the front door, shaking her head, huffing and puffing....

                         FRANK (VO)
               You wait until about nine o'clock
               and you ring the doorbell.

She opens the door and sees FRANK, crying and hysterical.

                         FRANK (VO)
               She opens it up, pissed as hell, but
               finds you sobbing your eyes out --

Frank looks up at her and says:

                         FRANK
               ...I can't believe what happened...

Frank and the Girl sit down on the couch together.

                         FRANK (VO)
               You explain between sobs that you hit
               a dog on the way over to pick her up
               and you had to rush it to the animal
               hospital but by the time you got there --

                         FRANK
               ...and it's paw was sticking out...
               and it was too late. It was too late.

She moves in and hugs him.

                         GIRL
               Ohhh, shhhh...shhh...Frank...

                                                          CUT TO:

76.   <u>INT. HOLIDAY INN/BANQUET ROOM - THAT MOMENT</u>   76.

Frank is cracking himself up. He continues.

                         FRANK
               I can't believe I'm telling you guys this,
               but the truly terrifying part is that: THIS WORKS.
               Any girl that calls herself your friend is <u>not</u>
               gonna let you be alone in a situation like that.
               Technique #2: Staging a fight.
               This is not knock down, drag out, crying
               screaming, yelling -- this is a simple,
               direct and subtle way of planting confusion
               into a girl's mind. Remember we are using
               reinforcement technique "G" with these women.
               Here's how:

                                                          CUT TO:

77.   <u>INT. GIRL'S HOUSE - NIGHT</u>   77.

The Girl picks up her phone and presses some numbers...

                          FRANK (VO)
               One day, she calls you up on the phone...

                                                        CUT TO:

78.   <u>INT. FRANK'S HOUSE - NIGHT</u>   78.

Frank picks up the phone.

                          FRANK
               Hello?

                          GIRL
               Hey, Frank. It's Cindy. I'm wondering
               if you wanna grab a bite and see a movie?

                          FRANK (VO)
               You very directly say:

                          FRANK
               "I don't think I have anything to say
               to you, Cindy."

Frank hangs up the phone.

                                                        CUT TO:

79.   <u>INT. GIRL'S HOUSE - THAT MOMENT</u>   79.

The Girl gets the dial tone. She looks completely confused and hurt.

                                                        CUT TO:

80.   <u>INT. HOLIDAY INN/BANQUET ROOM - BACK TO SCENE</u> .   80.

Frank speaking to the group:

                          FRANK
               Let her wonder what she did wrong.

CAMERA DOES A SLOW DOLLY IN. Frank's tone changes a bit, gets darker:

                          FRANK
               This is the way...because they will
               always wonder, "What did I do?"
               "What could I have done different?"
               "How should I behave to get this back?"
               And if they think that way -- then they
               are asking for you to hurt them and
               That Is What You Must Do. That is what
               you must do which is punish them many,
               many times over.

81.   INT. CEDARS SINAI MEDICAL CENTER - HALLWAY - DAY   81.

         CAMERA pushes in as LINDA walks towards us, down the same
         hallway we saw Jimmy Gator walking down earlier, she heads
         into an office --

                                                                 CUT TO:

82.   INT. DOCTOR'S OFFICE/RECPETION AREA - MOMENTS LATER   82.

         CAMERA pushes in on Linda as she enters, WHIPS over to a   *
         RECEPTIONIST who looks up;   *

                              RECEPTIONIST   *
                         Mrs. Partridge --   *

                              LINDA   *
                         I'm here and I need to see him.   *

                                                                 CUT TO:

83.   INT. DOCTOR'S OFFICE - MOMENTS LATER   83.

         Quick shots get them in the room: DR. LANDON (40s) sits
         across from LINDA, who's in semi-hysterics, pacing;

                              LINDA
                    -- he's fucking dying, he's dying
                    as we're sitting here and there
                    isn't a fucking thing -- jesus,
                    how can you tell me to calm down?

                              DR. LANDON
                    I can help you through this the
                    best I know how but there are certain
                    things you are gonna have to be
                    strong about and take care of, now
                    we can go over them, but I need to
                    know that you're listening to me, ok?

                              LINDA
                    I just, I just -- I just -- I'm just
                    in a fucking state, I know he's
                    going and it's like I don't know how
                    -- just tell me practical things --
                    What the fuck do I do with his body?
                    What happens when he dies? That next moment:
                    What? What do I do? Then What?

                              DR. LANDON
                    Well that's what Hospice will take care of
                    for you. They will send a nurse, someone
                    who can take care of all of that for you --

                              LINDA
                    He has Phil right now.

                         DR. LANDON
          Phil's one of the nurses from the service?

                         LINDA
          Yeah.

                         DR. LANDON
          If you're happy with Phil taking care
          of him and helping you, that's fine,
          but contact Hospice to arrange for the body --

                         LINDA
          -- you don't understand: it's more pain
          than before and the fucking morphine pills
          aren't working, he's -- past two days it's
          like he can't really swallow them and I don't
          know if they're going down -- I can't see inside
          his mouth anymore -- I'm up all night staring
          at him and I don't think the pills are going
          down and he moans and he hurts --

                         DR. LANDON
          We can fix that, because I can give
          you -- are you listening?

                         LINDA
          I'm listening I'm getting better.

                         DR. LANDON
          Do you wanna sit down?

                         LINDA
          I need to sit down.

                         DR. LANDON
          Ok. Linda: Earl is not gonna make it.
          He's dying. He is. He is dying very,
          very rapidly --

She breaks a bit more.

                         DR. LANDON
          Now the thing here is making that experience
          as painless and easy as possible for him,
          you understand? Now you need to get in touch
          with Hospice care because they can take care of
          all those practical things that you're asking
          me about -- they are who you call when he dies.

He writes a number on his bussiness card, hands it over as they speak;

                    DR. LANDON
          This is the number for Hopsice.
          Ok. Now. As far as the morphine pills go,
          there is something else to consider that
          can take the pain away that he is in,
          there is a very strong and very potent solution
          of liquid morphine....it's a little bottle,
          with an eye dropper and it's easy to get in
          his mouth and drop on his tounge and
          it will certainly diminish the pain that
          he is in but you have to realize that
          once you give it to him; there really
          is no coming back, I mean, it will certainly
          cure his pain, but he will float in and
          out of consciousness, even worse than he
          is now, Linda. I mean, any sign of the
          recognizable Earl will pretty much go away --

                    LINDA
          I -- how the fuck can I say anything
          to that -- I don't know what to say to that --

                    DR. LANDON
          The job here is to make him as comfortable
          as possible -- right now -- our job is to just
          try and make it as painless as possible.
          Right? You understand?

     CAMERA pushes into an EXTREME CLOSE UP on Dr. Landon's hands writing
     the perscription for the liquid morphine....hands it to Linda....

                                                       CUT TO:

84. INT. JIMMY'S JAGUAR - PARKED - DAY   84.

     CAMERA holds a CU on Jimmy sitting behind the wheel. He hesitates
     a moment, exits the car.

                                                       CUT TO:

85. EXT. CLAUDIA'S APARTMENT/STAIRWELL - MOMENTS LATER   85.

     CAMERA holds looking down a staircase. Jimmy enters FRAME, walks
     up to the second floor, stands a moment, then knocks.

                                                       CUT TO:

86. INT. CLAUDIA'S BEDROOM - THAT MOMENT   86.

     CAMERA DOLLIES in on the bed. Claudia's asleep. The MIDDLE AGED GUY is
     lying next to her in his underwear. He hears the door, wakes.

                                                       CUT TO:

87.   EXT./INT. CLAUDIA'S APARTMENT - THAT MOMENT   87.

Jimmy knocks again....after a BEAT...the door is opened by the MIDDLE
AGED GUY. He stands in his underwear.

                    MIDDLE AGED GUY
          Hello?

                    JIMMY
          Hello. Is Claudia here?

                    MIDDLE AGED GUY
          She's asleep.

BEAT.

                    JIMMY
          Are you her boyfriend?

                    MIDDLE AGED GUY
          You're Jimmy Gator, right?

                    JIMMY
          Yes. What's your name?

                    MIDDLE AGED GUY
          I'm Bob.

                    JIMMY
          You're her boyfriend?

                    MIDDLE AGED GUY
          No, I'm just a friend. What are you
          doing here, I mean...you know Claudia?

                    JIMMY
          I'm her father.

The Middle Aged Guy looks a bit confused.

                    JIMMY
          Can I come in?

                    MIDDLE AGED GUY
          Yeah. She's sleeping now, I mean --

Jimmy steps inside, looks around the place, sees the coke and some pot
and pills sitting out on the coffee table.

                    MIDDLE AGED GUY
          Want me to wake her up?

                    JIMMY
          I'll go....is it...back here?

The Middle Aged Guy points Jimmy to the back bedroom.

88.   INT. CLAUDIA'S BEDROOM — THAT MOMENT   88.

Claudia is asleep. Jimmy enters, stands near the edge of the bed.
After a moment, Claudia's eyes open, look over and see Jimmy.

                         CLAUDIA
              ...what the fuck is this...?

                         JIMMY
              It's me. Claudia. It's me.

She sits up a bit, covers herself, looks past him and sees the
Middle Aged Guy, sitting in his underwear in the living room,
watching them. She looks back to Jimmy;

                         CLAUDIA
              What do you want? Why are you here?

                         JIMMY
              I'd like to talk to you. Your boyfriend
              let me in, I just knocked on the door --

                         CLAUDIA
              He's not my boyfriend.

Jimmy hesitates a beat, then:

                         CLAUDIA
              Wanna call me a slut now, something?

                         JIMMY
              No. No.

She starts to move towards tears, nervousness;

                         CLAUDIA
              What the fuck do you want?

                         JIMMY
              I want to sit. I want to talk to you.

                         CLAUDIA
              Don't sit down.

                         JIMMY
              ...I want to....I want so many things, Claudia.
              Maybe we can just talk to straighten
              our things out....there are so many
              things that I want to tell you --

                         CLAUDIA
              I don't wanna talk to you.

JIMMY

Please. It doesn't have to be now.
Maybe we can make a date to sit down,
I didn't mean to walk in on you like this --

CLAUDIA

Why are you here, why are you doing this?
Coming in here -- you wanna call me a whore?

JIMMY

I don't want you to think that I'm that
way to you -- I'm not gonna call you
a slut or something --

CLAUDIA

Yeah, yeah right -- what the fuck are
doing? WHAT THE FUCK ARE YOU DOING IN MY HOUSE?

JIMMY

Don't yell, honey. Please don't go crazy --

CLAUDIA

I'M NOT CRAZY. Don't you tell me I'm crazy.

JIMMY

I'm not saying that, I'm sorry --

CLAUDIA

I'M NOT CRAZY. You're the one. You're
the one who's wrong. You're the one --

JIMMY

I have something, so much -- I'm sick, Claudia.
I'm sick.

CLAUDIA

Get out of here, get the fuck out of
my house --

JIMMY

Now STOP IT and LISTEN to me right now.
I AM DYING, I GOT SICK...now I fell
down and I'm Not...DON'T --

CLAUDIA

GET THE FUCK OUT.

JIMMY

I'm dying, Claudia. I have cancer.
I have cancer and I'm dying, soon.
It's metastasized in my bones and I --

CLAUDIA

FUCK YOU. FUCK YOU, YOU GET OUT.

JIMMY

I'm not lying to you, I'm not --

                         CLAUDIA
              FUCK YOU. YOU GET THE FUCK OUT OF HERE.

                         JIMMY
              baby, please, please --

                         CLAUDIA
              I'M NOT YOUR BABY, I'M NOT YOUR GIRL.
              I'm not your fuckin' baby --

She moves up in the bed, exposes a bit of her breast, tries to
cover herself --

                         JIMMY
              Please put your clothes on, please --

                         CLAUDIA
              YOU BURN IN HELL. You burn in hell
              and you deserve it -- YOU GET THE FUCK OUT.

                         JIMMY
              Honey.

                         CLAUDIA
              GET OUT.

BEAT. He stands a moment.

                         JIMMY
              Your mother wants to hear from you --

                         CLAUDIA
              GET THE FUCK OUT OF HERE.

He walks out of the bedroom, past the MIDDLE AGED GUY, who's
sitting on the couch.

                         JIMMY
              I'm sorry.

                         MIDDLE AGED GUY
              It's alright.

Jimmy exits. Claudia is shaking and crying and holding herself
in the covers of the bed.

The Middle Aged Guy snorts a line of coke, looks into her;

                         CLAUDIA
              Can you get your shit and leave, please?

                                              CUT TO:

89.   <u>INT. SOLOMON AND SOLOMON ELECTRONICS - DAY</u>   89.

       CAMERA pushes in as Donnie Smith runs in the door, brushes his
       hair back, etc. This is a "Good Guys" type electronics place.
       He rushes towards the back.

       ANGLE, DOOR TO BACK ROOM.
       CAMERA pushes in real quick and tilts down as Donnie reaches
       to his belt and his KEY HOLDER (one of those attached to string
       on the belt) He inserts the KEY.

                                                            CUT TO:

90.   <u>INT. BACK HALLWAY - SOLOMON AND SOLOMON - THAT MOMENT</u>   90.

       Donnie enters, walks swiftly down the hall to another door.
       Just before he reaches it, AVI SOLOMON (30s) appears at the
       end of the hall.

                              AVI
                    Don.

       Donnie stops short, looks. Avi gives him the "follow me" finger.

                              DON
                    Hey, Avi. I'll be right there.

       Avi goes back in the room he came from. Donnie does the
       KEY and CODE thing now on this door.

                                                            CUT TO:

91.   <u>INT. DRESSING ROOM/EMPLOYEE LOUNGE - MOMENTS LATER</u>   91.

       Donnie is changed into his Solomon and Solomon Electronics vest
       and name tag. He brushes himself up, sweating a bit. (Note:ON HIS BACK)

                              DONNIE
                    This is going to be ok. This is. This is.

                                                            CUT TO:

92.   <u>INT. SOLOMON'S OFFICE - MOMENTS LATER</u>   92.

       Donnie sitting across the desk from SOLOMON SOLOMON (40s) owner
       of the store. Avi, his brother, stands nearby.

                              DONNIE
                    ...please...

                              SOLOMON
                    Don't Donnie. Don't do it.

       Donnie swells up a bit, about to cry.

DONNIE
This is so fucked, Solomon.
I don't deserve this.

SOLOMON
Don't get strong, Donnie. This is making
sense, this making a lot of sense.
You are not doing the job, the job
I ask you to do, a job I give you.
Over and over and over and I'm sorry.
But I'm not gonna say I'm sorry that
much more.

DONNIE
Solomon: I am in the middle of so much.
So much in my life and this is --
If you do this, if you fire me: I Am Fucked.
I can't really explain much, but please,
please, I've worked here for four years,
four years I've given you and I'm, I'm,
I mean what? I'm sorry I was late.
I had a car accident. I accidentaly
drove into a seven-eleven. It was not
my fault.

AVI
Who's fault was it, Don?

SOLOMON
Avi, please, shut the fuck up for
one second. Don, how much further
do you want me to go in showing you,
showing you what I've done for you
in four years and what you've done
back? Do you want me to do it? I can.
The loans I've given, how much your sales
are, how late you are, over and over, loosing
the keys to the Covina store --

DONNIE
I don't have any money, Solomon.
If you fire me --

SOLOMON
-- I give you money, I give you a paycheck.
Your sales suck, Don. I give, I give.
When I find you, when I meet you,
what? I put you on the billboard,
I put you in the store, my salesman,
my fucking representation of Solomon
and Solomon Electronic, Quiz Kid Donnie Smith
from the game show --

DONNIE
I lent my name, my celebrity. Exactly --

SOLOMON
FUCK YOU. I pay you, I paid you.
I give you a fucking chance and
a chance and over and over, over you
let me down. I trust you with so much.
The keys to my store, the codes to my locks,
the life, the blood of my bussiness and
return is smashing in seven-eleven, late,
always late, loans -- I loaned you money
for your kitchen that you never did --

DONNIE
I paid you back.

SOLOMON
Two years! Two years later and out of your
paycheck, I never charge interest --

DONNIE
Solomon, please. Please. I am so fucked
here if you do this. This is the worst timing.
The worst timing I could ever imagine.
I need to keep working. I have so many
debts, so many things, I have, I have,
I have -- I have surgery -- I have my
oral surgery coming --

AVI
What surgery?

DONNIE
Oral surgery. Corrective teeth surgery.

SOLOMON
What is that?

DONNIE
Braces.

SOLOMON
Braces?

DONNIE
Yes.

SOLOMON
You don't need braces.

DONNIE
Yes I do.

SOLOMON
Your teeth are fine.

AVI
Your teeth are straight.

                    DONNIE
I need corrective oral surgery.
I need the braces.

                    AVI
Don, you got hit by lightning that
time in Tahoe, you went on vacation,
I don't think braces is a good idea --

                    DONNIE
I can't believe you're gonna do this
to me, the situation I'm in, I don't --
Avi: You know what? Being hit by lighting
doesn't matter for getting braces, ok?
Now Solomon, let me just ask you once:
Please. Please. Don't do this.

                    AVI
How are you paying for the braces, Donnie?

                    DONNIE
I don't know.

                    SOLOMON
And how much is braces?

                    DONNIE
It's...doesn't matter....

                    AVI
It's like five thousand dollars,
I've seen it, I know --

                    SOLOMON
You're pissing me off, Don. This is
so unbelievable -- so fucking stupid,
you're gonna spend five thousand dollars
on braces you don't need --

                    DONNIE
I've been a good worker --

                    SOLOMON
Don't do this, Don.

                    AVI
No need for braces, Donnie.

                    SOLOMON
Where are you getting the money for this?

                    DONNIE
I don't know.

                    SOLOMON
You were gonna ask me weren't you?

                    DONNIE
          I've been a good worker, Solomon.
          A hard and loyal --

                    AVI
          No need for braces, Donnie.

                    DONNIE
          THAT'S NONE OF YOUR BUSSINESS.
          I HAVE BEEN A GOOD WORKER, A GOOD AND
          LOYAL WORKER FOR YOU, YOU FUCKING ASSHOLE.

                    AVI
          HEY FUCK YOU DON WATCH IT NOW.

                    SOLOMON
          Give me your keys, Don.

                    DONNIE
          PLEASE DON'T DO THIS!

                    SOLOMON
          GIMME YOUR FUCKIN' KEYS.

     BEAT. Donnie tries to calm himself, hold back tears, stands up.
     He struggles with his KEY CHAIN and finally after a bunch
     of moments, hands over six or seven keys.

     CU. INSERT, KEYS. placed on the desk.

                                                  CUT TO:

93. <u>INT. APARTMENT COMPLEX/NORTH HOLLYWOOD - THAT MOMENT</u>   93 *

     CAMERA hangs inside bedroom w/Detectives and Investigators and
     County Coroner folks as we go through in a series of quick shots.
     (<u>Director's Note</u>: Very technical here. Snapshots, ECU's on body,
     procedure, etc.) * See County Coroner videotape.

94. IN THE LIVING ROOM   94 *

     CAMERA pushes in past DETECTIVES and OFFICERS who are exchanging
     information...CAMERA moves towards Jim Kurring, standing off a bit
     now, usless to the investigation as far as everyone else is concerned,
     but listening carefully to what they say:

                    OFFICER   *
          Identified as Porter Parker, aged 59.   *
          Better known as the dead guy in the closet.   *
          So says the building guy, this is her   *
          husband --   *

                    DETECTIVE #2   *
          -- he's doesn't live here, but he comes   *
          around, raises shit, screaming, yelling,   *
          something or other --   *

                    OFFICER   *
There's a son, apparently. And a kid.   *

                    DETECTIVE #1   *
<u>Her</u> son?   *

                    OFFICER   *
<u>Her</u> son, that's right...and the kid.   *
And they were here and around and   *
from late last night and through the   *
morning, it's screaming and yelling --   *

                    DETECTIVE #1   *
And Where Are They?   *

                    DETECTIVE   *
-- they are not to be found.   *

                    CORONER WOMAN   *
-- she's got six hundred dollars and   *
a large box of condoms next to the bed --   *

                    OFFICER #1   *
And three wedding rings.   *

                    DETECTIVE #1   *
Ok.   *

                    CORONER WOMAN
-- guys come in, out and around all day,
this is the building guy talking --

                    OFFICER
The building guy says The Son and The
Closet guy are always goin' at it --

                    CORONER WOMAN
That's right.

                    DETECTIVE #1
And what is she saying?

                    OFFICER
Not a god damn thing.

CAMERA lands CU on Jim Kurring.

95.   ANGLE, COURTYARD AREA - THAT MOMENT   95 *

Another set of Detectives/Officers/Investigators are standing
over Marcie, who sits handcuffed. She has her best, "I'm not
saying anything" face on. Again, they're OC througout;

>   OFFICER #2   *
>   Why did you kill him, Marcie?   *

>   DETECTIVE #3   *
>   Did you kill him?   *

>   OFFICER #2   *
>   Did he hurt you, did he do something?   *

>   DETECTIVE #4   *
>   How long's he been in there?

>   DETECTIVE #3   *
>   You're hurting yourself, Marcie.   *

>   OFFICER #3   *
>   You have the dead body of your husband   *
>   in the closet of your apartment, Marcie.   *

>   OFFICER #2   *
>   That Is Not Good.   *

>   DETECTIVE #3   *
>   You hit him with the ashtray,   *
>   you strangled him --   *

>   DETECTIVE #4   *
>   -- tell us he fell and hit his head,   *
>   but tell us something, Marcie.   *

>   OFFICER #2   *
>   Why did you kill him?   *

The Main Detective from previous steps into FRAME, says: *

>   DETECTIVE #1   *
>   -- Marcie: Where's your son? Marcie?   *
>   Marcie? Marcie tell us where your Son is now.   *
>   Marcie tell us where your son is.   *

CAMERA arrives CU on Marcie.

>   MARCIE
>   I wanna talk to my motherfuckin' lawyer.

96.   ANGLE, STREET OUTSIDE APARTMENT COMPLEX - LATER   96 *

The investigation is wrapping up now and CAMERA (STEADICAM)
moves with Jim Kurring as he heads towards his squad car,
talking into his WALKIE TALKIE. (Dir. Note: technical info re:
disturbance at adress/Jim takes call/etc.)

                    WALKIE VOICE
          ...4277 Tujunga...

                    JIM KURRING
          10-4.

Out of the group of neighborhood lookie-lo's comes a little black
kid who starts walking alongside Jim Kurring as they head away
from the scene -- this is DIXON, age 10. He's very small for his age
and he carries one of those boxes filled with Candy Bars he's trying
to sell. They walk/talk;

                    DIXON
          How much you pay me for my help?

                    JIM KURRING
          I think it's more complicated
          than that little man.

                    DIXON
          Put me on the payroll, find out,
          find out wassup --

                    JIM KURRING
          You don't just sign up to be a police
          officer -- it's about three years of
          training -- ok?

                    DIXON
          I'm trained, I'm ready to go, you wanna
          buy some candy to help underprivelaged
          youth in the --

                    JIM KURRING
          Sorry, little man.

                    DIXON
          You wanna take my statement, I'll
          perform for you, gotta get paid though,
          gotta get PAID.

                    JIM KURRING
          Why the hell aren't you in school?

                    DIXON
          No school today. My teacher got sick.

                    JIM KURRING
          They don't have substitute teachers
          where you go to school?

                    DIXON
          Nope. So what'd they find out in there?

                    JIM KURRING
          That's confidential information, little man.

                    DIXON
          Tell me what you know, I'll tell you
          what I know --

                    JIM KURRING
          No Can Do.

                    DIXON
          Leave this one to the detectives,
          they ain't gonna solve shit, I can
          help you, make you the man with a plan,
          give you the gift that I flow -- think
          fast -- you wanna know who killed that guy?

Jim Kurring stops at his Squad Car, turns to Dixon;

                    JIM KURRING
          Ok. Listen. You: c'mere.

                    DIXON
          No.

                    JIM KURRING
          You wanna disrespect an officer of the law?

                    DIXON
          I can help you solve the case,
          I can tell you who did it.

                    JIM KURRING
          Are you a joker? huh? Tellin' jokes?

                    DIXON
          I'm a rapper.

                    JIM KURRING
          Oh, you're a rapper, huh? You got a
          record contract?

                    DIXON
          Not yet -- "give you the clue for
          the bust if you show me some trust -- "

                    JIM KURRING
          Have you ever been to Juvenille Hall?

                    DIXON
          I ain't fuckin with you --

                    JIM KURRING
          Hey. Watch the mouth. Watch it.

                    DIXON
          C'mon, man, just watch me, watch
          and listen --

                    JIM KURRING
          Go. Hurry up. Let's go.

Dixon places his box of candy down and starts dancing around.
Jim Kurring stands beside his squad car.

                    DIXON
          Presence - with a double ass meaning
          gifts I bestow, with my riff, and my flow
          but you don't hear me though
          think fast, catch me, yo
          cause I throw what I know with a
          Resonance - fo'yo'trouble-ass fiend in
          weenin yo-self off the back of the shelf
          Jackass crackas, bodystackas
          dicktootin niggas, masturbatin' yo trigga
          butcha y'all just fake-ass niggas --

                    JIM KURRING
          -- watch the mouth, homeboy, I don't
          need to hear that word --

                    DIXON
          -- livin' to get older
          with a chip on your shoulder
          'cept you think you got a grip,
          cauze you hip gotta holster?
          Ain't no confessor, so busta, you best just
          Shut The fuck up, try to listen and learn --

                    JIM KURRING
          Alright, alright, cut it, coolio.
          That's enough with the mouth and
          the language.

                    DIXON
          I'm almost done.

                    JIM KURRING
          Finish it up without the lip.

                    DIXON
          Check that ego - come off it -
          I'm the profit - the proffesor
          Ima teach you 'bout The Worm,
          who eventually turned to catch wreck
          with the neck of a long time oppressor
          And he's runnin from the devil, but the
          debt is always gaining
          And if he's worth being hurt, he's worth
          bringin' pain in
          When the sunshine don't work, the Good Lord
          bring the rain in.

HOLD ON KURRING.

                    DIXON
          Now that shit will help you SOLVE the case.

                    JIM KURRING
          Whatever that meant, I'm sure it's
          real helpful Ice-T.

Kurring gets behind the wheel, Dixon hustles over;   *

                    DIXON   *
          Did you listen to me?   *

                    JIM KURRING   *
          I was listening --   *

                    DIXON   *
          -- I told you who did it and you're not   *
          listening to me.   *

                    JIM KURRING   *
          -- and I'm through playin' games.   *

Kurring closes his door and drives off...(Director's Note: Reference
notes for SOUND design here, carries over cut...)

                                                  CUT TO:

MUSIC QUE starts, builds over the following cut and through sequence;

97.   INT. SCHOOL LIBRARY - DAY   Sequence C   97.

CAMERA PUSHES IN SLOW on STANLEY as he sits at a desk...piles of
books spread out in front of him....

OVERHEAD ANGLE, LOOKING STRAIGHT DOWN ONTO:
All the books he has in front of him, we catch glimpses of things:

"How Things Work" "Forensic Studies" "The Guiness Book of World
Records" "The Natural History of Nonsense" "Weather" "Learned Pigs..."

INSERT, CU. IMAGES of the book about weather. CAMERA scans, dissolves
and moves around various images of ancient BAROMETERS, HYGROMETERS
from the 1700's. We see 16th Century French comic strips regarding
weather as cartoon characters. Aristotle pointing to the sky.
Scan past the words, "...our quest to understand and predict the
weather reaches back to the Stone Age..."

CU - Stanley's face as he reads. SLOW ZOOM IN.
CU - School Bell RINGS.
CU - He grabs his books.

                                                      CUT TO:

98.   EXT. SCHOOL - PICK UP AREA - MOMENTS LATER   98.

CAMERA (STEADICAM) follows behind Stanley as he heads, with all his
backpacks, towards Rick, who's waiting in the car --

                         RICK
                    C'mon, man.

                         STANLEY
                    You're late, not me.

                         RICK
                    You coulda been in front --

                         STANLEY
                    -- I didn't see you from the window.

Rick helps him get the bags in the car. CAMERA stays real TIGHT
following STANLEY'S FACE....he sits in the car....OC we hear Rick
getting in the driver's seat and starting the engine...little droplets
of RAIN start to fall on the windshield....

                         RICK (OC)
                    You ready to keep winning?

                         STANLEY
                    Sure.

STANLEY is driven away, OUT OF FRAME.

                                                      CUT TO:

99.   <u>EXT. SKY - DAY</u>   99.

     CAMERA looking straight up. It starts POURING RAIN real hard
     right INTO CAMERA....SLOW ZOOM IN....hold until it's just a
     WASH OF WATER.

     Title Card reads: <u>Temperature/Percipitation reading/</u>
                               <u>wind direction/weather info/humidity/etc</u>

                                        QUICK DISSOLVE TO:

100.   <u>EXT./INT. TELEVISION STUDIO - SECUIRTY ENTRANCE - MOMENTS LATER</u>   100.

     CAMERA (STEADICAM) follows behind Stanley and Rick as they run
     in from the rain, through some sliding glass doors, past a SECURITY
     GAURD who buzzes them into another set of doors --

     They enter a hallway with a bunch of production offices, walking
     swiftly, shaking their wet clothes....the contestant coordinator
     comes walking towards them: CYNTHIA (30s)

                            CYNTHIA
               There you are, there you are.
                           RICK
               Sorry we're late, Cynthia.

                          CYNTHIA
               Nothin' to it, no problem.
               How you doin' Stanley?

                          STANLEY
               I'm fine. Yes. I'm fine.

                          CYNTHIA
               Ready to go,go,go?

                          STANLEY
               Where's Richard and Julia?

                          CYNTHIA
               They're here, they're fine.
               In the dressing room.
                     (to Rick)
               See you later --

     Rick gives Stanley a pat on the head;

                           RICK
               Go to it, handsome.

                        STANLEY
               See you.

     CAMERA holds with Rick, does a 180 around him, he turns his
     back to us now, walks a bit, enters a door, into --

101.   THE PARENTS GREEN ROOM   101.

Rick greets the other two kids parents: RICHARD'S MOM (overweight, 50s)
and RICHARD DAD (same) JULIA'S DAD and JULIA'S MOM (50s)

                              RICK
              Who's ready to beat the record?

                         RICHARD'S MOM
              Jesus you scared us!

                          JULIA'S DAD
              That was close.

                              RICK
              It's fuckin cats and dogs out there --

                          JULIA'S DAD
              Cats and Dogs, indeed.

CAMERA picks up with a young PRODUCTION KID who drops some coffee
off for JULIA'S MOM...follow him back out into the hallway -- CAMERA
branches off from him -- moves down another corridor and picks back
up with STANLEY and CYNTHIA as they walk and talk;

                           STANLEY
              Where's the news department at this studio?

                           CYNTHIA
              It's upstairs.

                           STANLEY
              Have you ever been there?

                           CYNTHIA
              Sure, why?

                           STANLEY
              I'm wondering about the weather
              department. I'm wonderin' wether
              or not the weather people use outside
              meteorlogical services or if they
              have in-house instruments?

                           CYNTHIA
              I can check on that for you, maybe
              we can take a tour --

                           STANLEY
              Ok.

They pass CAMERA which picks up now with a woman MARY (40s)
This is Jimmy Gator's assistant...she walks to his dressing
room door and knocks --

                         JIMMY (OC)
              Come in.

Mary enters the room. Jimmy is getting dressed in his outfit
for the show* and starting to take shots of Jack Daniel's.

                          MARY
              Rose is on the phone and here's
              the cards for today --

                          JIMMY
              Fifteen minutes ago, where were
              those cards?

                          MARY
              I'm sorry.

                          JIMMY
              I need you to get me Paula --

                          MARY
              You want her right now?

                          JIMMY
              Yes. Now. Find her. She's somewhere
              in the building --

                          MARY
              We're on the air in twenty minutes, Jimmy.

                          JIMMY
              Find her, get her and tell her I want
              to talk to her, Mary. Fucking hell.

He picks up the phone.

                          JIMMY
              Hello?

                                                    INTERCUT:

102.   INT. JIMMY'S HOUSE - THAT MOMENT   102.

CAMERA PUSHES in on ROSE (Jimmy's wife) as she sits in the kitchen
on the phone to him. A MAID does some work in the b.g.

                          ROSE
              How you doing?

                          JIMMY
              I'm drinking.

                          ROSE
              Slowly or quickly?

                          JIMMY
              As fast as I can.

                    ROSE
Come home soon after the show.

                    JIMMY
I went to see her -- some fuckin'
asshole answers the door in his
underwear, he's fifty years old,
there's coke and shit laid out
on the table --

                    ROSE
-- did she talk to you?

                    JIMMY
She went crazy. She went crazy, Rose.

                    ROSE
Did you tell her?

                    JIMMY
I don't know. I have to go, I don't
have time and I have more drinking
to do before I go march --

                    ROSE
I love you.

                    JIMMY
Love you too..

                    ROSE
Bye.

HOLD with Rose.

                                              CUT TO:

103. EXT. CLAUDIA'S APARTMENT - THAT MOMENT   103.

CAMERA holds a moment on the building. JIM KURRING pulls his squad
car INTO FRAME, looks at the building.

                                              CUT TO:

104. INT. CLAUDIA'S APARTMENT - THAT MOMENT   104.

CAMERA dollies in quick on Claudia as she snorts a line of coke.
She has some music BLASTING.

                                              CUT TO:

105. EXT. CLAUDIA'S APARTMENT - THAT MOMENT   105.

CAMERA (STEADICAM) follows behind Jim Kurring as he heads up the
pathway, up the stairs and lands at her door. He knocks.

106.   <u>INT. CLAUDIA'S APARTMENT - THAT MOMENT</u>   106.

Claudia jumps -- turns her head to the door. She sniffs a bit,
yells over the blasting music;

                         CLAUDIA
                    ...Hello...?

                         JIM KURRING (OC)
                    LAPD. Open the door.

She looks through her peep-hole, sees Jim Kurring. She turns looks
at her coffee table: It's full of coke, pills and pot, etc.

                         CLAUDIA
                    uh...uh...What is it?

                         JIM KURRING
                    It's the LAPD, can you open the door, please?

Claudia rushes over to the table of drugs and starts to scoop
things up in her arms --

                         CLAUDIA
                    Just a minute....just a...I have
                    to get dressed -- (fuck,fuck,fuck)

                                              CUT TO:

107.   <u>EXT. MEDICAL BUILDING/SHERMAN OAKS - THAT MOMENT</u>   107.

CAMERA pushes in on LINDA'S MERCEDES as it pulls into a parking
structure. The RAIN is pouring down. She steps out of the car --

                                              CUT TO:

108.   <u>INT. MEDICAL BUILDING - MOMENTS LATER</u>   108.

CAMERA pulls back as Linda exits some elevators, heads down a hall --

                                              CUT TO:

109.   <u>INT. OFFICE/WAITING ROOM - MOMENTS LATER</u>   109.

She enters a psychologist's waiting room. Three or four chairs
and a LIGHT SWITCH that has a doctors name next to it.

ECU - She flips the switch and a red light goes on.

                                              JUMP CUT TO:

110.   INT. PSYCHOLOGIST'S OFFICE - MOMENTS LATER   110.

A small, comfortable office space. Linda is crying, talking,
pacing. The psychologist is a middle aged woman, DR. DIANE.
As they talk, Dr. Diane writes a perscription;

                    LINDA
          I hate doing this, coming here
          and not being able to talk --

                    DR. DIANE
          I understand, it's fine --
          I wish the circumstance was better.

                    LINDA
          I don't know what's gonna happen,
          I really don't -- I'm so fucking,
          I feel so over the top with everything.

                    DR. DIANE
          Mmm..Hmm. Running out of your
          medication at all, let alone at
          a time like this could be drastic,
          I'm glad you came in to see me,
          as short as this has been --

She hands over the perscriptions (x2) and is about to say another
word -- but Linda SNATCHES the two small pieces of paper from
her hand and heads for the door --

                    LINDA
          Thank you Doctor Diane --

                    SHRINK
          Good luck with everything.

ECU - Door slammed.

                                                    CUT TO:

111.   INT. EARL'S HOUSE - DEN - THAT MOMENT   111.

CAMERA holds on PHIL. SLOW ZOOM IN as he stands in front of
the television, flipping stations.

ANGLE, THE TELEVISION.
It's plays all sorts of various things. Phil stops a few beats
on each thing that looks vaguely like an infomercial.

He puts the remote down, exits the room. CAMERA stays a moment,
catches a glimpse of a promo for, "What Do Kids Know?"

It's VARIOUS IMAGES of Stanley and the other kids answering
questions, with a calendar showing they've been at it for over
seven weeks and total winnings moving towards $450,000.00

> PROMO ANNOUNCER
> Can they do it? Tune in live at three
> o'clock and see if Stanley Spector and
> his brilliant friends Richard and Julia
> can defeat todays adult challengers Mim,
> Luis and Todd -- they're moving towards
> A Half A Million Dollar Team Total and
> a "What Do Kids Know?" record --

                                                        CUT TO:

112.   INT. EARL'S HOUSE/KITCHEN - MOMENT LATER   112.

       Phil enters and picks up the phone. Dials a number. (Director's Note)

                                                        INTERCUT:

113.   INT. PINK DOT - THAT MOMENT   113.

       A young/Mexican GIRL (20's) takes orders for delivery at Pink Dot,
       sits in front of a little computer.

> PINK DOT GIRL
> Pink Dot.

> PHIL
> Hi. I'd like to get an order for delivery.

> PINK DOT GIRL
> Phone number.

> PHIL
> 818-753-0088.

> PINK DOT GIRL
> Partridge?

> PHIL
> Yeah.

> PINK DOT GIRL
> What would you like?

> PHIL
> I'd like to get an order of...um...peanut butter.

> PINK DOT GIRL
> Mmm.Hmmm.

> PHIL
> Cigarettes. Camel Lights.

> PINK DOT GIRL
> mmm.hmm.

                    PHIL
Water.

                    PINK DOT GIRL
Bottled Water?

                    PHIL
Um, no, y'know what? Forget the water,
just give me a loaf of bread...white
bread.

                    PINK DOT GIRL
Ok.

                    PHIL
And um....do you have Swank magazine?

                    PINK DOT GIRL
Yeah.

                    PHIL
Ok. One of those. Do you have Ram Rod?
The magazine, Ram Rod?

                    PINK DOT GIRL
Yeah.

                    PHIL
Ok. One of those. And...um...Barely Legal?

                    PINK DOT GIRL
yeah.

                    PHIL
Do you have that?

                    PINK DOT GIRL
yeah, I said. Is that it?

                    PHIL
That's it.

                    PINK DOT GIRL
Do you still want the peanut butter,
bread and cigarettes?

                    PHIL
Yes. What? Yes.

                    PINK DOT GIRL
Total is $15.29. Thirty minutes or less.

                    PHIL
Thank you.

Phil hangs up, looks to Earl. CU - EARL. He's asleep, uncomfortably.
CAMERA moves inside his chest.

QUICK DISSOLVE TO:

114. INT. EARL'S BODY - THAT MOMENT   114.

    CAMERA roams around a bit, watching the CANCER eat away at Earl's lungs.
    CAMERA MOVES BACKWARDS, pulling out;

QUICK DISSOLVE TO:

115. INT. HOLIDAY INN/BANQUET ROOM - THAT MOMENT   115.

    CAMERA pulls back from Frank, who heads offstage. The AUDIENCE is
    applauding him. The sidekick, DOC takes the mic and makes an
    announcement about the one hour break/snacks served in lobby/etc.

    Frank hops offstage, greets Captain Muffy and Gwenovier;

                    CAPTAIN MUFFY
           Chief, this is Gwenovier from the show,
           "Profiles," for the interview --

                    FRANK
           Hello, hello, I'm a bit out of breath
           from all this work --

                    GWENOVIER
           That's fine. It's nice to meet you.

                    FRANK
           Are we gonna tape some stuff now?

                    GWENOVIER
           If you're up to it, I've got us
           set up in a suite upstairs --

                    FRANK
           You got us a room so quick?

    Frank and Captain Muffy laugh at the joke.

                    FRANK
           I'm kidding of course.

CUT TO:

116.   <u>INT. HOTEL SUITE - MOMENTS LATER</u>   116.

Frank is getting his mic put on, Gwenovier has a small VIDEO CREW
with her. They both get touched up for the interview, Frank's
talking away;

> FRANK
> I swear to fucking-god, I do one-a-my
> seminars, I'm Superaman! I'm Batman!
> I'm like a fucking action hero the way
> I feel afterwards, like I could walk out
> this door, down the street, pick up any fuckin'
> pootie I see that has even one second to stop --

Gwenovier gives a little snap and finger gesture to her CAMERAMAN
to start rolling;

> GWENOVIER
> All it takes is one second?

> FRANK
> Just one look, one hesitation,
> one subtle gesture for me to know --
> And Bing-Bam-Boom I'm away on a
> tangent -- I get so fuckin' amped
> at these seminars and lemme tell you
> why: Because I Am What I Believe.
> I am what I teach, I do as I say,
> I live by these rules as religiously
> as I preach them: And you wanna know
> what? I'm gettin' pussy left, right,
> up, down, center and sideways.

> GWENOVIER
> I'm gonna start rolling --

> FRANK
> -- go, go, go. I'm givin' pearls here.
> And I'll tell you somethin' else:
> I'm not succeding in the bush because
> I'm Frank TJ Mackey. If anything,
> there are women out there that want
> to <u>destroy</u> me -- it makes it twice as
> hard for me, I run into some little
> muffin, knows who I am, knows my schemes
> and plans -- shit, she's gonna wanna
> fuck around, prove to her friends, say,
> "Yaddda-yadda-yadda, I saw that guy, he
> wasn't anything, didn't get me." So me?
> I'm runnin' on full throttle the whole
> fuckin' time. Dodging bullets left and
> right from terrorist blonde beauties.
> But I'll tell you this: The battle of
> the bush is being fought and won by Team
> Mackey. Can I have a cigarette?

> GWENOVIER
> Ok. So, lemme just ask you a couple
> questions to start --

Captain Muffy hands Frank a cigarette, lights it for him.

VIDEO CAMERA'S POV - It's zooms in to close up of Frank. He exhales;

> FRANK
> What do you want to know?

CUT TO:

117.   EXT. SMILING PEANUT BAR - THAT MOMENT   117.

CAMERA BOOMS DOWN and PUSHES IN on Donnie Smith's Honda Accord,
with damaged front end, as it pulls into a parking space.
It's POURING RAIN. (dir.note)

CAMERA lands in close. Donnie sits a moment. He plays his tape,
"Dreams," sings along a bit, pep talks himself, does some deep
breathing, says;

> DONNIE
> Make it happen, make it happen and go,go,go.

He gets out of the car real quick --

CUT TO:

118.   INT. SMILING PEANUT BAR - THAT MOMENT   118.

CAMERA (STEADICAM) pushes in as Donnie enters this dark little bar.
It's not too crowded. He takes off his wet coat, brushes his hair
back a bit and walks to an empty corner table --

Donnie takes his seat and looks over to the bar -- CAMERA swings a 180,
heads away from him -- it moves to the bar area and into:

A young, handsome BARTENDER BRAD (20s) is pouring drinks.

CAMERA picks up with a COCKTAIL WAITRESS (30s) who walks over and
brings us back to Donnie's booth --

> COCKTAIL WAITRESS
> Hello. You're back again, huh?

> DONNIE
> yeah, yes, hi, hello.

> COCKTAIL WAITRESS
> -- can I get you?

> DONNIE
> Diet Coke.

She exits. Donnie lights a cigarette -- CAMERA blends from 24fps
to 40fps -- he looks across the room -- CAMERA swings 180 back towards
the bar and pushes in towards --

Bartender Brad takes the order from the Cocktail Waitress.
He nods, turns from her and smiles to reveal <u>a full set of BRACES</u>.

ANGLE, DONNIE. CAMERA pushes in slow and he smiles, touches his
hand to his mouth.

DONNIE'S POV - The Bartender pours the coke, turns his attention towards
an old-freaky looking Thurston Howell/Truman Capote/Dorothy Parker
type guy (60s) at the end of the bar, who raises his glass, motions as
if to say, "Another one of these, please," while waving some money
and smiling/flirting with Brad the Bartender.

Donnie's face drops. CAMERA DOLLIES back a little bit and blends from
40fps to 24fps. The Cocktail Waitress arrives back;

                    COCKTAIL WAITRESS
          Diet Coke.

                    DONNIE
          I want a shot of tequila too.

                    COCKTAIL WAITRESS
          -- what kind?

                    DONNIE
          It doesn't matter.

Donnie GLARES across the bar at BRAD and THURSTON as they flirt.

                                                  CUT TO:

119. <u>INT. TELEVISION STUDIO/HALLWAYS - THAT MOMENT</u>   119.

CAMERA leads/follows the kids from the show; STANLEY, RICHARD
(overweight, 12) and JULIA (child-star-type 11). They're led by
CYNTHIA, down the corridors towards the main set --

                    JULIA
          Do you still have to do homework?

                    RICHARD
          Not as much as I used to. Ever since
          we started, I haven't really gone in to
          school that much because I've been getting
          more and more auditions --

                    STANLEY
          I don't have regular classes anymore.

                    RICHARD
          What do you do?

                    STANLEY
They just let me have my own study-time,
my own reading time in the library.

                    RICHARD
That's pretty cool.

                    JULIA
Do you have an agent, Stanley?

                    STANLEY
No.

                    JULIA
You should get one, I'm serious,
you could get a lot of stuff out of this --

                    STANLEY
Like what?

                    RICHARD
What do you mean, "like what?"
-- you could get endorsments and shit --

                    CYNTHIA
-- Richard.

                    RICHARD
Bite it, Cynthia. You could get free
things from people that want you to
endorse their products.

                    JULIA
Commercials, a sitcom, an MOW or something.

                    STANLEY
What's MOW?

                    JULIA
Movie Of The Week. I went up for
one this morning with Alan Thicke
and Corey Haim --

                    RICHARD
Was it a call back?

                    JULIA
No. But I probably will get a call back.

                    RICHARD
If we beat the record, you might get
a call back --

                    JULIA
I'll get it because I'm a good actress, Richard.

                         RICHARD
          Saucy-saucy.

                         CYNTHIA
          C'mon guys, settle down --

                         STANLEY
          Cynthia?

                         CYNTHIA
          What?

                         STANLEY
          How much time do we have?

                         CYNTHIA
          Not enough, what do you want?

                         STANLEY
          I should maybe go to the bathroom.

                         CYNTHIA
          Can you hold it?

                         STANLEY
          I don't know.

                         CYNTHIA
          Just hold it, you'll be fine.

They arrive and enter onto the stage -- CAMERA swings around, branches
away from them and BOOMS UP to reveal the set;

There is a LIVE STUDIO AUDIENCE that's being settled into their seats.

It's a three-camera set up with a FLOOR DIRECTOR roaming around,
shouting orders, etc.

There's a spot for the announcer, an old-pro named DICK JENNINGS (60s)
Dick is in the middle of doing bad-comedy warm up for the studio
audience. He's had a few drinks, etc.

The STAGE itself is a cross between JEAPORDY/NEWLEYWED GAME/PRICE IS
RIGHT. There's a podium for Jimmy Gator. One panel holds "The Kids,"
and one panel holds, "The Adults." There are chaser-lights all around
and some of the design feels left over from the early days of the show.

CAMERA hangs out with the KIDS as they are ushered into their panel,
which at this moment faces away from the audience and is behind a
curtain. Julia turns her head, sees something:

                         JULIA
          Here they come --

The ADULT CHALLENGERS are brought out by an assistant type and loaded
into their panel. The Adult Challengers are:

Black woman named MIM MacNEAL(40s)
White guy with glasses TODD GERONIMO (20s)
Puerto Rican guy named LUIS GUZMAN (40s)

The Adults give a couple small glares over to the Kids.

                    RICHARD (sotto)
          Yeah, yeah, yeah, keep lookin'
          tough-old folks.

                    STANLEY
          They look pretty smart, I think.

                    JULIA
          No they don't --

                    RICHARD
          What are they gonna do -- beat us?

                    STANLEY
          Maybe.

                    JULIA
          We're not going out two days before
          we set the record, it's not gonna happen.

                    RICHARD
          When they want us done, they'll call
          in the Harvard S.W.A.T team or some shit.

CAMERA lands in CU on Stanley. HOLD. BEAT. THEN:

                                             CUT TO:

120. INT. JIMMY'S OFFICE - THAT MOMENT   120.

Jimmy and a woman named PAULA (30s) sit in his office. SLOW DOLLY IN
ON EACH thru scene;

                    JIMMY
          You look great.

BEAT.

                    PAULA
          What the fuck is this, Jimmy?

                    JIMMY
          ...you know...

                    PAULA
          Did your wife find out?

                    JIMMY
          No.

                          PAULA
          Then what?

                          JIMMY
          It's just...too late for me to be
          fuckin' around. I gotta stop.
          I gotta clean my brain of all the
          shit I've done that I shouldn't have done --

                          PAULA
          -- that you shouldn't have done?
          That you regret, what? This? What's
          this? Fuck, man, c'mon. Treat me
          like an asshole, but treat me like
          an asshole.

                          JIMMY
          I don't wanna have to lie to anyone.
          I don't want to hurt anyone else, anymore.

She doesn't respond. BEAT. THEN:

                          JIMMY
          Thirty fuckin' years I've been with
          Rose, don't -- y'know -- with
          this, and I know what you think --

                          PAULA
          All your other fluzzies?

                          JIMMY
          Yeah. Yes.

                          PAULA
          You're making me feel so dirty and shitty.
          I feel like a big piece of shit right now.

BEAT.

                          PAULA
          Are you gonna tell her what you've done?

                          JIMMY
          Yes.

                          PAULA
          Will you say my name?

                          JIMMY
          If she asks me any question I want
          to tell her. I want to tell her
          everything I've done.

                          PAULA
          Well can you do me one favor and
          don't do that.

Jimmy doesn't answer.

> PAULA
> Come and tell me it's over and I'll
> walk away, Jimmy. I've fucked you
> behind your wife's back for three
> years, and you've fucked teenage girls
> behind mine for the same amount of
> time -- I'll walk away, you need something
> for your life, for your conscience,
> but don't put me in the middle --

> JIMMY
> I won't.

> PAULA
> What happend to you?

> JIMMY
> I got in trouble at school.

She stands and walks over to him, moves to give him a hug.

> PAULA
> Are you ok?

> JIMMY
> Fuck no.

There's a KNOCK at the door and then it's opened by BURT RAMSEY (60s)
He's the producer of the show; (WHIP TO HIM)

> BURT
> Ready to run. Paula.

> PAULA
> Burt.

Jimmy takes a quick shot, moves to Paula, gives her a tap on the
cheek and says;

> JIMMY (to Paula)
> You're a good one arentcha?

> CUT TO:

121.   INT. TELEVISION STUDIO/HALLWAY - MOMENTS LATER   121.

Burt and Jimmy walking and talking (STEADICAM);

                              BURT
                    You smell like trouble --

                              JIMMY
                    I'm fuckin' hammered, Burt.

                              BURT
                    You ok?

                              JIMMY
                    ooohhhhhh no.

                              BURT
                         (re: cards)
                    Good. You look these over?

                              JIMMY
                    It's been the same fuckin' thing for
                    thirty years, Burt --

                              BURT
                    These adults are tough enough, I think
                    you'll be surprised -- the Mexican's
                    a bit of a question mark --

Jimmy FALLS STRAIGHT TO THE FLOOR.

                              BURT
                    Fuck - fuck - fuck - Jimmy -

                                                           CUT TO:

122.   INT. CLAUDIA'S APARTMENT - THAT MOMENT. **   122.

Claudia finishes throwing her drugs into a dirty t-shirt and throwing
that dirty t-shirt into her laundry basket. Jim Kurring bangs away at
the door.

                              JIM KURRING (OC)
                    OPEN THE DOOR.

                              CLAUDIA
                    I'm coming!

She runs towards the door, takes a small fall on the way, recovers,
opens up;

                              CLAUIDA
                    Yeah. Hi. Hello.

REVERSE, CLOSE UP - JIM KURRING - 40fps.
CAMERA pushes in on him a little bit at his first sight of Claudia.

                    JIM KURRING
          ...yeah...

                    CLAUDIA
          I'm sorry, I had to get dressed.

Wider Angle reveals Jim Kurring, in a bit of a daze, standing with
his BILLY CLUB removed and at the ready. He stands back...they have
SHOUT above the music;

                    JIM KURRING
          -- you the resident here?

                    CLAUIDA
          Yes.

                    JIM KURRING
          You alone in there?

                    CLAUDIA
          Yes.

                    JIM KURRING
          No one else in there with you?

                    CLAUIDA
          No, what's wrong?

                    JIM KURRING
          You mind if I come in, check things?

                    CLAUDIA
          For what?

                    JIM KURRING
          Ok. For one thing, we're gonna
          need to turn that music down so
          we can talk, ok?

                    CLAUDIA
          I'm sorry.

She turns and Jim Kurring moves to replace his billy club, but misses
the holster and it FALLS straight to the floor, slides down the steps --

Claudia turns the music down, turns back and sees that he is gone.

Jim Kurring grabs his billy club from the bottom of the steps and
bounces back up and into the apartment as if nothing happend;

                    JIM KURRING
You live alone?

                    CLAUIDA
Yes.

                    JIM KURRING
What's your name?

                    CLAUIDA
Claudia.

                    JIM KURRING
Claudia What?

                    CLAUDIA
Wilson.

                    JIM KURRING
Ok. Claudia Wilson: You tryin' to go deaf?

                    CLAUDIA
What?

                    JIM KURRING
Did you hear what I said?

                    CLAUDIA
Yeah, but I don't know --

                    JIM KURRING
-- listenin' to that music so loud:
You Tryin' To Damage Your Ears?

                    CLAUDIA
No.

                    JIM KURRING
Well if you keep listenin' to the
music that loud you're not only
gonna damage your ears but your
neighbors ears.

                    CLAUDIA
I didn't realize it was that loud.

                    JIM KURRING
And that could be the sign of a damaged
ear drum, you understand?

                    CLAUDIA
Yeah.

                    JIM KURRING
You got the TV on too, keep those
on at that same time usually?

                              CALUDIA
          I don't know -- I mean. What is this?

                              JIM KURRING
          Have you been drinkin' today,
          doin' some drugs?

                              CLAUDIA
          No.

                              JIM KURRING
          I got a call of a disturbance, screaming
          and yelling, loud music. Has there been
          some screaming and yelling?

                              CLAUDIA
          Yes. I had someone come to my door,
          someone I didn't want here and I told them
          to leave -- so -- it's no big deal.
          They left. I'm sorry.

                              JIM KURRING
          Was it a boyfriend of yours?

                              CLAUDIA
          No.

                              JIM KURRING
          You don't have a boyfriend?

                              CLAUDIA
          No.

                              JIM KURRING
          Who was it?

                              CLAUDIA
          I was...he's gone...I mean it's not.
          It's over, y'know --

Jim Kurring snoops a bit, she rubs her nose, nervous. Jim Kurring
heads closer to bedroom --

                              JIM KURRING
          You mind if I check things back here?

                              CLAUDIA
          It's fine.

Jim Kurring heads into the bedroom, looks around, stands by the
laundry basket --

                              CLAUDIA
          What are you looking for?

                    JIM KURRING
          Claudia: Why don't you let me
          handle the questions and you handle
          the answers, ok?

                    CLAUDIA
          ok.

                    JIM KURRING
          You just move in here?

                    CLAUDIA
          About two years ago.

                    JIM KURRING
          Bit messy.

                    CLAUDIA
          Yeah.

                    JIM KURRING
          I'm a bit of a slob myself.

                    CLAUDIA
          Yeah.

                    JIM KURRING
          You and your boyfriend have a party
          last night?

                    CLAUDIA
          I don't have a boyfriend.

BEAT. Jim Kurring looks at Claudia and she looks back. HOLD.

                                        CUT TO:

123.   INT. SMILING PEANUT BAR - THAT MOMENT.   123.

Donnie sits in his booth after two tequila's. He's slightly fucked up.
He gets up, stumbles over to the bar and takes a seat uncomfortably
close to Thurston, who's now holding court among three or four other
PATRONS. Brad the Bartender is washing glasses, keeps half an eye on
things...Donnie to Thurston;

                    DONNIE
          You look like you've got money
          in your pocket.

                    THURSTON
          Maybe I'm just happy to see my
          friend, Brad there.

The PATRONS laugh a bit, Brad nods, Donnie doesn't laugh or look
anywhere but Thurston;

                    DONNIE
          Just throw some money around.
          Money, money, money.

                    THURSTON
          This sounds threatening.

                    DONNIE
          Do you have love in your heart?

                    THURSTON
          I have love all over. I even have
          love for you, friend.

                    DONNIE
          Is it real love?

                    THURSTON
          Well --

                    DONNIE
          -- the kind of love that makes you feel
          that intagible joy. Pit of your stomach.
          Like a bucket of acid and nerves running
          around and making you hurt and happy and
          all over you're head over heels....?

                    THURSTON
          Well you lost me with the last couple
          of cocktail words spoken, m'boy, but
          I believe it's that sort of love.
          Sounds nice to me.

                    DONNIE
          I have love.

                    THURSTON
          A very chatty-kind, you do, indeed, it seems.

                    DONNIE
          No. I mean, I'm telling you:
          I'm telling you that I have love.

                    THURSTON
          And I'm listening avidly, fellow.

                    DONNIE
          My name is Donnie Smith and I have
          lot's of love to give.

     BEAT.

                                        CUT TO:

124.   EXT. SHERMAN OAKS PHARMACY - THAT MOMENT   124.

         CAMERA holds wide angle on a pharmacy. It's still POURING RAIN.
         LINDA'S MERCEDES comes driving real fast into FRAME and slams it's
         brakes on, parks.

                                                              CUT TO:

125.   INT. SHERMAN OAKS PHARMACY - THAT MOMENT.   125.

         CAMERA pushes in on Linda as she enters, heads to the back for
         the perscription counter and a YOUNG PHARMACY KID behind the counter;

                         YOUNG PHARMACY KID
                     Hello.

                              LINDA
                     Hi.

         She hands over her three perscriptions. The Young Pharmacy Kid takes a
         long look at them, gives her a suspicious glance.

                         YOUNG PHARMACY KID
                     Wow. Lot-o-stuff here, huh?

         Linda nods. He goes to the back to the old-guy PHARMACIST and says
         a few words, points to Linda. Another suspicious look or
         two from the both of them...the PHARMACIST guy gets on the phone.

         ANGLE, LINDA. SLOW ZOOM IN. Blend from 24fps to 40fps.
         She just holds her breath and temper, looks down.

                                                              CUT TO:

126.   INT. TELEVISION STUDIO/STAGE - THAT MOMENT   126.

         CAMERA PUSHES in on a oversized STOPWATCH and the FLOOR DIRECTOR nearby;

                         FLOOR DIRECTOR
                     Thirty Seconds.

         CAMERA with the announcer DICK JENNINGS who walks to his post.

         CAMERA with the ADULT CHALLENGERS who talk a bit amongst themselves,
         CAMERA moves over to the KIDS. Richard looks over to Stanley;

                              RICHARD
                     The fuck is wrong with you?

                              STANLEY
                     I gotta go to the bathroom.

                              JULIA
                     Jesus Christ, Stanley.

                                                              CUT TO:

127.   <u>INT. PARENT'S GREEN ROOM - THAT MOMENT</u>   127.

CAMERA pushes in on the Parents;

>   RICK
> -- you cannot do that. You have to
> tone it. Don't be real agressive, just
> subtely abusive. You must say, "No.
> You are not leaving this house until
> that room is cleaned."

>   JULIA'S MOM
> Julia's room is the same way.

>   JULIA'S DAD
> Like a pig sty.   But it's the outfits
> that we're getting into now --

>   JULIA'S MOM
> You should have seen what she had
> on walking out the door --

>   JULIA'S DAD
> -- all dolled up.

>   JULIA'S MOM
> I said: "No. No. No. We are not
> going to a fashion show. You are
> going to school."

>   RICHARD'S MOM
> -- It's not a fashion show, it's school.

>   JULIA'S MOM
> It is <u>not</u> a fashion show.

CAMERA lands over on Rick, who's flipping through a brocheure
for a new MERCEDES.

>   RICK
> Let's make some fuckin' money, folks.

They all look to the Monitor.

                                              WHIP TO:

128.   INT. TELEVISION STUDIO/STAGE - THAT MOMENT   128.

CAMERA pushes in on JIMMY and BURT, behind the curtain. Jimmy drunk;

                         BURT
               You okay? huh? Jimmy?

                         JIMMY
               And the book says: "We may by through with
               the past, but the past ain't through with us."

                         BURT
               C'mon, Jimmy, snap up, snap up --

                         JIMMY
               In my sleep, Burt.

CAMERA pushes in on the FLOOR DIRECTOR as he counts off;

                         FLOOR DIRECTOR
               And...three...two...one....

He points his finger...CAMERA WHIPS over to DICK JENNINGS who says:

                         DICK JENNINGS
               Live from Burbank, California it's:
               "What Do Kids Know?"

CAMERA WHIPS RT. to the APPLAUSE signs, then WHIPS again to the AUDIENCE
that cheers, then WHIPS again to see the "What Do Kids Know?" sign as it
lowers over the stage. The THEME MUSIC kicks in and we're away;

Director's Note: We move between their TV CAMERA'S POV and our 35mm
CAMERA POV.

                         DICK JENNINGS (VO)
               Going into our thirty-third year on the air,
               it's America's longest running quiz show and
               the place where three kids get to challenge
               three adults and in the end see who's boss!

"The Kids" panel as it turns towards the Audience and lights up.

                         DICK JENNINGS (VO)
               Moving towards their eighth consecutive
               week as champions we have the kids:
               Richard, Julia and Stanley.

"The Adults" panel turns towards the audience and lights up.

                         DICK JENNINGS (VO)
               And our new adult challengers
               today are Todd, Luis, and Mim.

129.   ANGLE - BACKSTAGE - THAT MOMENT   129.
       Jimmy stands behind the curtain. CAMERA DOLLIES IN on his back. He
       holds his head down.

                          DICK JENNINGS (VO)
                Please say hello and welcome
                to the always ready host of
                "What Do Kids Know?" Your favorite:
                and my boss: Jimmy Gator!

       The curtain opens -- a spotlight SHINES DIRECTLY INTO CAMERA --
       Jimmy enters the stage.

                                            CUT TO:

130.   INT. EARL'S HOUSE - LIVING ROOM - THAT MOMENT   Sequence D   130.

       CAMERA pulls back from the TELEVISION and WHIPS to Phil watching.
       The CAMERA pushes past him and over to Earl, asleep in the bed.

       Jimmy Gator's opening bit continues OC over the following;

                         JIMMY GATOR (OC)
                Back again, again, again! I'm Jimmy Gator
                and believe it or not we are at the end
                of week seven, going towards eight for these
                three incredible kids --

                                       WHIP TO:

131.   INT. HOLIDAY INN SUITE - THAT MOMENT   131.

       CAMERA pushes in on Frank who's babbling away about "Seduce and
       Destroy," (Director's Note) then WHIP over to Gwenovier and her video
       crew as they all listen.

                         JIMMY GATOR (OC)
                -- who hello-hello, are just two days and
                two games from the "What Do Kids Now?" record
                for the longest winning streak in this shows
                thirty three year history --

                                       WHIP TO:

132.   INT. CLAUDIA'S APARTMENT - THAT MOMENT   132.

       CAMERA pushes in on Jim Kurring then WHIP to Claudia as they
       talk and he snoops, etc. (Director's Note: Ref. note pages)

                         JIMMY GATOR (OC)
                We're endorsed by the PTA and the
                North American Teacher's Foundation
                and we are try and do our best to hold
                standards high -- that's why we're the
                longest running quiz show in television
                history --

WHIP TO:

133. <u>INT. SMILING PEANUT - THAT MOMENT</u>   133.

CAMERA WHIPS from the TELEVISION above the bar which is playing
the quiz show and pushes over Donnie, staring at the monitor.
He shots another Tequila.

> JIMMY GATOR (OC)
> And let me say: With these three kids
> right here, I wouldn't be surprised if
> we've got a while to go, but today is
> a dangerous day --

WHIP TO:

134. <u>INT. SHERMAN OAKS PHARMACY - THAT MOMENT</u>   134.

CAMERA whips a ZOOMS in slow on Linda, holding her temper as the
Pharamcy guy suspiciously glance at her and make a call or two to
check on her perscriptions.

> JIMMY GATOR (OC)
> -- for I have met the three adult challengers
> backstage and they <u>are</u> quite a challenge
> for our youngsters -- SO LET'S GET THIS GAME
> OFF AND AWAY, EH?

WHIP TO:

135. <u>INT. JIMMY GATOR'S HOUSE - THAT MOMENT</u>   135.

CAMERA pushes in on ROSE as she watches her husband.

> JIMMY GATOR (OC)
> Let's jump right in, quick re-cap
> for those who don't know: Round One.
> Three Categories.

WHIP TO:

136. <u>INT. POLICE STATION - THAT MOMENT</u>   136*

CAMERA pushes in on MARCIE who's being processed and finger printed/
questioned. Two DETECTIVES nearby/OC throughout. A small   *
portable TELEVISION in the b.g., plays the show.

> DETECTIVE #1   *
> We want to know where your Son is, Marcie.   *
>
> DETECTIVE #2   *
> Jerome Samuel Hall. Did he have a fight   *
> with your husband? Where they fighting?   *
>
> DETECTIVE #1   *
> Maybe they had a fight, maybe it was an accident.   *
> Maybe it was an accident?   *

                        DETECTIVE #3   *
            Help him out, and help us get there   *
            before something else --   *

                        DETECTIVE #2   *
            Help us help your son, Marcie.   *

                                              WHIP TO:

137. INT. NORTH HOLLYWOOD APARTMENT - THAT MOMENT   137*

      CAMERA pushes in on the little kid, DIXON, who gave Jim Kurring
      the rap before. Sitting around with the friends who we saw
      earlier in one of their apartments. They're glued to the   *
      TELEVISION that plays the show.   *

      The BACK OF A FIGURE (black male) enters FRAME and taps Dixon's
      shoulder with a "let's go" motion and Dixon gets up and follows...
      CAMERA keeps going in towards the television --

                        JIMMY GATOR (OC)
            Steals are OK, escelating point scale
            from 25 to 250 so Let's Go Categories!

                                              WHIP TO:

138. INT. EARL'S HOUSE - LIVING ROOM - THAT MOMENT   138.

      CAMERA pushes in profile on PHIL. The DOORBELL RINGS and he jumps.
      The DOGS go crazy barking. Phil heads for the door, opens up.
      It's the PINK DOT GUY.

                        PHIL
                  Hi.

                        PINK DOT GUY
            $15.24.

139. ANGLE, EARL'S TELEVISION - THAT MOMENT.   139.
      A small bank of VIDEO MONITORS pops up and displays some categories;

                        JIMMY GATOR
            We have, "Authors" "The Deep Blue"
            and "Chaos vs. Superstring"

140. ANGLE, PHIL   140.
      He hands over a twenty dollar bill to the Pink Dot Guy. The DOGS
      go crazy barking and he tries to calm them down.

141. ANGLE, EARL'S TELEVISION   141.
      Jimmy behind the podium.

                        JIMMY GATOR
            Adults won a coin toss backstage and
            they'll have first choice: Todd.

                          TODD
              I'll take "Authors," Jimmy.

142.   ANGLE, PHIL   142.
       He dumps the bag out and goes straight for the Porno Magazines.
       He flips to the back of one, scanning quickly for something --
       XCU, his finger moves down the page, arrives at an AD for "Seduce and
       Destroy" that has a picture of Frank with a girl in a bikini and
       says, "Get Laid Now."

                          PHIL
              Got it.

143.   ANGLE, EARL'S TELEVISION - THAT MOMENT   143.
       Jimmy reads from his index cards. (tv slow zoom in)

                          JIMMY GATOR
              First question for 25. This
              female author's most famous work
              "O! Pioneers" --

144.   ANGLE, PHIL - THAT MOMENT   144.
       CAMERA pushes in super-quick as Phil picks up the phone and
       starts to dial the 1-800 number listed in the porno magazine.

                                                        CUT TO:

145.   INT. GAME SHOW STAGE - THAT MOMENT   145.

       CAMERA does a super fast WHIP and DOLLY in to STANLEY as he presses
       his buzzer:

                          STANLEY
              Willa Cather.

       CAMERA PUSHES IN ON JIMMY.

                          JIMMY
              For 25. Best known for the "tragedy and
              blood" genre, this author-playwright --

       CAMERA WHIPS and PUSHES IN ON STANLEY.

                          STANLEY (buzzes)
              Thomas Kyd.

                          JIMMY
              This French playwright and actor joined
              the Bejart troupe of actors --

                          STANLEY (buzzes)
              Moliere.

                          JIMMY
              I'm gonna need a full name, Stanley.

STANLEY
Jean Baptiste Poquelin Moliere.

CAMERA WHIPS to the adults who instantly look un-happy:

LUIS (to Todd)
What the fuck is this?

CUT TO:

146.   INT. PARENTS GREEN ROOM - THAT MOMENT   146.

CAMERA pushes in on Rick as he sits back and smiles.

RICK
My little fucker -- I have no idea where
he gets this stuff.

CUT TO:

147.   INT. VAN NUYS OFFICE SPACE - THAT MOMENT   147.

CAMERA pushes in on a geek named CHAD (20s) who answers a phone.
He has a small computer in front of him. This is the bolier-room-
answering-phones-for-orders headquarters for "Seduce and Destroy."

Five or six other guys sit around desks, answering phones and working
computers, etc. There are posters of Frank all around and some
maps and some charts, etc.

CHAD (into phone)
"Seduce and Destroy," thisz Chad,
can I have your home phone number with
area code, please?

CUT TO:

148.   INT. EARL'S HOUSE - KITCHEN - THAT MOMENT   148.

CAMERA pushes in on Phil, on the phone.

PHIL
Hi, hello, great. This is Seduce and Destroy?

CHAD
It is. Can I have your home phone number
with area code?

PHIL
Well I don't want to order anything, you see.
I have a situation, a situation just come
up that's really pretty serious and I'm
not sure who I should talk to or
what I should do but could you maybe
put me in touch with the right person
if I explain myself?

                              CHAD
                    I'm really only equipped to take orders --

                              PHIL
                    Well can you connect me to someone else?

                              CHAD
                    Well what's the situation?

                              PHIL
                    Well, ok. Lemme see how I explain
                    this without it seeming kinda crazy,
                    but here go: I'm, my name is Phil
                    Parma and I work for a man named
                    Earl Partridge -- Mr. Earl Partidge.
                    I'm his nurse. He's a very sick man.
                    He's a dying man and he's sick and he's
                    asked me to help him, to help him find
                    his son -- Hello? Are you there, hello?

                              CHAD
                    I'm here, I'm listening.

                              PHIL
                    OK. See: Frank TJ Macky is Earl
                    Partridge's son....

                                                        CUT TO:

149.   INT. HOLIDAY INN SUITE - THAT MOMENT   149.

      Frank and Gwenovier doing the interview;

                              GWEN
                    Where are you from originally?

                              FRANK
                    Around here.

                              GWEN
                    the valley?

                              FRANK
                    Hollywood, mainly.

                              GWEN
                    And what did your parents do?

                              FRANK
                    My father worked in televison.
                    My mother -- this is gonna sound
                    silly to you -- she was a librarian.

                              GWEN
                    Why does that sound silly?

                              FRANK

Well I guess it doesn't.

                    GWEN
Does you mother still work?

                    FRANK
She's retired.

                    GWEN
Are you close?

                    FRANK
She's my mother.

                    GWEN
What does she say about, "Seduce
and Destroy."

                    FRANK
"Go Get 'Em, Honey."

                    GWEN
And your father?

                    FRANK
He passed away.

                    GWEN
I'm sorry.

                    FRANK
people die.

                    GWEN
I wouldn'tve asked --

                    FRANK
Not a problem.

                    GWEN
And you ended up at UC Berkely --

                    FRANK
From '84 to '89.

                    GWEN
Psychology major?

                    FRANK
Right.

                    GWEN
Do you have your masters?

                    FRANK
...this close...

                              GWEN
                        In five years?

He winks and clicks his teeth.

                              FRANK
                    Muffy, can I get another ciggy?

                                                        CUT TO:

150.   INT. PHARMACY - THAT MOMENT   150.

The YOUNG PHARMACY KID is stacking some stuff away while waiting
for the PHARMACIST to finish filling the perscription.

                        YOUNG PHARMACY KID
                    Cats and Dogs out there, huh?

                              LINDA
                    mmmhmm.

                        YOUNG PHARMACY KID
                    Must have alot goin' on for all that
                    stuff you got back there, eh? You could
                    have quite a party all that stuff....

Linda looks down. HOLD. BEAT. THEN:

                        YOUNG PHARMACY KID
                    You been on Prozac long? Dexadrine?

                              LINDA
                    ...I don't....

                        YOUNG PHARAMCY KID
                    Interesting drugs. Dexadrine's basically
                    speed in a pill. Y'know? But I guess
                    a lot of doctors are balancing out
                    the prozac with the dexadrine, eh?
                    That Liquid Morphine'll knock you down,
                    out, around, up and down someone's
                    not careful.....can't mix those up, y'know...
                    ...Must have a lot goin' in your life for
                    all that stuff there.

The Older Pharamacist DINGS his bell and the Young Pharmacy Kid
gets the bag and starts to ring it up. SLOW ZOOM IN ON LINDA as
he babbles away;

                        YOUNG PHARAMCY KID (OC)
                    Strong, strong stuff here, boy...wow....
                    What exactly you have wrong, you need this stuff?

LINDA snaps. She starts to tremble and cry and build --

                    LINDA
          You motherfucker...you motherfucker....
          YOU FUCKING ASSHOLE, WHO THE FUCK ARE YOU?
          WHO THE FUCK DO YOU THINK YOU ARE?

                 YOUNG PHARMACY KID
          -- what-what-what, ma'am -- I --

                    LINDA
          I COME IN HERE - YOU DON'T KNOW,
          YOU DON'T KNOW WHO THE FUCK I AM
          OR WHAT MY LIFE IS AND YOU HAVE THE
          FUCKING BALLS, THE INDECENCY TO ASK
          ME A QUESTION ABOUT MY LIFE --

Linda PUSHES a large DISPLAY over on it's side, SMASHES things on the
counter, throws things around, basically goes nuts. The Older
Pharamacist comes rushing to the front to try and calm things --

                 OLDER PHARMACIST
          Please, lady, why don't you just calm down --

                    LINDA
          And FUCK YOU TOO. Don't you call me "lady."
          I come in with these things, I give it
          over to you, you doubt, you make your
          phone calls, check on me, look suspicious,
          ask questions, "I'm sick." I HAVE SICKNESS
          ALL AROUND ME AND YOU FUCKING ASK ME MY LIFE?
          WHAT'S WRONG? HAVE YOU SEEN DEATH IN YOUR BED
          IN YOUR HOUSE? And where is your fucking
          decency? That I'm asked questions "WHAT'S WRONG?"
          You suck my dick, that's what's wrong and you,
          you fucking call me "lady." You SHAME ON YOU.
          SHAME ON YOU. SHAME ON BOTH OF YOU.

She THROWS a crumpled STACK OF MONEY at them both, grabs the
PERSCRIPTION and heads for the door --

                                                    CUT TO:

151. INT. LINDA'S MERCEDS - MOMENTS LATER   151.

     She slams the door. She's shaking and crying.

     CU - Pharmacy bag ripped open.
     CU - Bottle cap of Dexadrine popped off.
     CU - Linda's mouth as she swallows back the pills.

                                                    CUT TO:

152. EXT. PHARMACY/STREET - THAT MOMENT   152.

     CAMERA BOOMS down on her Mercedes as it peel out and off --

                                                    CUT TO:

153.   <u>INT. EARL'S HOUSE/VAN NUYS OFFICE SPACE - THAT MOMENT</u>   153.

Continue w/intercut between Phil and Chad on the phone. BEAT, THEN:

                          CHAD
          Why don't they have the same last name?
          They don't have the same last name.

                          PHIL
          I know -- and I can't really explain that,
          but I have a feeling there's something,
          some situation between them, like they don't
          really know each other much or well, something
          like they don't talk much anymore --

                          CHAD
          Uh-huh.

                          PHIL
          Does this sound weird?

                          CHAD
          Well I'm not sure why you're calling me.

                          PHIL
          There's no number for Frank in any
          of Earl's stuff and he's pretty out
          of it -- I mean, like I said, he's
          dying, y'know. Dying of Cancer.

                          CHAD
          What kind of Cancer?

                          PHIL
          Brain and Lung.

                          CHAD
          My mother had breast cancer.

                          PHIL
          It's rough. I'm sorry, did she make it?

                          CHAD
          Oh, she's fine.

                          PHIL
          Oh that's good.

                          CHAD
          It was scary though.

                          PHIL
          It's a helluva disease.

                          CHAD
          Sure is. So why call me?

CAMERA pushes in on Earl, asleep in the bed, breathing becomes
a bit irregular. HOLD on him. 30fps.

                    PHIL
          I know this all seems silly.
          I know that maybe I sound ridiculous,
          like maybe this is the scene of the
          movie where the guy is trying to get
          ahold of the long-lost son, but this
          is that scene. Y'know? I think they
          have those scenes in movies because they're
          true, because they really happen.
          And you gotta believe me: This is really
          happening. I mean, I can give you my
          phone number and you can call me back
          if you wanna check with whoever you can check
          this with, but don't leave me hanging on this --
          please -- please. See: See:
          See this is the scene of the movie where
          you help me out --

                                              CUT TO:

154. INT. HOLIDAY INN SUITE - THAT MOMENT   154.

Frank and Gwenovier doing the interview, CAMERA DOLLIES IN SLOW ON EACH:

                    GWENOVIER
          -- see, I thought you grew up here
          in the valley --

                    FRANK
          Like I said, yeah --

                    GWEN
          And you went to Van Nuys High, right?

                    FRANK
          I don't how much I went -- but I was
          enrolled. I was such a loser back then.
          I was -- misguided, pathetic -- I was very fat.
          Not even close to what I am today.
          Not the Frank TJ Mackey you're eager to talk
          to because I was swimming in what was as
          opposed to I wanted.

                    GWEN
          Where does that name come from?

                    FRANK
          What name? My name?

                    GWEN
          It's not your given name, right?

                    FRANK
My mother's name, actually.
Good question. You've done you're research.

                    GWEN
And "Frank?"

                    FRANK
"Frank" was my mother's father.

                    GWEN
Ok. That's why. I had trouble locating
your school records at Berkely and UCLA.
Your name change -- they had no official
enrollment --

                    FRANK
Oh, yeah. No, no, no. They wouldn't --

                    GWEN
They wouldn't?

                    FRANK
no, no, no. Certainly not. I wasn't
officialy enrolled, that's right.
Was that unclear?

                    GWEN
Kind of.

                    FRANK
I wouldn't want that to be misunderstood:
My enrollment was totally unoffical because
I was, sadly, unable to afford tuition up
there. But there were three wonderful men
who were kind enough to let me sit in on
their classes, and they're names are:
Macready, Horn and Langtree among others.
I was completely independent financially,
and like I said: One Sad Sack A Shit.
So what we're looking at here is a true
rags to riches story and I think that's
what most people respond to in "Seduce,"
And At The End Of The Day? Hey -- it may not
even be about picking up chicks and sticking your
cock in it -- it's about finding What You Can Be
In This World. Defining It. Controling It and
saying: I will take what is mine. You just happen
to get a blow job out of it, then hey-what-the-fuck-
why-not? he.he.he.

                                        CUT TO:

155. INT. GAME SHOW SET - THAT MOMENT.   155.

        CAMERA pushes in on Jimmy Gator. A BELL is ringing.

                        JIMMY GATOR
                End of Round One! Excellent work ladies
                and germs, let's see the scores on the boards:
                Kids up a leg with 2025, Adults down a bit
                with 1200. We'll be back for Round Two
                and a Ring-Dang-Do --

        A sudden and LOUD WISHTLE sounds.

                        JIMMY GATOR
                HELLO! Musical Bonus Question before we
                go to break and the lucky team is --

        Jimmy opens an ENVELOPE and reads:

                        JIMMY GATOR
                Kids in the lead and they get a chance
                to pull further and farther ahead -- with
                the following secret bonus musical question:
                I will read you a line from an opera
                and you are to give me the same line
                in the language in which the opera
                was originaly written and for a bonus
                25 you can sing it. Here's the line:
                "*Love is a rebellious bird that nobody
                 can tame, and it's all in vain to call it,
                 if it chooses to refuse.*"

        CAMERA PANS and DOLLIES over to the KIDS and moves in close on Stanley;

                        STANELY
                Well that was..uh..in French...and that
                was in the opera, "Carmen." And that
                goes...um...
                        (sings)
                *L'amour est un oiseau rebelle
                Que nul ne peut apprivoiser,
                Et c'est bien en vain qu'on l'appelle,
                S'il lui convient de refuser.*

        The AUDIENCE applauds and the "Carmen," que carries over the
        following scene;

                                                        CUT TO:

156.   INT. CLAUDIA'S APARTMENT - THAT MOMENT   Sequence E   156.

Jim Kurring and Clauida continued. He walks into the KITCHEN area
and sees a pot of coffee.

                         JIM KURRING
               got some coffee brewing, huh?

                         CLAUDIA
               Yeah...it's not...it's been on for a bit --

                         JIM KURRING
               I like iced coffee, generally, but a day
               like this, rain and what not, I enjoy
               a warm cup --

                         CLAUDIA
               -- do you wanna cup?

                         JIM KURRING
               That's great, thank you.

She starts heating/preparing him some coffee.

                         CLAUDIA
               I don't know how fresh it's gonna be --

                         JIM KURRING
               Oh, it'll be fine, I'm sure, Claudia.

                         CLAUDIA
               You take cream or sugar?

                         JIM KURRING
               That'd be fine. So, Claudia, lemme just say,
               so I can get my role of LAPD officer
               out of the way before we enjoy our
               coffee (I never like to talk shop over coffee)
               I'm not gonna write you up or anything,
               I'm not gonna give you a citation here --
               but the real problem we have is that there
               are people around here, people that
               work from their homes, people tryin' to get
               some work done, and if you're listenin' to
               your music that loud: They're incovenienced
               by that. If you had a job you'd probably
               understand, but I see you like listenin'
               to your music and that's fine, you're just
               gonna wanna keep it down at a certain volume,
               maybe memorize what number you see on the
               dial and just always put it to that --
               If it's the middle of the day -- that's
               what I do -- just put it on two and a half
               and that's a good listening level, alright?
               I see you like listenin' to your music loud,
               but, hey, forget about the neighbors, you
               end up damaging your own ears ok?

                        CLAUDIA
          Yeah.

                        JIM KURRING
          Arlight, then. Cheers.

They clink coffee cups. He makes a sour face at the taste;

                        JIM KURRING
          Is this boyfriend bothering you?

                        CLAUDIA
          I don't have a boyfriend.

                        JIM KURRING
          The gentleman who came to the door --

                        CLAUDIA
          -- is not my boyfriend.

                        JIM KURRING
          Many times, in domestic abuse situations
          the young lady is afraid to speak,
          but I have to tell you that, being
          a police officer, I've seen it happen:
          Young woman afraid to speak, next thing
          you know, I'm gettin' a call on the radio,
          I got a 422 --

                        CLAUDIA
          It's not -- what's a 422?

                        JIM KURRING
          It's where situations like these
          lead, Claudia, unless you do something
          about it early, if and when the police
          call and come for help. Now there
          are certain measures you can take --

                        CLAUDIA
          It's not my boyfriend -- and it's
          not anything -- it's over. Really.
          It's not. He won't come back.

                        JIM KURRING
          I don't wanna have to come back here
          in an hour and find that there's
          been another disturbance.

                        CLAUDIA
          You won't. You won't have to.

                        JIM KURRING
          But I wouldn't mind comin' back in
          an hour just to see your pretty face!

They laugh.

                    CLAUDIA
          I'm gonna run to the bathroom real quick.

                    JIM KURRING
          Okey-doke.

She exits. HOLD A BEAT with him.

                                             CUT TO:

157. <u>INT. CLAUDIA'S BEDROOM - MOMENT LATER</u>   157.

      She enters, gets the coke from the laundry basket -- and sets
      some up, snorts it back --

                                             CUT TO:

158. <u>INT. CLAUDIA'S KITCHEN NOOK - THAT MOMENT</u>   158.

      Jim Kurring looks over his shoulder and sees that she's gone.
      He quickly moves to the kitchen and dumps the coffee in the sink
      and then quickly sits back down. End Carmen Que.

                                             CUT TO:

159. <u>INT. GAME SHOW SET - THAT MOMENT</u>   159.

      CAMERA on Jimmy, behind the curtain, during the Commercial Break.
      He takes a shot of Jack Daniels that Mary has brought out for him.

                    JIMMY
          I can't fuckin' do this.

                    MARY
          Are you alright?

                    JIMMY
          Fuck. I think I'm gonna throw up, I think.
                (beat)
          I haven't thrown up since I was
          twenty years old.

Jimmy stumbles over to a corner a bit;

160. ANGLE, GAME SHOW SET.   160.
      Stanley is trying to flag down Cynthia, who stands off in the
      wings, she finally comes over;

                    CYNTHIA
          Stanley, what's the problem?

                    STANLEY
          I have to go to the bathroom, Cynthia.

                    CYNTHIA
          Jesus Christ, Stanley, you can't
          go to the bathroom now. You have
          exactly one minute before we're back
          on the air, this is NOT the time to go
          to the bathroom.

                    STANLEY
          I'm, I need to go, I'm gonna --

                    RICHARD
          Why does this kinda shit always happen, Stanley?

The Adult Challengers look over at the Kids section;

                    LUIS
          What's the problem over there?

                    RICHARD
          Mind yer bussiness --

                    MIM
          Watch your mouth, little man.

                    JULIA
          Why don't you mind your own bussiness?

                    CYNTHIA
          Alright, stop it, cool down, cool it. Please.
          Now: Stanley, you wait until the next commercial break
          and you can go then -- Just Hold It.
                    (to Adults)
          Don't taunt the kids --

                    LUIS
          I just asked what was going on --

                    CYNTHIA
          Don't start trouble, Luis.

161. ANGLE, BACKSTAGE.   161.
      CAMERA pushes in on Jimmy from behind as he throws up in a corner.
      Mary pets his back. He throws up a lot of BLOOD. She snaps fingers
      to a stage hand to bring some towles and a glass of water --

                    OC VOICE
          Two minutes, everyone, we're back in two!

                                        CUT TO:

162.   <u>EXT. LAW OFFICE BUILDING/PARKING STRUCTURE - THAT MOMENT</u>   162.

    Linda's Mercedes pulls out of the rain and to a parking
    structure. CAMERA PUSHES IN real fast, she takes a ticket.
    CU'S (Director's note - three ecu's ticket take green button)

                                                          CUT TO:

163.   <u>INT. LINDA'S MERCEDES - MOMENTS LATER</u>   163.

    CU's on Linda. She pops three or four more DEXADRINE.

                                                          CUT TO:

164.   <u>INT. LAW OFFICE BUILDING/HALLWAY - THAT MOMENT</u>   164.

    Linda off the elevators...CAMERA pushes in with her....

                                                          CUT TO:

165.   <u>INT. LAWYER'S OFFICE - THAT MOMENT</u>   165.

    CAMERA whips around, RECEPTIONIST --

                        LINDA
            I'm Linda Partridge to see Alan Kligman.

                                              CUT TO:

166.   <u>INT. SEDUCE AND DESTROY CONDO - THAT MOMENT</u>   166.

    CAMERA pushes in quick on a young girl named JANET. (This is the GIRL
    from Frank's flashback's.) She answers the phone in this converted
    condo into office headquarters for "Seduce and Destroy." Frank TJ Mackey
    paraphenallia, propoganda and literature all over the place;

                      JANET
          "Seduce and Destroy," thisz Janet.

                                          INTERCUT:

167. <u>INT. VAN NUYS OFFICE SPACE - THAT MOMENT</u>   167.

    CAMERA pushes in on Chad, on the phone;

                          CHAD
                Hey, Janet, it's Chad.

                         JANET
                What's wrong?

                         CHAD
                Nothing's wrong, I just got some
                guy on the phone on my other line,
                he's says he works for this guy,
                this guy who's Frank's father --

                         JANET
                -- no,no,no what is this? who?
                What's this guy's name?

                                          CUT TO:

168. <u>INT. EARL'S HOUSE - THAT MOMENT</u>   168.

    CAMERA (HAND HELD) with Phil, phone to his ear, on hold (we can
    hear Frank's commercial playing on the receiver, ref. notes.)

    Earl is MOANING in pain, the DOGS are barking at the noise.

    Earl continues to hallucinate and remains in major pain, but at
    the same time he's very, very weak. There are moments of stregnth
    that pop and push into him and he's very angry with Phil, continues
    to scream for someone named, "Lily," and generally treats Phil like
    an enemy.

                         EARL
              LILY. FUCK. LIL, PLEASE. LILY.

    Phil moves into the kitchen and gets the bottle of MORPHINE PILLS.
    He drops them, the crash on the floor, picks them all up, except one...

    ...which one of the Mutt Dogs walks over to and eats. Earl SCREAMS.

                                            CUT TO:

169. <u>INT. SEDUCE AND DESTROY CONDO - THAT MOMENT</u>   169.

    CAMERA on Janet on the phone, listens, says:

                         JANET
              ...mmm.hmmm. mmm..hmm. Alright.
                Put him through and lemme see
                what's goin' on --

                                          CUT TO:

170.   INT. VAN NUYS OFFICE SPACE - THAT MOMENT   170.

CAMERA on Chad. He puts Janet on hold and clicks over to Phil:

> CHAD
> Phil, you there?

INTERCUT:

171.   INT. EARL'S HOUSE - THAT MOMENT   171.

CAMERA on Phil, tending to Earl, who moans away. (Bit less pain now.)
The Mutt/Morphine Dog is starting to get a bit wobbly.

> PHIL
> Yeah, hey. Chad.

> CHAD
> Alright, so I'm gonna transfer
> you over to Frank's assitant, Janet
> she's gonna see what she can do --

> PHIL
> Thank you, Chad, and good luck
> to you and your mother --

> CHAD
> Thank you. Thank you very much.

Chad clicks a line and confrences Janet and Phil.

> JANET
> Hello?

> CHAD
> Ok. Janet you have Phil Parma --

> JANET
> Hello, Phil.

> PHIL
> Hi, hi, thank you for taking my call --

CAMERA holds with EARL for a quick BEAT, THEN:

CUT TO:

172.　　**INT. GAME SHOW - BACKSTAGE - THAT MOMENT**　　　172.

Jimmy finishes cleaning himself up and he looks to Mary:

> JIMMY GATOR
> I have Cancer, Mary.

She doesn't know what to say.

> JIMMY GATOR
> I have about two months, I have no time.
> It's in my bones and I don't have a chance.
> And I'm fucked. I had a stroke last week --

> MARY
> ...Jimmy...

The OC call from FLOOR DIRECTOR.

> FLOOR DIRECTOR
> Ten Seconds.

Jimmy walks from behind the curtain to the "Adult" contestants, takes his mark and waits for the countdown -- CAMERA moves over to Stanley who watches Jimmy closely and sees him stumble a bit, recognizes that something is wrong. Floor Director counts, 3-2-1 --

> CUT TO:

173.　　**INT. SMILING PEANUT BAR - THAT MOMENT**　　　Sequence F　　173.

CAMERA pulls back from the TELEVISION above the bar, playing the show. We see Jimmy start to chat w/and do intro's for the adults. (Director's Note: This runs through scene and a complete script is avail/will be shot.)

Donnie and Thurston and the Patrons continued;

> DONNIE
> ....do you know who I am?

> THURSTON
> You're a friend of the family I presume?

> DONNIE
> What? What does that mean?

> THURSTON
> Nothing special, just a spoke in
> the wheel.

> DONNIE
> You talk in rhymes and riddles and
> ra...rub-adub --- but that doesn't mean
> anything to me, see....see...see I used
> to be smart....I'm Quiz Kid Donnie Smith.
> I'm Quiz Kid Donnie Smith from the tv --

                    THURSTON
Might of been before my time.

                    PATRON #1
I remember you. I remember. In the 60's right?

                    DONNIE
I'm Quiz Kid Donnie Smith.

                    THURSTON
...like you said...

                    PATRON #1
Smart Kid! Fuck, yeah, he-he. You got
hit by lightning that one time, right?

                    DONNIE
So what?

                    PATRON #1
I heard about that.

                    PATRON #2
Did it hurt?

                    DONNIE
Yes.

                    THURSTON
But you're alright now, so what's the what?

                    DONNIE
What?

                    THURSTON
That's right.

                    DONNIE
I used to be smart but now I'm just stupid.

                    THURSTON
Brad, dear?

Brad turns and looks:

                    THURSTON
Who was it that said: "A man of genius
has seldom been ruined but by himself."

                    DONNIE
          (to himself)
-- Samuel Johnson.

                    BRAD
I don't know.

Donnie looks up at Brad. Brad smiles with his braces, Donnie looks
away quick --

                    THURSTON
          It was the lovely Samuel Johnson who
          also spoke of a fella "Who was not only
          dull but a cause of dullness in others."

                    DONNIE
          "The" cause of dullness in others --

                    THURSTON
          Picky, picky.

                    DONNIE
          -- and lemme tell you this: Samuel Johnson
          never had his life shit on and taken from
          him and his money stolen -- who took his
          life and his money? His parents?
          His mommy and daddy? Make him live this life
          like this -- "A man of genius" gets shit on
          as a child and that scars and it hurts and
          have you ever been hit by lighting? It hurts
          and it doesn't happen to everyone, it's an
          electrical charge that finds it's way across
          the universe and lands in your body and your
          head -- and as for "ruined but by himself,"
          not if his parents take his friggin' life and
          his money and tell you to do this and do that and
          if you don't? well, what --

                    PATRON #1
          You're parents took your money you won
          on that game show?

                    DONNIE
          Yes they did.
               (turns quick to Thurston)
          What does that mean, "spoke in the wheel?"

                    THURSTON
          Things go round 'n round, don't they?

                    DONNIE
          Yes they do, they do, but I'll make
          my dreams come true, you see? I will.

                    THURSTON
          This sounds Sad as a Weeping Willow.

                    DONNIE
          I used to be smart but now I'm just stupid.

                    THURSTON
          Shall we drink to that?

Donnie looks to the television for a moment, starts to tear up,
CAMERA pushes in slow to an EXTREME CLOSE UP. He repeats line's from
his days on "What Do Kids Know?" and does his best Jimmy immitation;

> DONNIE
> "If a brick weighs one pound plus one
> half brick -- how much does the brick weigh?"
> "Well if subtracting the half of brick from
> the whole brick you got one half of brick,
> equals one pound so therefore the brick
> equals two pounds --" "A little more than
> kin and less than kind," is Hamlet to Claudius.
> "The sins of the father laid upon the children,"
> is Merchant of Venice but borrowed from Exodus
> 20:5 and "win her with gifts if she respects not
> words," is Two Gentleman from Verona.
> Where? Who? How and Why, Kids?

> THURSTON
> "Why don't you shut the fuck up," is me to you,
> Chapter Right Here, Verse Right Now.

> CUT TO:

174. <u>INT. GAME SHOW SET - THAT MOMENT</u>   174.

CAMERA on the set with Jimmy walking over to the "Kids" panel;

> JIMMY GATOR
> KIDS! Are you guys glued to those
> seats or what? Are you ever leaving?
> You're getting close to the record,
> do you get more nervous as we go along?

> RICHARD
> A litte --

> JULIA
> -- yeah....

> JIMMY GATOR
> -- kids at school must be real
> excited for you, eh?

> JULIA
> Oh, yeah...yeah...

> RICHARD
> Sure.

> JIMMY GATOR
> Stanley the Man! How are you?

> STANLEY
> I'm fine. Yes.

                         JIMMY GATOR
              You're fast becoming a celebrity.
              How are you handling it all?

                           STANLEY
              Ohh, it's all fine. It's all.
              Nice. I'd just like to keep
              going....keep getting on....

                         JIMMY GATOR
              Sure, sure...that's fine, then...there...with.....

Jimmy starts to loose his grip on the proceedings a bit, slows
his pace down....Stanley notices....

                         JIMMY GATOR
              Well you've got..many..things, many
              things happening and on the way....

ANGLE, BURT.
CAMERA PUSHES IN on Burt as he sees Jimmy start to zone out a bit.

                                                    CUT TO:

175.   INT. JIMMY GATOR'S HOUSE - THAT MOMENT   175.

       CAMERA pushes in on Rose, sitting in the kitchen, watching the
       television. She holds her breath and tears a bit, noticing
       Jimmy start to fade.

                                                    CUT TO:

176.   INT. GAME SHOW STAGE - THAT MOMENT   176.

       Back to Stanley and Jimmy. Jimmy repeats himself;

                           JIMMY
              What were you saying, Stanley?

                           STANLEY
              I was saying...thinking maybe I'd get
              my own quiz show someday, Jimmy.
              Just like you!

The AUDIENCE laughs. Jimmy clicks back with a chuckle and
a "isn't that cute," smile to the crowd and he walks over to
his podium; CAMERA stays for a moment with Stanley, notices him
continue to grab his crotch and make a face....

                           JIMMY
              OK, OK, here we go: Steeper questions,
              bigger payoff, individual challenges with
              musical and audio pockets, no-steal-lock-out's,
              let's get it on in Round Two, Categories are:

                                                    CUT TO:

177.   <u>INT. HOLIDAY INN SUITE - THAT MOMENT</u>   177.

Frank and Gwenovier doing the telvision interview. CAMERA DOLLIES
IN SLOW ON EACH:

                FRANK
-- that's right, that's right, and what I'M
saying, that none of my competitors can say is
this: That there is no need for insight or
understanding. Things of the past! Gone, Over, Done.
Do you realize how fucking miraculous this is?
How fucking razor sharp and cutting edge and
ahead of it's time this concept is? I'm
talking about eliminating <u>insight</u> and <u>understanding</u>
as human values. GOD DAMN I'M GOOD. There is
no need for INSIGHT. There is no need for
UNDERSTANDING. I have found a way to take
<u>any</u> subjective human experience -- in other
words -- all the terrible shit or all the
great shit that you've had happen to you in
your life -- and quickly and easily transform
it in the unconscious mind through the subtle
and cunning use of language. The "listener-patient"
(in other words: The Chick) settles into a very
light, very delicate, conversationally induced
state: NOT A TRANCE, mind you, but a STATE.
A state that is brand new. The System's state.
What did I do? I REALIZED that concept and put
it into practical "get my dick hard and fuck it" use.
I'm gonna build a state for the seducer and the
seducee to live, vote, breath, pay takes and party
'till dawn. I'm gonna teach methods of language that
will help anyone get a piece of ass, tit and tail --

                GWENOVIER
Let's talk about --

                FRANK
I just realized this is for television,
isn't it? I can't swear up and down
like I just did.

                GWENOVIER
It's fine. I can bleep it out.

                FRANK
I warned you -- I get on a roll...

                GWENOVIER
-- let's talk more about your background --

                FRANK
Muffy -- coffee?

Muffy moves to pour a cup, Gwen looks down at her clipboard, then:

                    GWENOVIER
I'm confused about your past is the thing.

                    FRANK
Is that still lingering?

                    GWENOVIER
-- just to clarify --

                    FRANK
So boring, so useless --

                    GWENOVIER
I would just want to clear some things up:

                    FRANK
          (Muffy delivers coffee)
Thank you, Muffy. Funny thing is:
This is an important element of,
"Seduce and Destory:"
"Facing the past is an important way
in not making progress," that's something
I tell my men over and over --

                    GWENOVIER
This isn't meant --

                    FRANK
-- and I try and teach the students to
ask: What is it in aid of?

                    GWENOVIER
Are you asking me that?

                    FRANK
Yes.

                    GWENOVIER
Well, just trying to figure out who you are,
and how you might have become --

                    FRANK
In aid of what?

                    GWENOVIER
I'm saying, Frank, in trying to
figure out who you are --

                    FRANK
-- there's a lot more important things
I'd like to put myself into --

                    GWENOVIER
It's all important --

                    FRANK
Not really.

GWENOVIER
It's not like I'm trying to attack you --

FRANK
This is how you wanna spend the time,
then go, go, go -- you're gonna
be surprised at what a waste it is --
"The most useless thing in the world
is that which is behind me," Chapter Three --

GWENOVIER
We talked earlier about your mother.
And we talked about your father and his death.
And I don't want to be challenging or
defeatist here, but I have to ask and
I would want to clarify something -- something
that I understand --

FRANK
I'm not sure I hear a question in there?

GWENOVIER
Do you remember a Miss Simms?

FRANK
I know alotta women and I'm sure
she remembers me.

GWENOVIER
She does. From when you were a boy.

FRANK
Mm. Hm.

GWENOVIER
She lived in Tarzana.

FRANK
An old stomping ground -- is this
the "attack" portion of the interview,
I figured this was coming sooner
or later -- Is "the girl" coming in for the kill?

GWENOVIER
No, this is about getting something
right and claryfying one of your answers
to an earlier question --

FRANK
Go ahead and waste your time.

GWENOVIER
I was told that your mother died.
That your mother died when you were young --

> FRANK
> And that's what you've heard?

> GWENOVIER
> I talked to Miss Simms. Miss Simms
> was your caretaker and neighbor
> after your mother died in 1980.

BEAT. Frank goes silent.

> GWENOVIER
> In my research I have you listed as
> the only son of Earl and Lily Partridge.
> (beat)
> And what I learned from Mrs. Simms is that
> your mother passed away in 1980.
> (beat)
> See: It's my understanding that the information
> supplied by you and your company and answers
> to question's I've asked are incorrect, Frank.
> And if I'd like to get to the bottom of who you
> are and why you are then I think your family
> history -- you're accurate family history...well:
> ....this seems important...Frank...?

VIDEO CAMERA POV - THAT MOMENT
Frank lights his cigarette. CAMERA zooms into CU.

> FRANK
> Are you asking me a question?

> GWEN
> Well I guess the question is this:
> Do you remember Miss Simms?

BEAT. HOLD, THEN:

                                                    CUT TO:

178. <u>INT. GAME SHOW SET - THAT MOMENT</u>   178.

Jimmy asks questions. Stanley is visibly uncomfortable;

> JIMMY   *
> Kids, Adults, I'd like you to put   *
> yourself at a picnic. Place yourself   *
> there with your family and friends   *
> if you'd like -- you'll hear three   *
> musical notes and you are to tell me   *
> what it might represent that you'd   *
> find at a picnic -- The First Three Notes: *

OC we hear three musical notes. The "Adults" panel lights up,   *
Todd answers;   *

       TODD   *
  Well, Jimmy, I know this, I have perfect   *
  pitch, you see -- and that would be A-D-E.   *
  And that would represent lemonade.   *

       JIMMY   *
  For 250. Next notes, please: *

OC musical notes: E-G-G.   *

       TODD (buzzes)   *
  Got it. That's E-G-G which would be "egg."   *

Richard and Julia glance at Stanley, like "why the fuck aren't you answering these questions?" He looks straight ahead.

       JIMMY   *
  For 500 and the Third Set Of Notes: *

OC musical notes: B-E-E.   *

       TODD (buzzes)   *
  That's B-E-E -- and don't get stung.   *

The "Adults" are now within 200 points of the "Kids," on the scoreboard.

                  CUT TO:

179. <u>INT. LAWYERS OFFICE - THAT MOMENT</u>   179.

Linda seated across from a lawyer, ALAN KLIGMAN (50s) She's visibly shaking and fucked up.

       KLIGMAN
  You don't want any water?

       LINDA
  No...I just...(starts crying a bit)
  I'm so fucked up here Alan, I don't
  know...there's so much...so many things --

       KLIGMAN
  Are you on drugs right now?

       LINDA
  If I talk to you...y'know...if I tell
  you things...then you're a lawyer, right?
  You can't say things, you can't tell anyone,
  it's like the privelage, right?
  Attorney-client, you understand?

       KLIGMAN
  Not exactly, Linda. I'm not sure where
  you're going with this --

                        LINDA
          Like a shrink, like if I go to see
          a shrink, I'm protected, I can say
          things -- fuck -- I don't know what I'm doing --

                        KLIGMAN
          Linda, you're safe. Ok. It's alright.
          You're my friend. You and Earl are my clients
          and what you need to talk about won't leave
          this room, you have something you have to say --

                        LINDA
          -- I have something to tell you.
          I have to tell you something.
          I want to change his will, can I change
          his will?...I need to ---

                        KLIGMAN
          You can't change his will. Only
          Earl can change his will.

                        LINDA
          No, no....no, you see...I never loved him.
          I never loved him, Earl. When I started,
          when I met him, I met him and I fucked
          him and I married him because I wanted
          his money, do you understand?
                        (beat)
          I'm telling you this now...this I've never
          told anyone...I didn't love him.
          And now....I know I'm in that will,
          I know, I was there with him, we were
          all there together when we made that
          fucking thing and all the money I'll
          get -- I don't want it -- Because I love
          him so much now...I've fallen in love
          with him now, for real, as he's dying,
          and I look at him and he's about to
          go, Alan, he's dead...he's moments...
                        (beat)
          I took care of him through this, Alan.
          And What Now Then?

                                                CUT TO:

180.   INT. GAME SHOW STAGE - THAT MOMENT   180.

          CAMERA pushes in on Jimmy.

                        JIMMY
              Let's listen:

          There's an OC VOICE that speaks the clue;

> VOICE
> "Hello, Mary. How are you and the
> seven kids? As you probably heard by
> know, we sure gave that Pope a run for
> his money --"

The "Adults" buzz. Jimmy looks to Mim.

> MIM
> Well: That would be General Robert
> E. Lee. His wife Mary Park Custiss.
> And he did have seven children and he
> would be talking about Pope, who he defeated
> at the Battle of Monasses --

CUT TO:

181. INT. PARENTS GREEN ROOM - THAT MOMENT   181.

CAMERA pushes in on Rick, who sits back, starting to get real
pissed that Stanley isn't answering these questions.

> RICK
> C'mon, c'mon, c'mon, snap out of it.

CUT TO:

182. INT. GAME SHOW STAGE - THAT MOMENT.   182.

CAMERA moves from the AUDIENCE over to the Stage, listening
to another question that is spoken by the OC voice -- this
time in French;

> VOICE (in French)
> "Hello, Josephine,
> I'm speaking from Egypt --"

The Adults buzz again and Mim answers;

> JIMMY
> Mim --

> MIM
> Well that would be Napolean speaking
> to Josephine.

> JIMMY
> That's right!

ANGLE, BURT. He stands off, looking at the scoreboard as the
Adults have now pulled ahead by 200 points...he mumbles and
grumbles to himself.

CUT TO:

183.   <u>INT. LAWYER'S OFFICE - THAT MOMENT</u>   183.

Linda continued with the lawyer, Kligman.

                    LINDA
          I don't want him to die, I didn't love him
          when we met, and I've done so many bad things
          to him that he doesn't know, things I want
          to confess to him, but now I do: I love him.
          I love him so much and I can't stand -- he's going.

                    KLIGMAN
          What kind of medication are
          you on right now, Linda that's --

                    LINDA
          This is not any fucking medication
          talking, this isn't -- I don't know.
          I don't know -- Can you give me nothing?
          You have power of attorney, can you see him,
          can you, in this final fucking moment, go see
          him and make sure --- change the fucking
          will -- I don't want any money, I couldn't
          live with myself, this thing I've done --
          I've fucking done so many bad things --
          I fucked around. I fucked around on him,
          I fucking cheated on him, Alan. You're his lawyer,
          our laywer, THERE, I'm his wife, we are married.
          I broke the conract of marriage, I fucking
          cheated on him, many times over, I sucked
          other men's cocks and fuck - fuck - fuck -
                  ....fuck....
          Other Things I've Done..

                    KLIGMAN
          Adultery isn't illegal -- it's not something
          that can be used in a court to discredit
          the will or -- Linda. Linda. Calm down.

                    LINDA
          I can't.

                    KLIGMAN
          You don't have to change the will,
          if what you want to do is get nothing
          you can renounce the will when it's time.

                    LINDA
          Where will the money go?

                    KLIGMAN
          Well. Considering that there's no one
          else mentioned in the will...we'd
          have to go to the laws of intestacy,
          which is -- as if someone died without a will --

                    LINDA
          What does that mean?

                    KLIGMAN
          The money would go to Frank. The court
          would put the money in the hands of a relative --

                    LINDA
          -- that can't happen. Earl doesn't
          want him to have the money, the things.

                    KLIGMAN
          -- unless Frank is specifically ommitted
          as a beneficiary that's what will happen.

                    LINDA
          This is so over-the-top and fucked-up
          I can hardly stand it.

                    KLIGMAN
          Linda, you just have to take a moment
          and breath and one thing at a time --

                    LINDA
          Shut the fuck up.

                    KLIGMAN
          I'm trying to help, Linda --

                    LINDA
          Shut the fuck up. Shut the fuck up.

                    KLIGMAN
          You need to sober up.

                    LINDA
          Now you must really shut the fuck up, please.
          Shut The Fuck Up.

                    KLIGMAN
          Linda --

                    LINDA
          I have to go.

She heads for the door.

                    KLIGMAN
          Let me call you a car, Linda.

                    LINDA
          Shut the fuck up.

She's out the door.

                                        CUT TO:

184. <u>INT. GAME SHOW STAGE – THAT MOMENT</u>   184.

Three MEN in TUXEDOS and HARMONICAS have taken a place near
the band. Jimmy, reading from his cards, introduces them and
asks the following question:

(Note: Jimmy's speech is starting to slur a bit more at this
point. His motor skills seem to be fading quickly.)

                    JIMMY
          Imagine you are attending a jam session
          of classical composers and they have
          each done an arrangment of the classic
          favorite, "Whispering." Here are three
          variations on the theme, as three classic
          composer's might have written it -- you are
          to name the composer. The First:

The Harmonica Fella's play an arrangment....CAMERA pushes in close
on STANLEY and TITLS DOWN CLOSE TO HIS PANTS....

Stanley begins to piss his pants. He trembles and shakes and
holds back tears as the wet stain gets bigger.

OC through this we hear the Adults answer the question:

                    TODD (OC)
          Well, Jimmy that sounded to me
          like Brahms, a bit like his Hungarian
          Dance Number Six, I believe.

                    JIMMY (OC)
          Excellent. Next number:

The Harmonica Fella's play another arrangment of "Whispering"
that sounds like Ravel's "Bolero."

Stanley moves his arms down to his sides to cover his crotch
and pull at his pants -- <u>and his BUZZER goes off with a brush
of the side of his arm</u> --

                    JIMMY
          Stanley the Man -- answer:

Stanley. HOLD. He starts to cry. Julia and Richard look over
at him and see his pants and they start to laugh a bit.

                    STANLEY
          ...I don't know the answer...

Jimmy starts to STUDDER and SHAKE a bit....holds a tight grip on
the podium;

> JIMMY GATOR
> That is not right! That's not right,
> Stanley, the answer is...Ravel....Ravel....
> ....xhjksndlsmnop.....

CAMERA WHIPS and pushes over to the FLOOR DIRECTOR.

> FLOOR DIRECTOR
> What the fuck is wrong with him?
> (into headseat)
> What do you wanna do here, he's
> fading fast --

CUT TO:

185.   INT. BOOTH - THAT MOMENT   185.

The main booth with monitors and board, etc. The DIRECTOR and
and ASSITANT watch the monitors;

> DIRECTOR
> I need a better cutaway, go to the
> black chick, Camera Three, Camera Three
> the black chick --

A monitor sees the video camera zoom in on Mim as a cutaway but
her face is like, "What the fuck is going on?"

CUT TO:

186.   INT. GAME SHOW SET - THE FLOOR - THAT MOMENT   186.

Jimmy is, with a lot of trouble, trying to que the Harmonica
Fella's with the next question....

...Burt walks over quickly to the Floor Director...

> BURT
> Get the technical difficulty card up --

...CAMERA pushes over to Stanley, who's crying and shaking....

...CAMERA pushes in on Jimmy, who stumbles back from his
podium and falls to the ground....taking the podium with him....

....CAMERA pushes in on Burt and the Floor Director...

> BURT
> Cut it, go to the card, go to
> the fucking card --

CUT TO:

187. INT. BOOTH - THAT MOMENT   187.

        The DIRECTOR snaps his fingers to an ASSISTANT at the board.

                            DIRECTOR
                Go to the card, now -- go --

        CU - MONITOR IMAGE.
        The card that reads, "Technical Difficulty," comes up and holds.

                                                        CUT TO:

188. INT. CLAUDIA'S APARTMENT - THAT MOMENT   188.

        CAMERA pushes in real quick on Claudia SNORTING COKE from her   *
        hand in the bedroom -- she rushes back into the kitchen area --   *

                            CLAUDIA
                Ok, ok. I'm back.

                            JIM KURRING
                This is, for not a fresh cup, a great
                cup of coffee, Claudia --

                            CLAUDIA
                Thank you.

        She sits down, ready to talk, lights a cigarette.

                            CLAUDIA
                What do you wanna talk about?

                                                        CUT TO:

189. INT. GAME SHOW STAGE - THAT MOMENT   189.

        Burt, Mary and Assistants and folks run over to Jimmy. He stands,
        doesn't realize what's happend and mumbles, "what the fuck, what the..."

        The AUDIENCE is murmuring, standing and watching the scene.

                                                        CUT TO:

190. INT. HALLWAY - THAT MOMENT   190.

        CAMERA leads RICK as he comes charging out of the green room
        and races down the hallway.--

                                                        CUT TO:

191. <u>INT. GAME SHOW SET – THAT MOMENT</u>   191.

CAMERA with the "Kids" panel as Richard and Julia looking at Stanley.

                    RICHARD
          Did you piss your fuckin' pants, Stanley?

                    STANLEY
          Shut up -- shut up --

Cynthia walks over;

                    CYNTHIA
          What happend, what's going on?

                    STANLEY
          NOTHING. NOTHING HAPPEND. GO AWAY.

                    CYNTHIA
          Don't tell me to go away, Stanley.
          I am the Co-ordinator in this show
          and you will answer the questions
          that I ask, you understand?

Rick comes over;

                    RICK
          What's the problem, what's the problem here?

                    STANLEY
          I'm fine. nothing.

                    RICK
          Why didn't you answer those questions?

                    STANLEY
          I didn't know the answer --

                    RICK
          Bullshit. Bullshit. You know the
          answer to every goddamn question and
          I knew the answer to those questions
          and I'm not half as smart as you are so
          What Happened?

                    STANLEY
          I don't know.

                    RICHARD
          He pissed his pants.

                    RICK
          Did you -- did you --

                    STANLEY
          I didn't I'm fine, I'm fine.

                    RICK
          Stand up.

                    STANLEY
          I said I'm fine.

Rick grabs Stanley a bit and sees a large WET STAIN in Stanley's pants.

                    RICK
          ...oh Jesus, what the fuck...?

                    STANLEY
          I'm fine. I'm fine, I just wanna
          keep playing --

                    RICK
          Why did you do this?

192. ANGLE, JIMMY. THAT MOMENT.   192.
      Jimmy is sweating.

                    JIMMY
          I had a stroke, I think I had a stroke.

                    BURT
          Call 911. Call 911 right now.

                    JIMMY
          No, no, no. I'm fine. It's small,
          I wanna keep going --

                    BURT
          no, no, c'mon Jimmy we need to call
          this quits and you need to see a doctor.

                    JIMMY
          I'm telling you right now, I'm fine.
          I lost my goddamn balance and I couldn't
          see a moment, but I'm ok.

                    BURT
          Call 911, Mary, do it right now.

                    JIMMY
          You fuckin' don't do that. You don't do it,
          you cocksucker. I'll fuckin' kill you
          with my barehands. Go. get the fuck
          fuck -- we're going back and we finish
          the show --

                    BURT
          Jimmy you look like you're about
          to fuckin' die right here --

                    JIMMY
          Shut it. Shut yer fuckin' mouth.

193.　ANGLE, RICK and STANLEY.　　　　　　　　　　　　　　　　　193.

　　　　　　　　　　　　　　RICK
　　　　　　Are we gonna keep going with this game?

　　　　　　　　　　　　　　STANLEY
　　　　　　Yes.

　　　　　　　　　　　　　　RICK
　　　　　　You're two fuckin' days from the
　　　　　　record, get through this and I'll
　　　　　　do anything for you, you just gotta
　　　　　　get through this --

　　　　　　　　　　　　　　STANLEY
　　　　　　Alright.

　　　　　　　　　　　　　　RICK
　　　　　　hang in there, ok. I love you.

Rick walks away with Cynthia...

...Dick Jennings has sobered up a bit and is doing bad, "calm
down/comedy/everything's cool" stuff for the Audience....

...Jimmy and Burt and Mary stand up and a MAKE UP person runs over
with some water and cleans him up a bit. Burt moves away --

　　　　　　　　　　　　FLOOR DIRECTOR
　　　　　　What are we doing?

　　　　　　　　　　　　　　BURT
　　　　　　This is fuckin' stupidity, we'll get
　　　　　　back on and go through it --

The Floor Director starts throwing directions in his headset and
to the camera people, etc.

　　　　　　　　　　　　　　　　　　　　　　　CUT TO:

194.   INT. HOLIDAY INN SUITE - THAT MOMENT.   Sequence G   194.

CAMERA holds on Frank and starts a SLOW DOLLY IN.   Gwenovier remains OC.

                    GWENOVIER (OC)
          Frank...Frank...what are we gonna do here?
          Are we having a staring contest?
                    (beat)
          Do you have anything to say?

                    CAPTAIN MUFFY (OC)
          I think maybe we should rap this up, Chief --

Frank SNAPS his fingers and signals Captain Muffy to stay quiet.

                    GWENOVIER (OC)
          I'm not trying to attack you, Frank.
          I think that if you have something that
          needs to be cleared up...Well, then...
                    (beat)
          I was told that your father, (your father
          is Earl Partridge,) that he left you and
          your mother and you were forced to take care
          of her during her illness...that you took
          care of your mother as she struggled with Cancer....
                    (beat)
          And Miss Simms became your caretaker after
          your mother died...Frank...Frank...
                    (beat)
          Frank, can you talk about your Mother?
                    (beat)
          Frank....can you?

CAMERA LANDS CU. ON FRANK.   HOLD, THEN:

                                                   CUT TO:

195.   INT. CLAUDIA'S APARTMENT - THAT MOMENT   195.

Claudia and Jim Kurring talking. She's rubbing her jaw, blabbing
away and he's listening with a grin;

                    CLAUDIA
          --- yeah, yeah, I get in it in my ear.
          It's TMJ is what it's called technically.

                    JIM KURRING
          What's that stand for?

                    CLAUDIA
          Tempural-something-mandibular,
          thing with something, I dunno.
          But it affects my ear, I don't even
          know if I have TMJ exactly but just
          very tight, like - it's like a muscle
          spasm and it's just gets so clenched --

She's interupted by the call on his RADIO. He takes the call.
(Director's Note: Technical blah-blah-blah,etc.)

>   JIM KURRING
>   This is my job.

>   CLAUDIA
>   We were just gettin' warmed up.
>   We were just getting started.

>   JIM KURRING
>   Well if you listen' to that music
>   too loud again and that fella returns
>   maybe we'll share another cup of coffee --

>   CLAUDIA
>   If you're not here for a 422 --

>   JIM KURRING
>   No. No. Don't joke about that.
>   That's not funny, Claudia. Please, now.

>   CLAUDIA
>   I'm sorry.

>   JIM KURRING
>   Ok, then. Keep your chin up and your
>   music down, alright?

>   CLAUDIA
>   Yes. I will. It was nice to meet you
>   Officer Jim.

>   JIM KURRING
>   Just Jim.

>   CLAUDIA
>   yeah, good, ok.

>   JIM KURRING
>   Bye, bye, Claudia.

>   CLAUDIA
>   Good bye.

She closes the door. HOLD.

                                              CUT TO:

196. <u>EXT. CLAUDIA'S APARTMENT - THAT MOMENT</u>   196.

Jim Kurring stands outside the door for a moment. He hesitates
a moment, then....he's about to knock....His RADIO goes off...he turns
it down real quick --

                                              CUT TO:

197. <u>INT. CLAUDIA'S APARTMENT - THAT MOMENT</u>   197.

Claudia hears the RADIO go off and stands back a bit from her
door...hold a moment...then there's a KNOCK...she opens up:

CAMERA DOLLIES IN A LITTLE ON JIM KURRING.

                          JIM KURRING
          I'm sorry, Claudia.

                          CLAUDIA
          What is it? Did you forget something?

                          JIM KURRING
          No, no. I was wondering...man oh man.
          I think I feel like a bit of a scum-bucket
          doing this, considering that I came here
          as an officer of the law and the situation
          and all this but I think I'd be a fool
          if I didn't do something I really want
          to do which is to ask you on a date.

                          CLAUDIA
          You wanna go on a date with me?

                          JIM KURRING
          Please, yes.

                          CLAUDIA
          Well...is that illegal?

                          JIM KURRING
          No.

                          CLAUDIA
          Then...I'd like to go...What do you want to do?

                          JIM KURRING
          I don't know. I haven't thought about
          it -- you know what -- that's not
          true -- I have thought about it. I've
          thought about going on a date with you
          since you opened the door.

                          CLAUDIA
          Really?

                          JIM KURRING
          Yeah.

                          CLAUDIA
          I thought you were flirting with me
          a little.

He laughs and she laughs and then:

                    CLAUDIA
Do you wanna go tonight? I mean,
are you working?

                    JIM KURRING
No, I'm off tonight. I would lov-like,
to go tonight, I can pick you up,
I can pick you up here at about what
time? What time?

                    CLAUDIA
Eight o'clock?

                    JIM KURRING
What about ten o'clock, is that
too late? I don't get off and then --

                    CLAUDIA
Oh sure yes, that's fine, late dinners
are good. Should I get dressed up or -- ?

                    JIM KURRING
No, no, just casual maybe, maybe
I thought -- there's a spot I like to go,
it's real nice that overlooks a golf course
and the course is lit up at night --

                    CLAUDIA
Billingsley's?

                    JIM KURRING
Yeah, You know it? You know Billingsley's?

                    CLAUDIA
It's my favorite place --

                    JIM KURRING
Oh, see? This is great. Ten o'clock.

                    CLAUDIA
Great, bye.

                    JIM KURRING
Bye.

She closes the door.

                                        CUT TO:

198.   <u>INT. HOLIDAY INN/SEMINAR ROOM - THAT MOMENT</u>   198.

       CAMERA pushes in on DOC, who's speaking to a group of Frank's
       disciples. He's blah-blah-blahing about Seduce and Destory, etc.

                              DOC
                    Not true. Not true. And you know what?
                    Even if you don't get to pump her,
                    you can still practice honing your skills
                    on a femenist --

                              DISCIPLE
                    -- I know --

                              DOC
                    -- and you need to do that.

                              DISCIPLE
                    I will.

                              DOC
                    No, you <u>need</u> to do it.

       His CEL PHONE rings and he excuses himself.

                              DOC (into phone)
                    Thisz Doc.

                                                          INTERCUT:

199.   <u>INT. SEDUCE AND DESTROY CONDO - THAT MOMENT</u>   199.

       CAMERA on JANET. She's on the phone. It rings.

                              JANET
                    Doc it's Janet.

                              DOC
                    What's up?

                              JANET
                    I have to talk to Frank, is he nearby?

                              DOC
                    He's doing the interview with the lady --

                              JANET
                    I need you to interupt him, I need
                    to get him on the phone with me right away --

                              DOC
                    What happend?

                              JANET
                    Doc, go get Frank and put him on the phone.

                                                          CUT TO:

200.　INT. HOLIDAY INN SUITE - THAT MOMENT　200.

CAMERA pushes in on Gwenovier and Frank. (Dead on Singles.)

                    GWENOVIER
          C'mon, Frank. What are you doing?

                    FRANK
          What am I doing?

                    GWENOVIER
          Yeah.

                    FRANK
          I'm quietly judging you.

                                        CUT TO:

201.　INT. GAME SHOW STAGE - THAT MOMENT　201.

CAMERA pushes in on the FLOOR DIRECTOR again who counts down;

                    FLOOR DIRECTOR
          And...three...two...one ---

He points to Jimmy, who pops into shape, looks into the TV CAMERA.

                    JIMMY GATOR
          What a day and what a round, going
          back and in for me and the final
          speed round to determine who's who
          today -- scores on the board's Kids:
          9225. Adults: 11,000. And this game is
          not out of reach for the Kids...can they
          hang in there and break the record? (etc,etc)
          Elders! Who's the lucky so and so?

Mim from the "Adults" speaks into her mic.

                    MIM
          It's gonna be me, Jimmy.

                    JIMMY
          C'mon down here, Mim.

She stands up and crosses over to Jimmy. This is for a ONE ON ONE
final section speed round. One Kid vs. One Adult.

202.　ANGLE, STANLEY.　202.
CAMERA pushes in on him and lands in CU.

He takes his shirt out of his pants and tries to pull it down enough to
cover the large wet stain in his pants.

203. ANGLE, JIMMY AND MIM   203.
     They chat about the game so far, etc. "They're quite a challenge, etc."

204. ANGLE, STANLEY and RICHARD and JULIA.   204.
     Stanley can't pull his shirt down enough to cover. He turns to
     Richard and Julia;

                         STANLEY
                    I don't wanna go, I can't do it this time.

                         RICHARD
                    -- the fuck are you talking about?

                         JULIA
                    You have to go, Stanley. You're the
                    smartest.

                         STANLEY
                    I don't wanna do it. Why can't one
                    of you do it --

                         RICHARD
                    Stanley if you don't fuckin' stand up
                    and go over there I'm gonna beat your ass --

                         STANLEY
                    I'm sick of being the one, the one who
                    always has to do everything, I don't
                    want to be the one always --

                         JIMMY (OC)
                    KIDS!

     Jimmy looks over to the "Kids" panel.

                         JIMMY
                    Do I even have to ask? Stanley, get
                    your butt over here --

     Stanley looks like a deer in headlights. The AUDIENCE applauds.

                                                              CUT TO:

205. INT. SMILING PEANUT BAR - THAT MOMENT   205.

     The TELVISION above the bar holds this moment where Stanley won't
     move. DONNIE is seriously fucked up now and the CAMERA pushes in
     on him. He glances around, up the television, sees Stanley. BEAT.

     Thurston and the other folks around chat away, etc;

                         DONNIE
                    ...I'm sick....I'm sick here now....

     They continue to chat, trying to ignore him now;

                    DONNIE
I confuse melancholy and depression sometimes....

                    THURSTON
Mmm.Hmm.

                    DONNIE
You see?

                    THURSTON
Why don't you run along now friend,
your dessert is getting cold.

                    DONNIE
I'm sick.

                    THURSTON
Stay that way.

                    DONNIE
I'm sick and I'm in love.

                    THURSTON
You seem the sort of person who confuses the two.

                    DONNIE
That's right. That's the first time
you're right. I CONFUSE THE TWO
AND I DON'T CARE.

Donnie looks to Brad, then:

                    DONNIE
HEY. HEY.

Brad looks. Donnie stands up, backs away from the bar as he talks;

                    DONNIE
I love you. I love you and I'm sick.
          (beat)
I'll talk to you....I'll talk to you
tommorrow. I'm getting corrective oral
surgery tomorrow. For my teeth. For my
teeth and for you....for you so we can speak.
You have braces. Me too. Me too. I'm getting
braces, too. For you. For you, dear Brad.
And I don't have any money. And I don't have
any money now....but I'll get it...I will for
you, Brad. I love you, Brad. Brad the Bartender. .
          (beat, crying now)
You wanna love me back? Love me back and I'll
be good to you. I'll be god damn good for you.
And I won't be mad if you don't know who said what.
I won't punish you if you get the answer wrong.
I can teach and tell you: Samuel Johnson.

> THURSTON
> Brad, honey, you have a special
> seceret crush over here I think, don't
> take him too lovely -- he might get hurt --

> DONNIE
> You mind your own bussines.

> THURSTON
> Gently, son --

> DONNIE
> Brad, I know you don't love me now --

> THURSTON
> "It's a dangerous thing to confuse
> chidlren with angels..."

> DONNIE
> -- and you wanna know the common element for
> the entire group, like he asks...I'll tell you
> the answer: I'll tell you, 'cause I had that
> question. I had that same question....Carbon.
> In pencil led, it's in the form of graphite
> and in coal, it's all mixed up with other
> impurities and in the diamond it's in hard form.
>   (Jimmy impersonation)
> "Well...all we were asking was the common
> element, Donnie...but thank you for all that
> unnecessary knowledge...ahhh, Kids! Full of
> usless thoughts, eh?" Thank you. Thank you.
>   (beat)
> And the book says: "We may be through with
> the past but the past is not through with us."
>   (to Thurston)
> And NO IT'S NOT DANGEROUS TO DO THAT.

Donnie has backed away, close to the bathroom. He heaves a bit,
cries, turns and runs for the bathroom --

                                                    CUT TO:

206. INT. SMILING PEANUT/BATHROOM - THAT MOMENT   206.

OVERHEAD ANGLE, LOOKING STRAIGHT DOWN ONTO:
Donnie bursts in the bathroom and starts to vomit and moan, etc.

                                                    CUT TO:

207.   INT. POLICE CAR - MOVING - THAT MOMENT   207.

It's pouring RAIN still. Jim Kurring is talking to himself, doing
"Cops." (Dial: Ref. improv. notes/sweet girl/excited/date/job)

Jim Kurring interupts himself and notices something (very blurry,
through the RAIN....)

JIM'S POV: A young BLACK MALE (late 20s) is standing on the street,
about to jay-walk.

The Young Black Male, at the site of Kurring, turns around and walks
back the direction he came, deciding against the jay walk.

Jim Kurring looks in his rear view mirror and sees that the Young
Black Male is now RUNNING back towards something --

                                                           CUT TO:

208.   EXT. STREET - THAT MOMENT   208.

Jim Kurring's POLICE CAR makes a U-turn.

                                                           CUT TO:

209.   INT. CLAUDIA'S APARTMENT - THAT MOMENT   209.

Claudia snorts a line of coke, comes up and looks at her televison;
It's playing, "What Do Kids Know?"

                                                           CUT TO:

210.   INT. GAME SHOW SET - THAT MOMENT   210.

Stanley doesn't move. He says to Jimmy:

                         STANLEY
              I'm going to pass, Jimmy.

    ANGLE, JIMMY. He doesn't know what to do and he's a bit out of it.

                         JIMMY
              Stanley, passing to one of the
              other kids --

                         RICHARD
              We want Stanley to go, Jimmy.

                         STANLEY
              I don't want to go.

BEAT.

                                                           CUT TO:

211. **INT. HOLIDAY INN/LOBBY - THAT MOMENT**   211.

CAMERA (STEADICAM) follows/leads DOC as he walks from the Seminar area
to the elevators...this is one continuous shot...as he gets into the
elevator's and rides up, talking on the cel phone.

                          DOC
          I'm walking towards the elevator's, Janet.

                          JANET (OC)
          Fine. Phil, you still there?

                          PHIL (OC)
          Yeah I'm here.

                          JANET (OC)
          I wanna ask you one question, Phil:
          Have you talked to anyone else about
          this? About Frank and Earl?

                          PHIL (OC)
          No I haven't.

                          JANET (OC)
          Alright, good, I'd like to keep
          it that way -- all the security and
          what not, you understand? This could
          be a delicate situation for Frank and
          the family --

                          DOC (OC)
          What happend?

                          JANET (OC)
          Doc, just - don't, how close are you?

                          DOC (OC)
          I'm about to get off the elevator --

The Elevator doors DING and OPEN and Doc steps out -- heads down the
hallway towards the suite --

                          JANET (OC)
          Phil, hang in just one more minute
          ok? I'm gonna put you on hold -- Doc
          you still there?

                          DOC
          Yeah, I'm here, I'm off the
          elevator, walking down the hall, now --

                                             CUT TO:

212.   <u>INT. GAME SHOW SET - THAT MOMENT</u>   212.

Stanley doesn't move. Jimmy tries to hold it all together;

                    JIMMY
          Richard, Julia, kids? What's it
          gonna be, we need a player for one
          on one --

                    RICHARD
          We want Stanley to play, Jimmy and
          we're not sure why he won't --

                    STANLEY
          I don't want to play. I always
          play, I always answer the questions
          and I don't wanna do it anymore --

CAMERA pushes in on Burt, who snaps at Cynthia:

                    BURT
          What the fuck is he doing, what's
          wrong with him?

                    CYNTHIA
          I have no idea.

                                        CUT TO:

213.   <u>INT. HOLIDAY INN - HALLWAY - THAT MOMENT</u>   213.

CAMERA (STEADICAM) following Doc as he walks swiftly down the
hallway towards the suite --

                                        CUT TO:

214.   <u>INT. EARL'S HOUSE - THAT MOMENT</u>   214.

CAMERA on Phil on the phone. He sits watching Earl. 30fps. PUSH IN.

                                        CUT TO:

215.   <u>INT. EARL'S HOUSE - GARAGE - THAT MOMENT</u>   215.

It's black. The GARAGE DOOR opens....Linda's MERCEDES is pulling in
out of the POURING RAIN....

                                        CUT TO:

216. <u>INT. BOOTH - THAT MOMENT</u>   216.

The DIRECTOR and his ASSISTANT and other folks in the booth;

                         DIRECTOR
               This fuckin' kid ain't gettin'
               up and we don't have a show, live
               television, ladies and gents --

                                                    CUT TO:

217. <u>INT. PARENTS GREEN ROOM - THAT MOMENT</u>   217.

The other parents snap at Rick. CAMERA DOLLIES in on him slow.

                        JULIA'S MOM
               What the hell does he think he's doing?

                       RICHARD'S DAD
            Is this a <u>point</u>? is this <u>a game</u>?

                          RICK
               GET THE FUCK UP, KID.

                                                    CUT TO:

218. <u>INT. HOLIDAY INN SUITE - THAT MOMENT</u>   218.

CAMERA on Frank. He looks at his watch, then:

                          FRANK
               Time's up. Thank you for the interview.

                        GWENOVIER
               So you sat it out, that's what you did?

                          FRANK
               You requested my time and I gave it
               you, you called me a liar and made accusations.
               And you say, "If I'd known I wouldn't have
               asked," then it's not an attack? Well,
               I don't wanna be the sort of fella who doesn't
               keep his word. I gave you my time, Bitch.
               So fuck you now.

Frank heads out of the room quick. CAMERA leading him in CU.

                        GWENOVIER
               You're hurting a lot of people, Frank --

                          FRANK
               -- fuck you.

He's out the door with Captain Muffy in tow.

                                                    CUT TO:

219. INT. HALLWAY - THAT MOMENT   219.

CAMERA moving quick with Doc towards the room. Frank and Captain Muffy
step out of the room and Doc holds up the Cel Phone....stops.

                              DOC
              Frank, there's a situation on the phone --

                                                          CUT TO:

220. INT. EARL'S HOUSE - THAT MOMENT   220.

The DOGS go crazy barking and Phil jumps a bit. They hear the garage
door and run towards it. The Morphine Dog runs into a wall.

Phil turns his head (40fps)

                                                          CUT TO:

221. INT. GAME SHOW SET - THAT MOMENT   221.

CAMERA on Stanley. BEAT. HOLD.

                         JIMMY (OC)
              I need a player, Kids....c'mon now.
                         (to Audience)
              The indescision of a child, ladies
              and germs!

The AUDIENCE laughs a bit and chuckles.

                         STANLEY
              This isn't funny. This isn't "cute."
              Jimmy -- Jimmy -- we're not a toy --
              we're not dolls, here. This isn't
              funny you see, the way we're looked at
              if you think that we're cute Because What?
              What? I'm made to feel like a freak
              if I answer questions and I'm smart or
              I have to go to the bathroom. What Is That?
                         (starts to cry)
              And what is that, Jimmy, I'm asking?
              I'm asking what is that, Jimmy?
              I'm asking you that -- ?

CAMERA pushes in a bit on him.

                         JIMMY
              Well I'm not sure, Stanley.

                                                          CUT TO:

222.   <u>EXT. APARTMENT BUILDING/LA RIVER - THAT MOMENT</u>   222.

CAMERA (STEADICAM) follows Jim Kurring as he walks around the side of
an apartment building, looking for the BLACK MALE....he snoops a bit,
holding his flashlight as it's just about dark....the side of the
building runs along the L.A River.....he starts in towards something...

A very LOUD GUNSHOT IS HEARD and HITS on the side wall of the
apartment, right next to Jim Kurring's FACE....

...he ducks for cover, looses balance and falls down, in the mud,
sliding down the embankment next to the L.A. River --- another
GUN SHOT is heard....

Kurring reaches for his REVOLVER <u>which is not in it's holster</u> --

                                                         CUT TO:

223.   <u>INT. SMILING PEANUT/BATHROOM - THAT MOMENT</u>   223.

CAMERA zooms in from overhead angle as Donnie continues to
throw up violently.

                                                         CUT TO:

224.   <u>INT. HOLIDAY INN - STAIRWELL - THAT MOMENT</u> (INTERCUT)   224.

CAMERA holds on Frank in close up, he's on the phone.
Doc and Captain Muffy stand with him in the stairwell.

                         JANET (OC)
                I'm sorry, Frank. I didn't know
                what you would want here, what you
                would want me to do -- I'm -- I asked
                him all the right questions,
                he's his nurse, he's sitting right
                there with him and he's -- I mean,
                I can hear him in the background --
                your father --

                         FRANK
                Is he at the house?

                         JANET (OC)
                I asked him the exact adress and he
                gave it -- I know that this must
                be hard, you having to hear this --

                         FRANK
                Don't give me things, Janet just tell
                me the thing, the information --

                         JANET (OC)
                I'm sorry.

                                                         CUT TO:

225. <u>INT. EARL'S GARAGE - THAT MOMENT</u>   225.

Linda parks the car and leaves the ENGINE RUNNING. BEAT.
We can hear the DOGS BARKING OC....HOLD.

                                                        CUT TO:

226. <u>INT. GAME SHOW SET - THAT MOMENT</u>   226.

Stanley is continuing. He's hyperventilating.

                    STANLEY
          We are not on display. I am not a doll.
          I AM NOT A DOLL...I'M NOT SILLY AND CUTE.
          I'M SMART SO THAT SHOULDN'T MAKE ME SOMETHING,
          SOMETHING SO PEOPLE CAN WATCH HOW SILLY IT
          IS THAT HE'S SMART? I KNOW. I KNOW THINGS.
          I KNOW. I HAVE TO GO TO THE BATHROOM I HAVE
          TO GO TO THE BATHROOM AND I HAVE TO GO.

                    JIMMY
          I'm sorry, Stanley.

Stanley embarresed now.

                    STANLEY
          I'm sorry, I'm sorry, I didn't mean to do this.

                                                        CUT TO:

227. <u>INT. PARENTS GREEN ROOM - THAT MOMENT</u>   227.

RICK is standing now....he VIOLENTLY throws a chair against the
wall and it SHATTERS into a hundred pieces --

                    RICK
          FUCK. FUCK. FUCK. FUCK.

                                                        CUT TO:

228. <u>EXT. APARTMENT/LA RIVER EMBANKMENT - THAT MOMENT</u>   228.

It's FLOODING with RAIN....Jim Kurring is without gun and he's
scared shitless....and he can't see...and he's running for cover
in some bushes....CAMERA is HAND HELD and wild, following and
falling with him....MUD and RAIN and SHIT everywhere.....

His POV...across a bridge...he sees the slight FIGURE as it flees....
(could be the Black Male, but hard to tell in a quick glimpse) he then
sees another SMALLER FIGURE scuttle away...

He doesn't run....he stays...holds....

                                                        CUT TO:

229. INT. CLAUDIA'S APARTMENT - THAT MOMENT   229.

CAMERA pushes in on her cocaine on the table, TILTS up to her FACE, watching the show, then WHIPS RT. and pushes in towards the MONITOR.

ON THE MONITOR.
Stanley is crying....

                                                              CUT TO:

230. INT. GAME SHOW SET - THAT MOMENT   230.

CAMERA on Stanley.

                         STANLEY
              I don't mean to cry, I'm sorry.

                         JIMMY
              It's okay, Stanley. It's alright.

CAMERA with Burt as he walks to the Floor Director...

                         BURT
              Take us off the air, go to the
              the credits --

The Floor Director starts to speak some things into the headset.

                                                              CUT TO:

231. INT. EARL'S GARAGE - THAT MOMENT   231.

Linda rolls down the windows in the closed garage with the engine running...fumes start to fill the garage...she starts to cry and lights a cigarrette...the bag of perscriptions sits next to her...

                                                              CUT TO:

232. INT. STAIRWELL - THAT MOMENT (INTERCUT)   232.

Frank on the phone with Janet, Captain Muffy and Doc in stairwell.

                         FRANK
              I haven't spoken to this asshole in
              ten years....what did I do....?
              What did I do today for this? For all
              of this? ....what....is this....
              ....Is This A Movie.....?

                                                              CUT TO:

233.   INT. GAME SHOW SET - THAT MOMENT   233.

The MONITORS in the place go to a Still Card that has the
"What Do Kids Know?" logo...and the titles start to roll on it.

Stanley notices and he RUNS from the podium, towards backstage...

...Jimmy is standing next to Mim....he holds on to her a moment....
loosing his balance again....

....Burt and Cynthia rush the stage....

Stanley dissapears from the stage...

                                                        CUT TO:

234.   INT. EARL'S HOUSE - THAT MOMENT   234.

Phil still on the phone, Earl is asleep. He stands up and heads for
the garage -- hears the sound of the engine running -- dogs are
continuing to bark like crazy --

                                                        CUT TO:

235.   INT. GARAGE - THAT MOMENT   235.

Linda in CU. She hesitates a moment. THEN: She quickly
shuts off the engine, GRABS the bag of LIQUID MORPHINE --

                                                        CUT TO:

236.   INT. EARL'S HOUSE - THAT MOMENT   236.

CAMERA leads/follows Linda as she enters, approaches Phil;

                         PHIL
                   Linda --

                         LINDA
               What are you doing?

                         PHIL
               I've got Frank...Frank Earl's son.
               He's...he asked me to get him and I did --

                         LINDA
               Hang up the phone.

                         PHIL
               No, Linda, you don't understan --

                         LINDA
               PUT THE FUCKIN' PHONE DOWN, HANG IT UP.

She SLAPS his FACE HARD. The PHONE FALLS to the ground.

                                                        CUT TO:

237. INT. STARIWELL - HOLIDAY INN - THAT MOMENT (INTERCUT)   237.

Frank on the cel phone to Janet --

                    FRANK
               Put him on --

Janet clicks Frank over and there's a MOMENT of BLUR/NOISE (Linda and
Phil, screaming and static) and then it's gone --

                                                        CUT TO:

238. INT. EARL'S HOUSE - THAT MOMENT   238.

Linda screaming at Phil.

                    LINDA
          You don't do that, you don't call him,
          you don't know to get involved in the
          bussiness of his, of his of my family.
          this is the family, me and him do you
          understand? You understand? NO ONE ELSE.
          THERE IS NO ONE ELSE. That man, his son
          does not exist. HE IS DEAD. HE IS DEAD
          and WHO TOLD YOU TO DO THAT?

                    PHIL
          Earl asked me, Linda, please, Linda,
          I'm sorry -- Earl asked me --

                    LINDA
          BULLSHIT. BULLSHIT HE DIDN'T ASK YOU,
          HE DOESN'T WANT HIM, HE DOESN'T
          WANT TO TALK TO HIM, SO FUCK YOU THAT
          HE ASKED THAT. THERE IS NO ONE BUT ME
          AND HIM.

She breaks down, more, more, more.

                                                        CUT TO:

239. INT. STAIRWELL - THAT MOMENT (INTERCUT)   239.

Frank listens on the phone to dead air....hold a long moment, then:
He hands the phone back to Doc;

                    FRANK
               There's no one there.

Frank walks away quick. CAMERA leads him out of the stairwell
and down the hallway...HOLD ON HIS FACE CLOSE.

                                                        CUT TO:

240.   <u>INT. GAME SHOW STAGE – THAT MOMENT</u>   240.

CAMERA (STEADICAM) follows Mary as she runs over to Jimmy.

                          JIMMY
              Take me outta here, Mary...I gotta
              go, I gotta go home to Rose, please, please.

She leads him away. CAMERA moves over to BURT who's dealing with
the situation -- RICK comes running over, looking for Stanley.
"Where is he? Where the fuck did he go?" Burt tries to calm him down.

CAMERA moves over to Cynthia who's dealing with Richard and Julia
and Mim and Luis and Todd.

                          CYNTHIA
              Let's go, c'mon, get up --

                          RICHARD
              Did we win or lose, I mean -- ?

                          CYNTHIA
              I don't know, Richard, they need
              to talk it over --

                          LUIS
              You lost, kid. They go to the score
              at the time it was called --

                          JULIA
              That's not an official rule.

                          LUIS
              That's the way it goes.

                          RICHARD
              Bullshit. Who says that, what rule book,
              in what sport? This is different, it's a quiz show,
              they don't go by sports rules --

                          MIM
              Let's all just settle down --

                          CYNTHIA
              Richard, shut it and keep it down.

                          RICHARD
              If he hadn't pissed his pants, we woulda
              won. We fucking had this game.

                          LUIS
              You didn't have shit, kid.

CAMERA with Jimmy and Mary as they head off, down the HALLWAY
and towards some elevators -- He's really out of it --

                                              CUT TO:

241. <u>INT. CLAUDIA'S APARTMENT - THAT MOMENT</u>   241.

She sits in front of the coke and in front of the television.

CU. TELEVISION IMAGE - THAT MOMENT

A still card with the "What Do Kids Know?" logo and the credits
still running. At the end a logo that reads:

<u>This has been a Big Earl Partridge Production</u>

CUT TO:

242. <u>EXT. WASH AREA/APARTMENT - DAY</u>   242.

CAMERA (HAND HELD) with Jim Kurring. He's searches around
frantic for his revolver....looking everywhere...RAIN IS POURING.

He does tearful "cops" dial. Ref: "I'm not goin' back
to the Station House without my god damn gun." etc.

CUT TO:

243. <u>EXT. STREETS/BURBANK - THAT MOMENT</u>   243.

CAMERA tracks with Stanley as he runs and runs down the streets
in the RAIN. CAMERA holds a ECU as we move.

CUT TO:

244. <u>EXT. SMILING PEANUT/PARKING AREA - THAT MOMENT</u>   244.

Donnie walks out and gets in his car -- he goes to start it,
but it won't start. HOLD outtside the car. Rain pouring down.

He gets out and walks. A Pedestrian walking in to the bar recognizes
him and smiles, says:

PEDESTRIAN
Smart Kid Donnie Smith! Quiz Kid! He.He.

Donnie keeps walking straight past.

CUT TO:

245. <u>INT. EARL'S HOUSE - THAT MOMENT</u>   245.

Linda is bedside with Earl. She cries her eyes out. She
speaks to him in mumbles about "...sorry..." "...my love..."
"...you've lived a long, good life..." She prepares the
bottle of liquid morphine and sets it next to the him...HOLD.

Earl comes out of it a bit, pets her head, mumbles a few words that don't make sense. Phil in the b.g. Linda can't administer the drops, she turns quickly to Phil;

> LINDA
> listen...listen to me now, Phil:
> I'm sorry, sorry....I slapped your face.
> ...because I don't know what I'm doing...
> ...I don't know how to do this, y'know?
> You understand? y'know? I...I'm...I do things
> and I fuck up and I fucked up....forgive me, ok?
> Can you....just...

> PHIL
> ....it's alright....

> LINDA
> Tell him I'm sorry, ok, yes, you do that,
> now, I'm sorry, tell him, for all the things
> I've done...I fucked up and I'm sorry....
> And I'm Gonna Turn Away And Walk Now And Not
> Look At Him Not See My Man, My Earl, I'll
> leave now...and tell him it's ok and I'm ok.
> The whole thing was ok with me -- and I know.

She turns quick and walks out of the house.

HOLD ON PHIL. He paces around a moment or two, looks at the side table.

CU - THE BOTTLE OF LIQUID MORPHINE.
It's ready to go.

CU - PHIL. He looks at it.

                                            CUT TO:

246. <u>INT. HOLIDAY INN - SEMINAR ROOM - THAT MOMENT</u>   246.

CAMERA holds on the image of a slide that reads:

<u>"How To Fake Like You Are Nice And Caring"</u>

Frank steps into FRAME. HOLD. OC we hear the audience applaud.

> FRANK
> Welcome back. Back from break.
> I hope you guys stayed away from those
> little nacho bits I saw out there...
> I know...I know...hey, you're not payin'
> for the snacks....

Slight laughter. Frank slows down.

                    FRANK
        "How To Fake Like You Are Nice and Caring."
        This is...obviously...quite an important
        section...I mean, let's face it...face the
        facts...Men Are Shit, right? I mean,
        that is what they all say. We've all done
        bad things...bad things that no woman
        has ever done...that's what they say.
        We As Men are taught to apologize: "I've done wrong."
        "I'm sorry." "My needs as a man made me..."
        Something, something...bullshit....well what
        I would like to say....

Frank references some note cards, a bit of a daze is clear now:

                    FRANK
        If you feel, made to feel like you need
        them, like -- like you can't live if
        you're without them or you need, what?
        They're pussy? They're love? Fuck that.
        Self Sufficient, gents. That's the truth.
        What you are -- we are -- you need them
        for what? To fucking make you a piece of
        snot rag? A puppett? huh? Hear them
        bitch and moan? bitch and moan --
        and we're taught one thing -- go the other
        way -- there is No Excuse I will give you,
        I'm not gonna apologize -- I'm not gonna
        apologize for my NEED my DESIRE...my, the
        things that I need as a man to feel comfortable...
        You understand? You understand? You need
        to say something, "my mommy hit me or
        daddy hit me or didn't let me play soccer,
        so now I make mistakes, cause a that -- something,
        so now I piss and shit on it and do this."
        Bullshit. I'm sorry. ok. yeah. no. fuck.
        go. fuck. alright. go make a new mistake.
        maybe not, I dunno...fuck....

Frank drops the microphone and walks off stage...Audience rumbles
with confusion, etc. Doc and Captain Muffy frantic, etc. Frank
heads off -- slight look across the reception hall to see Gwenovier --

He's gone.

                                        CUT TO:

247. <u>INT. EARL'S HOUSE - THAT MOMENT</u>   <u>Sequence H</u>   **247.**

    CAMERA on Earl. He opens his eyes a bit....looks over to Phil.

                         EARL
               Phil...Phil...

    Phil comes over and takes a seat next to him.

                         EARL
               I'm onna try and talk...I'm atryan
               say some thing some thing...

    Earl begins to talk. (<u>Director's Note</u>: Following is the story
Earl tells, it is to be more broken and elliptical, factoring
in Earl's state of mind and health, etc, but here's the concept
in its entirety;)

                         EARL
               Do you know Lily? Phil..do you know her?

                         PHIL
               No.

                         EARL
               ...Lily...?

                         PHIL
               No.

                         EARL
               She's my love...my life...love of it...
               In school....when you're 12 years old.
               In school, in six grade....and I saw her
               and I didn't go to that school...but we met.
               And my friend knew her...I would say,
               "What's that girl?" "How's that Lily?"
               "Oh, she's a bad girl...she sleeps with
               guys..." My friend would say this....but
               then sometime...I went to another school, you see?
               But then...when high school at the end, what's
               that? What is that? When you get to the end?

                         PHIL
               Graduation?

                         EARL
               No, no, the grade...the grade that you're in?

                         PHIL
               Twelve.

                        EARL
        Yeah...So I go to her school for that
        for grade twelve...and we meet...she
        was fuckin...like a doll...porcelain
        doll...and the hips...child bearing
        hips...y'know that? So beautiful.
        But I didn't have sex with anyone,
        you know? I was not...I couldn't
        do anything...always scared, y'know...
        she was...she had some boyfriends...they
        liked her y'know...but I didn't like that.
        I couldn't get over that I wasn't a man,
        but she was a woman. Y'see? Y'see I didn't
        make her feel ok about that....I would
        say, "How many men you been with?"
        She told me, I couldn't take it...take that
        I wasn't a man....because if I hadn't had
        sex with women...like as many women as
        she had men...then I was weak...a boy....
        But I loved her...you understand?
        ....well, of course, I wanted to have
        sex with her...and I did and we were
        together....we met...age twelve, but then
        again...age seventeen...something, somethin...
        I didn't let her forget that I thought she
        was a bad...a slut....a slut I would call
        her and hit her....I hit her for what she
        did...but we married...Lily and me and we
        married...but I cheated on her...over and
        over and over again...because I wanted
        to be a man and I couldn't let her be
        a woman...a smart, free person who was
        something...my mind then, so fuckin'
        stupid, so fuckin....jesus christ, what
        would I think...did I think....?
        ...for what I've done...She's my wife for
        thirty eight years...I went behind her...
        over and over...fucking asshole I am
        that I would go out and fuck and come
        home and get in her bed....and say
        "I love you..." This'z Jack's mother.
        His mother Lily...these two that I had
        and I lost .... and this is the regret that
        you make...the regret you make is the
        something that you take...blah...blah...blah...
        something, something....
                        (beat)
        Gimme a cigarettee....?

Through the following Phil tries to give Earl a cigarette,
which Earl can't get to his mouth, but then mimes that he's
smoking as he starts to get more and more delusional, etc.

149

                    EARL
          She had cancer...from her...in her
          stomach....and I didn't go anywhere
          with her...and I didn't do a god thing...
          for her and to help her....shit...this
          bitch...the beautiful, beautiful bitch
          with perfect skin and child bearing
          hips and so soft...her namewasLilysee?
                    (beat, fading)
          He liked her though he did, his mom,
          Frank/Jack...he took care of her and she died.
          She didn't stick with him and he thinks
          and he hates me, ok...see...I'm...that's
          then what you get?
          ....are you still walkin' in that car...?

                    PHIL
          What? Say it again...walking in the car?

                    EARL
          ....getthat on the tv....there...

Earl starts to break down in tears, streaming out of his eyes,
his body isn't moving at all;

                    EARL
          ...mistakes like this are not ok...
          sometimes you make some, and ok...not
          sometimes to make other one....know
          that you should do better....I loved Lily.
          I cheated on her. For thirty five years.
          And I have this son. And she has cancer.
          And I'm not there. And he's forced to take
          care of her. He's fourteen years old to take
          care of his mother and watch her die on him.
          Little Kid. And I'm not there. And She Dies.
          And I Live My Life. And I'm Not Fair.
          Thirty eight years and she has cancer and
          I'm gone...I leave...I walk out, I can't
          deal with that...who am I? Who the fuck
          do I think I am to go and do a thing?
          Shit on that and that lovely person.
          I'll go away...I'll go away...I can't
          hold this..you gotta take this fuckin'
          pen outta my hand...you fuckin' piss, cocksucker...
          ....atke this....

Phil mimes as if he's taking a pen from Earl's hand.

                    PHIL
          I got it.

CAMERA stays with PHIL. Hold on him as Earl continues a moment.
SLOW DOLLY IN.

> EARL
> OH FUCK...THIS FUCKIN STORY HAS FALLEN APART
> and I don't even think I can...I got no
> punchline -- we had good times later,
> the best times, the love of my life,
> thirty eight years -- but never the respect
> and the...she knew what I did...she knew...
> all the stupid things I've done....but the
> LOVE was stronger than anything you can think up.

CAMERA LANDS CU ON PHIL. Earl's Voice continues over the following:

                                                    CUT TO:

248.   EXT. JIMMY GATOR'S HOUSE - THAT MOMENT/EVENING   248.

Jimmy and Mary pull up in the pouring rain. Rose comes out and
they help him in the house.

> EARL'S VOICE
> ...The attachment....I loved her so much.
> And I didn't treat her and the goddamn
> regret...THE GODDAMN REGRET...and I'll die...

                                                    CUT TO:

249.   INT. JIMMY GATOR'S HOUSE - THAT MOMENT/EVENING   249.

Rose and Mary help Jimmy to the couch and get him situated.

> EARL'S VOICE
> Now I'll die and I'll tell you: what?
> The biggest regret of my life:
> I let my love go.....

                                                    CUT TO:

250.   INT. CLAUDIA'S APARTMENT - THAT MOMENT/EVENING   250.

Claudia in the shower. Claudia brushing her hair in the mirror.
Claudia attempting to look nice. Claudia, dressed for the date,
sits in front of the coke and looks at it;

> EARL'S VOICE
> ...I ruined my love...jesus...jesus christ.
> what did I do....and I had to get away...?
> something, something to do....I can't explain.
> ....I love her so much....leave her there....
> and to punish...punish her....

                                                    CUT TO:

251. <u>INT. POLICE CAR - THAT MOMENT/EVENING</u>   251.

Jim Kurring on the radio of his squad car, reports the gun missing.
(Technical language here.)

                    EARL'S VOICE
          ....and the punishment for what? What?
          ...nothing....and I'm so embarresed....
          so embarresed for what I've done...

                                              CUT TO:

252. <u>INT. WASH AREA/APARTMENT BUILDING - THAT MOMENT/EVENING</u>   252.

Other OFFICERS assist in the search for the missing gun. They are out
with flashlights, etc. A severe search of the area is underway. Jim
Kurring is clearly getting a lot of shit from the other officers, etc.

                    EARL'S VOICE
          I'm seventy five years old and embarresed.
          ....million years ago...my fuckin REGRET
          AND GUILT AND....these things...don't
          let anyone tell you that you shouldn't
          regret anything....don't do that...don't....

                                              CUT TO:

253. <u>INT. POLICE STATION/REPORT WRITING ROOM - LATER/EVENING</u>   253*

CAMERA pushes in on Jim Kurring, in civilian clothes now, filling
out a Loss Report. CU's on the form. OC voices of officers making
fun of him, etc. CAMERA continues a bit past him, views, through
some window, MARCIE...across the way in a detaining room.

                    EARL'S VOICE
          ...you fuckin' regret what you want...
          ...use that....use that....

253A <u>INT. HOLDING ROOM - THAT MOMENT</u>   253A*

CAMERA pushes in on Marcie. She's crying and looking down.
She lifts her head, speaks to an UNSEEN OFFICER nearby, guarding
her cell;

                    MARCIE
          I wanna confess what I've done.

                                              CUT TO:

254. <u>INT. SCHOOL LIBRARY - THAT MOMENT/EVENING</u>   254.

Stanley breaks a window. Stanley reaches in and unlocks a lock.
Stanley rummages around the dark school library. He's soaking
wet...he accumulates a bunch of books and starts to search for
stuff....CU - Dissolve images, optical, etc. (child performers,etc)

                    EARL'S VOICE
          ....use that regret for you any way
          you want...you can use that ok....
          someone says not to regret or think about
          the past, something, mistakes we make.....bullshit.

                                                    CUT TO:

255. <u>INT. DONNIE SMITH'S APARTMENT - THAT MOMENT/EVENING</u>   255.

Donnie takes some KEYS out of a kitchen drawer and puts them
on his key chain. Donnie places the keys on one by one....

                    EARL'S VOICE
          ....this is a long way to go for no
          punch...a little moral....story I say...
          Love. love. love....this fuckin' life....
          ohhhhhhh, love.....

                                                    CUT TO:

256. <u>EXT. EMPTY PARKING LOT - THAT MOMENT/EVENING/NIGHT</u>   256.

CAMERA holds a wide angle. Linda's Mercedes is parked.

                                                    CUT TO:

257. <u>INT. LINDA'S CAR - THAT MOMENT/EVENING/NIGHT</u>   257.

Linda takes some pills. Then she takes some more...then she takes
some more....then she swallows a whole bottle of pills...she
drinks from a small bottle of Vodka....swallows every last pill.....

                    EARL'S VOICE
          ...it's so fuckin' hard....and so long....
          life ain't short it's long....Life is long,
          goddamnit -- god damn....whatd I do?
          Whatd I do? ohhhh what'dIdo?

                                                    CUT TO:

258. <u>INT. FRANK'S CAR - THAT MOMENT/NIGHT</u>   258.

CAMERA holds CU on Frank. He just sits. BEAT. THEN.

WIDER ANGLE, THAT MOMENT.
Reveal that Frank's car is sitting out front of Earl's house.

The Mexican Nurse that we saw earlier in the film, who Phil
relieved, walks past his car and up to Earl's house...

CUT TO:

259. <u>INT. EARL'S HOUSE – MOMENTS LATER/NIGHT</u>   259.

Phil quietly stands in the front doorway, sotto words with the
Mexican Nurse, who keeps outside.

                    PHIL
        It's ok...I'm gonna stay...stay it out.

The Mexican Nurse nods, understands. Phil turns back into the house.

                                              CUT TO:

260. <u>INT. EARL'S HOUSE – THAT MOMENT/NIGHT</u>   260.

CAMERA CU on the bottle of liquid morphine. Phil's hand comes
into FRAME and takes it....TILT up to his face.

Phil is in tears....he dips the baby dropper in the bottle.....

Earl is out of breath, painfully....Phil hesitates, then:

CU – <u>The liquid morhphine is dropped into Earl's mouth.</u>

                                              CUT TO:

261. <u>INT. CLAUDIA'S APARTMENT – THAT MOMENT/NIGHT</u>   261.

She looks at the coke in front of her. She hesitates. Her stereo is
playing a song....it plays softly, then gets a bit louder....

She leans down and SNORTS the fat line of COKE. HOLD on her....she
starts to sing along with the song....

                    CLAUDIA
        "..it's not what you thought when you
        first began it...you got what you want....
        now you can hardly stand it though by now
        you know, it's not going to stop....."   *

The SONG continues. The following has each of the principles
half singing along with the song, who's lead vocal will stay
constant throughout.

                                              CUT TO:

262. <u>INT. JIM KURRING'S APARTMENT – THAT MOMENT</u>   262.

CAMERA PUSHES in slowly on Jim Kurring. He sits on the bed, dressed up
and ready to go. He starts to sing along to the song as well.

                    JIM KURRING
        ...it's not going to stop...it's not   *
        going to stop 'till you wise up..."   *

                                                    CUT TO:

262A <u>INT. JIMMY'S HOUSE - OFFICE - THAT MOMENT</u>   262A*

     CAMERA moves in towards Jimmy, alone, sitting in his office, singing. *

                         JIMMY GATOR   *
                 "You're sure there's a cure and you   *
                 have finally found it...."   *

                                                    CUT TO:

263. <u>INT. DONNIE'S APARTMENT - THAT MOMENT</u>   263.

     CAMERA pushes in on Donnie Smith as he starts to sing.

                         DONNIE SMITH
                 "You think....one drink...will shrink
                 'till you're underground and living down,
                 but it's not going to stop..."

                                                    CUT TO:

264. <u>INT. EARL'S HOUSE - THAT MOMENT</u>   264.

     CAMERA DOLLIES in on Phil, holding back his tears and singing
     along to the song...as he sits over Earl....

                            PHIL
                 "It's not going to stop...it's not
                 going to stop...."

     CAMERA moves over to Earl, eyes closed, starts to sing as well...

                            EARL
                 "...it's not going to stop 'till   *
                 you wise up..."

                                                    CUT TO:

265. <u>INT. EMPTY PARKING LOT - THAT MOMENT</u>   265.

     CAMERA DOLLIES in on LINDA. She's passed out in her car, head
     pressed against the glass, but she starts to sing along....

                            LINDA
                 "...prepare a list of what you need
                 before you sign away the deed, 'cause
                 it's not going to stop..."

                                                    CUT TO:

266. <u>INT. FRANK'S CAR - PARKED - THAT MOMENT</u>   266.

CAMERA pushes in a bit on Frank, singing along.

                   FRANK
      "...it's not going to stop...it's not
      going to stop....it's not gonna
      stop 'till you wise up, no it's not
      gonna stop..."

                                      CUT TO:

267. <u>INT. SCHOOL LIBRARY - THAT MOMENT</u>   267.

CAMERA pushes in, (light coming up from the book he reads)
optical, glimpse what he reads....then pulls back from STANLEY.

                 STANLEY
      "..till you wise up, no it's not
      going to stop, so just....give up."

PULL BACK.

                                      CUT TO:

268. <u>EXT. SKY - NIGHT</u>   <u>Sequence I</u>   268.

The rain stops. Suddenly and quickly it's over. Clear as a bell. HOLD.

Title card: <u>Weather information,etc</u>.

                                      CUT TO:

269. <u>INT. CLAUDIA'S APARTMENT - STAIRWELL - NIGHT</u>   269.

The door opens and Claudia looks really nice. Jim Kurring smiles
and says hello.

                                      CUT TO:

270. <u>EXT. CLAUDIA'S APARTMENT - MOMENTS LATER</u>   270.

Jim Kurring opens the door for Claudia and she gets in.
He runs around and they drive off.

                                      CUT TO:

271.   INT. DONNIE'S APARTMENT - THAT MOMENT   271.

Donnie takes the KEYS and puts on big dark coat and looks
in the mirror.

                          DONNIE
              You know, you know, you know. Go,go,go.

                                                      CUT TO:

272.   INT. DONNIE'S APARTMENT - STAIRWELL - THAT MOMENT   272.

Donnie knocks on his neighbor's door. A little OLD LADY opens up;

                        LITTLE OLD LADY
                  Donnie, oh, Donnie --

                          DONNIE
              Hello, dear...I need a favor.

                                                      CUT TO:

273.   EXT. DONNIE'S APARTMENT - CAR PORT - THAT MOMENT   273.

Donnie comes down and gets in the little old lady's
Buick Regal and starts it up.

                                                      CUT TO:

274.   EXT. EARL'S HOUSE - THAT MOMENT   274.

Frank gets out of his car and walks up to the house.
He rings the doorbell.

                                                      CUT TO:

275.   INT. EARL'S HOUSE - THAT MOMENT   275.

The DOGS go crazy barking. Phil walks away from Earl and answers
the door. Frank standing there. Phil looks a bit surprised and
fumbles a moment...They stand in doorway and speak very quietly;

                          PHIL
              Hello. Frank. Frank TJ Mackey.

                          FRANK
              ...are you Phil...?

                          PHIL
              Yeah. I was trying to get in touch
              with you. We got dissconnected.

                          FRANK
              I got your message. That you were
              trying to get me -- right?

                PHIL
Yes. I didn't know how to find you.
Earl asked me, so I looked through
the adress books and there was no number,
nothing --

                FRANK
Is Linda here?

                PHIL
She's not here, she went out.
I'm sorry. This is all just so,
I don't know what, what to do -- your
Dad asked me to try and track you down.
To get you and I did, I called the number --
Do you wanna come in?

                FRANK
Yeah....let's...maybe just stand.

                PHIL
These Dogs'll calm down -- you just
have to come in --

He steps in the door and the dogs start to settle down a bit.

                PHIL
He's in here.

                FRANK
Let's just wait one minute and stay here, okay?

                PHIL
Ok.

BEAT. They stand in the foyer and the dogs eventually calm down
and go away. BEAT.

                FRANK
How long have you taken care of him?

                PHIL
For six months. I'm the day nurse...

                FRANK
Uh-huh. What's going on?

                PHIL
He's...I'm sorry...so sorry...I've seen
this before, you know and you don't....
He's going very fast....Frank...um....

                FRANK
Is he in pain?

                    PHIL
          I just...he was...but I gave him,
          I just had to give him a small dose of
          liquid morphine. He hasn't been able to
          swallow the morphine pills so we now,
          I just had to go to the liquid morphine...
          For the pain, you understand?

                    FRANK
          ...uh-huh...

BEAT. Silence, then:

                    FRANK
          How long...you think?

                    PHIL
          Um...soon....tonight...I think, yes?
          Tommorrow...I mean...very soon...very...

                    FRANK
          When did he go off chemo?

                    PHIL
          About three weeks ago.

                    FRANK
          ....have you ever seen this..I mean,
          never mind, you said --

                    PHIL
          I work as a nurse, for a proffesion --

                    FRANK
          Uh. huh.

                    PHIL
          I'm really sorry.

                    FRANK
          He's in here -- ?

                    PHIL
          Yeah.

Phil starts to guide him, Frank holds him back,.

                    FRANK
          No, let's just wait one minute,.
          let's just stand here one minute or so --

BEAT. They stand. HOLD.

                    PHIL
          I've heard your tapes on the phone.

                         FRANK
                    Oh yeah.

                         PHIL
                    When they put me on hold, to
                    talk to you...they play the tapes.
                    I mean: I'd seen the commercials
                    and heard about you, but I'd never heard
                    the tapes ....

                         FRANK
                    Uh. huh.

                         PHIL
                    It's interesting.

                         FRANK
                    Mmm.

     Long pause. Then:

                                                              CUT TO:

276. OMIT**(Scene changed to Sc. 277A)   *
276A INT. LAMPLIGHTER – THAT MOMENT   276A*

     CAMERA with Stanley, sitting alone in a booth with a Coke and a cookie.
     He's reading a book. BEAT, HOLD, THEN:

     CAMERA pans/dollies away and booms up -- moving across the   *
     restaraunt -- across the way, sitting in a booth by the opposite . *
     window, out of view from Stanley;   *

     Dixon, the little kid from earlier, sitting in a booth with a   *
     young black male, WORM (20s) This is clearly the back figure   *
     we've been seeing glimpses of --   *

     ANGLE, AT THE BOOTH.   *
     Dixon eats some pudding. Worm mumbles to him, various jabs.   *
     "...sit up straight..." "...world is hard..." "..little brat..."   *

     HOLD. Worm glances across the coffee shop -- he sees Stanley.   *

     Worm HOLDS his look, thinks a moment. He looks up at the   *
     WOMAN behind the counter...she's doing a crossword puzzle.   *

     Worm looks back to Dixon, subtle mumbles and gestures and   *
     few moments later, Dixon stands from the booth and exits the   *
     coffee shop.   *

     HOLD w/WORM. He sticks a finger down his throat, makes himself   *
     well with tears. He stands up OUT OF FRAME.   *

     ANGLE, COUNTER NEAR STANLEY.   *
     Worm sits into FRAME, near to Stanley. Stanley glances up, they   *
     make a quick moment of eye contact, then look away. BEAT. HOLD.   *

                                                              CUT TO:

277. OMIT**(Scene changed to Sc.276A)
277A EXT. PARKING LOT/BEHIND LAMPLIGHTER - MOMENTS LATER   277A*

    CAMERA follows Dixon as he walks towards an old beat up PARKED CAR.
He stops, hesitates, looks across the way --

    LINDA'S MERCEDES is parked.

    He hestitates a moment, looks left and right and all around
and then he starts to walk over to the car...

    AT LINDA'S CAR. Dixon sees that she's passed out, knocks on
the window...

                   DIXON
        Lady...hey Lady...Lady....you ok?
        you alive...huh...hey....?

    He looks around again, then gets in the passenger's side of the
car, shakes her some more.....

                   DIXON
        Lady. Lady. Hey wake up. Lady?

    Dixon reaches down and takes her PURSE, takes the MONEY out of the
WALLET and then reaches for her CEL PHONE and dials 911.

                   DIXON
        Hello? Hello? I have an emergency
        situation -- this lady -- this lady
        seems like she's dead -- hello?
        She's in the parking lot -- (etc. gives
        information reagrding location. etc.)

    Then he gets out, walks back across parking lot...and into the
concealed parked car he came from --

                               CUT TO:

278. INT. JIMMY'S HOUSE - LIVING ROOM - THAT MOMENT   278.

    Jimmy and Rose. They're on the couch. Lights dim. Sitting, talking.
She hands him a pill from a bottle with a drink.

                   JIMMY
        I don't think I want that.

                   ROSE
        It'll take the pain away.

                   JIMMY
        It's not really pain.

    She sets it on the coffee table, sits down. Drinks a drink herself.

                    JIMMY
          I gotta ask you for a cigarette, 'cause
          I don't wanna spend six hours tryin'
          to get it to my mouth --

She lights a cigarette, puts it in his hand and he struggles
a bit with his hand/eye coordination....beat, then;

                    JIMMY
          How do we do this, then?

                    ROSE
          We just do it...we do it and we figure it
          out and we do as we do, I guess...

                    JIMMY
          Do you love me, Rose?

She smiles and moves closer to him.

                    ROSE
          You're my handsome man.

                    JIMMY
          I'm a bad person.

                    ROSE
          No. No.

                    JIMMY
          No, I mean: I'm telling you this, now.
          You see? You see....I want to make
          everything clear and clean...and
          apologize for me....for all the stupid
          things I've done....that will eat me up....

                    ROSE
          You feel like you want to be forgiven
          for your sins? Honey, you're not on
          your death bed, yet....this kinda talk's
          gonna get you in trouble --

                    JIMMY
          --- don't. don't. Please. Just...
          listen to me...honey....
                    (beat)
          ...I've done...I've cheated on you.

Rose doesn't move much. Hold.

                    JIMMY
          I've cheated on you and it kills me
          and the guilt of what I've done...I don't
          want you to think...maybe you knew,
          I think that maybe you've known...
          So I hope that I'm not saying this for
          me...for me to make myself feel better
          about what I've done...but for making
          you not feel like you're sitting there
          like a jerk...you've been the good one...
          You understand...I'm so sorry for all I've done
          wrong...and this is pathetic...what?
          "Dying man, confess the sins" something?
          Is it selfish for me to say this? To
          say what I've done...I feel better already.
          I do...do you hate me?

Rose takes a long moment, then:

                    ROSE
          ...No...I don't hate you.
                    (beat)
          Do you want talk...do you really
          want to <u>talk</u> to me and say things
          and get things figured out, Jimmy?

                    JIMMY
          Yeah.

                    ROSE
          The question isn't wether or not
          you cheated on me, the question is
          how many times have you cheated on me?

                    JIMMY
          Will that help?

                    ROSE
          Yeah.

                                        CUT TO:

279.   <u>INT. BILLINGSLEY'S - THAT MOMENT</u>   279.

In a secluded table in this dark steak place. Jim Kurring and
Claudia. CAMERA does a slow push in on a 2-shot.

                    CLAUDIA
          Did you ever go out with someone
          and just....lie....question after
          question, maybe you're trying to
          make yourself look cool or better
          than you are or whatever, or smarter
          or cooler and you just -- not really
          lie, but maybe you just don't say everything --

                    JIM KURRING
          Well, that's a natural thing, two people
          go out on a date, something. They want
          to impress people, the other person...or
          they're scared maybe what they say will
          make the other person not like them --

                    CLAUDIA
          So you've done it --

                    JIM KURRING
          Well I don't go out very much.

                    CLAUDIA
          Why not?

                    JIM KURRING
          I've never found someone really that
          I think I would like to go out with.

                    CLAUDIA
          And I bet you say that to all the girls --

                    JIM KURRING
          No, no.

                    CLAUDIA
          You wanna make a deal with me?

                    JIM KURRING
          ok.

                    CLAUDIA
          What I just said...y'know, people
          afraid to say things....no guts to
          say the things that they...that are real
          or something...

                    JIM KURRING
          ...yeah...

                    CLAUDIA
          To not do that. To not do that that
          we've maybe done -- before --

                    JIM KURRING
          Let's make a deal.

                    CLAUDIA
          Ok. I'll tell you everything and
          you tell me everything and maybe
          we can get through all the piss
          and shit and lies that kill other
          people....

He laughs a bit uncomfortable...repeats her line;

                    JIM KURRING
          Wow....huh..."...piss and shit..."

                    CLAUDIA
          What?

                    JIM KURRING
          You really use strong language.

                    CLAUDIA
          I'm sorry --

                    JIM KURRING
          -- no, no, it's fine. Fine.

                    CLAUDIA
          I didn't mean...it's seems vulgar
          or something, I know --

                    JIM KURRING
          It's fine.

                    CLAUDIA
          I'm sorry.

                    JIM KURRING
          ...nothing. I'm sorry...

                    CLAUDIA
          No, I'm sorry. I'm saying I'm sorry.
          I talk like a jerk sometimes --

                    JIM KURRING
          -- well I'm a real...y'know, straight
          when it comes to that...curse words
          I just don't use much --

                    CLAUDIA
          I'm sorry.

BEAT.

> CLAUDIA
> I'm gonna run to the bathroom for
> a minute...maybe just --

> JIM KURRING
> ok.

> CLAUDIA
> ok.

She goes. HOLD with him for a moment.

CUT TO:

280.   EXT. SOLOMON and SOLOMON ELECTRONICS - THAT MOMENT   280.

CAMERA is around back with Donnie in the Buick Regal.
He parks, gets out, looks around the empty place.

CAMERA tracks with him towards a back loading dock area.
He puts a large HAT on his head, to cover his face.

He takes one of the KEYS from the key chain and uses it to
get in a door in back. He enters.

CUT TO:

281.   INT. SOLOMON AND SOLOMON ELECTRONICS - THAT MOMENT   281.

Donnie in a back corridor. He walks down through some BOXES
and assorted MERCHANDISE towards another door. He pulls his
hat down some more, moves swiftly.

He arrives at another door and does a KEY PAD CODE thing and
also uses ANOTHER KEY from the key chain.

ANOTHER BACK CORRIDOR
Donnie enters, walks towards Solomon's office and does another
Key Pad Code and Lock thing and enters --

282.   SOLOMON'S OFFICE   282.
Donnie enters, takes a quick beeline to behind the desk and
under the floor, under a rug....he kneels down....

DONNIE'S POV
he pulls the rug back and there's a SAFE. He does the combination
and opens it up.

IN THE SAFE.
There's five stacks of five thousand dollars for a total of
$25,000. In addition, some jewelry and some papers, etc.

CU - DONNIE
he starts to take the money, putting into a plastic shopping bag.

CUT TO:

283.   <u>INT. EARL'S HOUSE - THAT MOMENT</u>   283.

Frank and Phil stand in the foyer. They're quiet a moment, then:

> FRANK
> So....Phil....um...I think I'm gonna
> step in and try and see him and say
> something if he can...talk...I mean:

> PHIL
> ...ok...

> FRANK
> Can you stand...back...maybe, I mean...
> just a little bit...in the room is
> ok, but back from us a little...

> PHIL
> yeah.

Frank walks slowly into the Living Room and over to Earl's
bedside. He's holding back his tears. He sits. Earl
is eyes closed, breathing a bit irregular....HOLD.

> FRANK
> ...Dad...Dad...hey...Earl?

He tries to wake him a bit, but Earl is not moving.

> FRANK
> ...hey...Dad...Dad can you wake up
> a minute....Dad....?

He turns to Phil, crying now, says:

> FRANK
> He's not waking up.

CUT TO:

284.   <u>INT. JIMMY'S HOUSE - THAT MOMENT</u>   284.

CAMERA holds CU on Jimmy.

> ROSE
> How many times....it's ok...just say...
> Just say ...

> JIMMY
> I don't even remember...many...twenty...
> maybe more...not much more...twenty times.

BEAT.

> ROSE
> I don't hate you, Jimmy. But I have
> a couple questions that I wanna ask....

> JIMMY
> I'll answer anything.

> ROSE
> Was there anyone that I know?

> JIMMY
> Yes.

> ROSE
> Who?

> JIMMY
> Rose, I don't --

> ROSE
> hey.

> JIMMY
> Paula. Ellen.

She laughs a bit, rolls her eyes.

> JIMMY
> That's it.

> ROSE
> No one else that I know?

> JIMMY
> No.

> ROSE
> How long with Ellen?

> JIMMY
> Just once.

> ROSE
> How long with Paula?

> JIMMY
> Two years...three years...

> ROSE
> What about now?

> JIMMY
> It's over. I talked to her
> this morning.

> ROSE
> Is it over 'cause you're sick?

                    JIMMY
          It's over becuase...for all the
          right reasons I hope, what I said.

                    ROSE
          Do you have any children with anyone?

                    JIMMY
          What? No, Rose, jesus, no --

                    ROSE
          Well maybe.

                    JIMMY
          I don't.

                    ROSE
          Do you feel better now that you've said this?

                    JIMMY
          I don't know....

                    ROSE
          I'm not mad. I am, but I'm not. Y'know?

                    JIMMY
          I love you so much.

                    ROSE
          I'm not through asking my questions.

Jimmy laughs a bit, smiles.

                    ROSE
          Why doesn't Claudia talk to you, Jimmy?

                    JIMMY
          Why, well I think we've, we both
          don't know...what do you mean?

                    ROSE
          I think that you know.

                    JIMMY
          Maybe...I don't...

BEAT. HOLD.

                                             CUT TO:

285. EXT. VENTURA BLVD. - THAT MOMENT   285.

     CAMERA tracks with an AMBULANCE rushing down the street.

                                             CUT TO:

285A <u>INT. LAMPLIGHTER - THAT MOMENT</u>   285A*

Through the window, the AMBULANCE passes in the b.g., heading   *
nearby...and OC we hear the siren throughout scene;   *

....Stanley looks up at Worm, who's crying harder now, they make   *
another moment of eye contact. BEAT, THEN: *

                    WORM   *
          Hi.   *

                    STANLEY   *
          Hi.   *

                    WORM   *
          ..sorry...   *

                    STANLEY   *
          It's ok.   *

BEAT.

                    STANLEY   *
          Are you alright?   *

Worm looks up.   *
                                                        CUT TO:

286. <u>EXT. EMPTY PARKING LOT - THAT MOMENT</u>   286.

The AMBULANCE arrives at Linda's Mercedes and the PARAMEDICS
hop out, open the doors, call direction and try to speak with
her and revive, etc. CAMERA is HAND HELD and moving frantically
with them;

                    PARAMEDICS (various)
          Hello, hello, can you hear us, huh?
          Stay with us, can you hear me...etc. etc.

287. ANGLE, ACROSS THE PARKING LOT.   287.
      Dixon is hiding way across the way in the shadowed, hidden
      parked car, watching the paramedics. All the while he counts
      the money from Linda's wallet.

                                                        CUT TO:

288. <u>INT. BILLINGSLEY'S BATHROOM - THAT MOMENT.</u>   288.

CAMERA with Claudia, she snorts some coke off her hand in the stall.
She takes a quick look in the mirror, walks out --

                                                        CUT TO:

289.   <u>INT. BILLINGSLEY'S - THAT MOMENT</u>   289.

CAMERA tracks with Claudia as she walks back to the table...she
comes up from behind Jim Kurring and leans in quick...KISSES
HIM ON THE CHEEK and then quickly sits down across from him;

                         CLAUDIA
             I wanted to do that.

Jim Kurring smiles, shaken a bit.

                         JIM KURRING
             Well.

                         CLAUDIA
             That felt good to do...to do what
             I wanted to do.

                         JIM KURRING
             Yeah.

                         CLAUDIA
             Can I tell you something?

                         JIM KURRING
             Yeah, of course.

                         CLAUDIA
             I'm really nervous that you're
             gonna hate me soon. That you're
             gonna find stuff out about me
             and you're gonna hate me --

                         JIM KURRING
             -- no, like what, what do you mean?

                         CLAUDIA
             You're a police officer. You have
             so much, so many good things and
             you seem so together...so all straight
             and put together without problems.

                         JIM KURRING
             I lost my gun.

                         CLAUDIA
             What?

JIM KURRING

I lost my gun after I left you today
and I'm the laughing stock of a lot
of people. I wanted to tell you that.
I wanted you to know...and it's on my mind
and it makes me look like a fool and
I feel like a fool and you asked that
we should say things, that we should
say what we're thinknig and not lie
about things and I'll tell you that, this:
that I lost my gun and I'm not a good
cop...and I'm looked down at...and I know
that....and I'm scared that once you
find that out you might not like me.

CLAUDIA

Oh my god, Jim. Jim, that was so --

JIM KURRING

I'm sorry --

CLAUDIA

That was so great what you just said.

JIM KURRING

I haven't been on a date since I
was married and that was three years
ago....and Claudia...whatever you
wanna tell me, whatever you think
might scare me, won't...and I will
listen...I will be a good listener
to you if that's what you want...and
you know, you know...I won't judge you....
I can do that sometimes, I know, but
I won't...I can...listen to you and you
shouldn't be scared of scaring me off
or anything that you might think I'll
think or on and on and just say it and
I'll listen to you....

CLAUDIA

You don't how fuckin' stupid I am.

JIM KURRING

It's ok.

CLAUDIA

You don't know how crazy I am.

JIM KURRING

It's ok.

CLAUDIA

I've got troubles.

                    JIM KURRING
          I'll take everything at face value.
          I'll be a good listener to you.

                    CLAUDIA
          Ohhhh I started this, didn't I,
          didn't I, didn't I, fuck.

                    JIM KURRING
          Say what you want and you'll see --

                    CLAUDIA
          Wanna kiss me, Jim?

                    JIM KURRING
            Yes I do.

They lean across the table and kiss each other. CAMERA DOLLIES
IN SUPER QUICK as their lips touch.

                                             CUT TO:

290. INT. SOLOMON AND SOLOMON ELCTRONICS - THAT MOMENT   290.

      Donnie finishes taking the money from the safe....

      ...Donnie walks back one of the corridors and heads through
      a door...(again using the key and code)....

      ...Donnie enters into the warehouse area and heads for
      the door to outside....

      ...He puts the key into the lock and opens the door....but he
      takes a small stumble back and the key chain that's attached to
      his belt gets stuck, causing him to fall back, down and to the
      ground...with the KEY SNAPPING OFF IN THE LOCK....

      ..the door is about to shut on him but he stops it with his
      foot....he gets up, grabs the money...leaves with the
      broken key still left in the lock...

                                             CUT TO:

291. EXT. SOLOMON AND SOLOMON PARKING LOT - THAT MOMENT   291.

      Donnie gets in the Buick Regal and drives away.

                                             CUT TO:

292. EXT. EMPTY PARKING LOT/LINDA'S MERCEDES - THAT MOMENT   292.

      CAMERA (HAND HELD) is in the middle of the PARAMEDICS dealing with
      Linda....they find the pill bottle...they put her on a gurney...they
      search for ID, come up only with the registration for the car and some
      papers in the glove box....they get her into the ambulance....

                                             CUT TO:

293.   <u>INT. LAMPLIGHTER - THAT MOMENT</u>   293.

Stanley finishes his cookie. Worm, sitting across from
him starts to cry a little, very quietly. He hides it best he can.

Stanley looks up here and there from his books. They make another
moment of eye contact....then:

> WORM
>
> Hi.

> STANLEY
>
> Hi.

> WORM
>
> ..sorry...

> STANLEY
>
> It's ok.

BEAT.

> STANLEY
> Are you alright?

Worm looks up.

                                               CUT TO:

294.   <u>INT. JIMMY'S HOUSE - THAT MOMENT</u>   294.

Jimmy and Rose. HOLD. THEN:

> ROSE
> ...say it, Jimmy...

> JIMMY
> Do you know the answer to this?

> ROSE
> I'm asking you. I'm asking you
> if you know why Clauida will not
> speak to you....please, Jimmy....tell me.

> JIMMY
> I think that she thinks I may
> have molested her.

Rose doesn't flinch.

                         JIMMY
          She thinks terrible things that
          somehow got in her head...that I might
          have done something. She said that
          to me last time...when it was...ten
          years ago she walked out the door,
          "You touched me wrong..." "I know that."
          Some crazy thought in her, in her head...

                         ROSE
          Did you ever touch her?

                         JIMMY
          ...No....

HOLD. BEAT. Rose asks again;

                         ROSE
          Jimmy, did you touch her?

                         JIMMY
          I don't know.

Rose starts to cry a bit. So does Jimmy.

                         ROSE
          ...Jimmy...

                         JIMMY
          I really don't know.

                         ROSE
          But you can't say....

                         JIMMY
          I don't know what I've done.

                         ROSE
          Yes you do....you do and you won't say.

                         JIMMY
          ...I don't know...

She stands up and walks to a small table and gets her car keys
and her jacket....

                         JIMMY
          What...? ...no...no, please...

She stands above him.

                         ROSE
          You deserve to die alone for what you've done.

                         JIMMY
          <u>I don't know what I've done.</u>

                              ROSE
              Yes you do.

                              JIMMY
              Stay here, please don't leave me,
              please, please, if I said I knew
              would you stay?

                              ROSE
              No.

                              JIMMY
              I don't know what I've done.

                              ROSE
              You should know better.

She leaves.

                                                        CUT TO:

295.   INT. BILLINGSLEY'S - THAT MOMENT   295.

       CAMERA CU on Claudia as she pulls back from the kiss. HOLD.
       She starts to cry....through her tears, then:

                              CLAUDIA
              ....now that I've met you....
              Would you object to never seeing me again?

CU. JIM

                              JIM KURRING
              What?

                              CLAUDIA
              Just say no.

                              JIM KURRING
              I won't say, no, wait, Claudia --

ECU - The two of them. Tight, tight 2-shot. She gets up and walks out,
he follows -- grabs her arm and she whispers, forcefully:

                              CLAUDIA
              Let me go, leave me, let me go, it's ok, please.

                              JIM KURRING
              please, what is it, please --

                              CLAUDIA
              just let me walk out, ok?

She leaves in tears. He watches her walk.

                                                        CUT TO:

296.   EXT. VENTURA BLVD. - THAT MOMENT   296.

        CAMERA is travelling with the PARAMEDICS who are driving real fast.
        They approach a RED LIGHT at an intersection....

        ....they breeze through it, but the CAMERA PANS and moves over to
        Donnie's BUICK REGAL that's stopped at the intersection....

        CAMERA moves into a CU of him behind the wheel. He's paniced. HOLD.

                            DONNIE
                    What am I doing? What am I doing?
                    What the fuck am I doing?

        Donnie looks at the large bag of money in the passenger's seat
        next to him...he panics some more...

                            DONNIE
                    WHAT THE FUCK AM I DOING?

297.   WIDE ANGLE, THAT MOMENT   297.
        Donnie's Buick Regal makes a u-turn and heads back the direction
        it came ---

                                                        CUT TO:

298.   INT. EARL'S HOUSE - THAT MOMENT   298.

        Frank and Earl. Earl opens his eyes a bit.

                            FRANK
                    Dad...dad it's me...it's Frank...
                    It's Jack....It's Jack....Dad....

        Earl can barely make it but he touches Frank....Frank holds
        his Dad's hand....Phil steps up closer....

                            FRANK
                    I'm here. I'm here now. What do you want?
                    Do you want anything?

                            PHIL
                    I don't think, he can't...

                            FRANK
                    ...just wait...Dad...you want
                    something...can you say...

                            EARL
                    ....fuck...fuck...fuck...

        Earl is in PAIN and his hallucination make him a bit angry.

                            EARL
                    ...thismssm....

>   FRANK
>   Oh, Dad. It's ok. jesus. ok.
>   it's ok...I'm here with you now, please.
>   i'm sorry...it's ok. alright..ok.

                                              CUT TO:

299. EXT. VENTURA BLVD - THAT MOMENT   299.

     CAMERA with the Buick Regal. It moves past CAMERA, which PANS
     and DOLLIES over to --

     THE LAMPLIGHTER COFFEE SHOP. Looking inside, through the window
     to see Stanley and Worm, sitting....talking...

     CAMERA GOES INSIDE THE LAMPLIGHTER COFFEE SHOP.

                                         QUICK DISSOLVE TO:

300. INT. LAMPLIGHTER - THAT MOMENT   300*

     Worm is in tears, talking to Stanley. SLOW ZOOM IN.

>   WORM
>   ....you have it...easy....you know?
>   You have a father who loves you, huh?

>   STANLEY
>   Yes.

>   WORM
>   You know what it's like to come home
>   scared, scared that maybe if you don't
>   have the money you're supposed to
>   go out each day and get that you're gonna
>   get beaten....by a belt...he hits me
>   with a belt, Stanley....
>   (beat)
>   I'm supposed to sell those candy bars,
>   and if I don't, I come home without
>   the money....

>   STANLEY
>   ....Why does he do it...?

>   WORM
>   Cause he hates me....he hates me so much.

>   STANLEY
>   It's not right.

>   WORM
>   I hate it.

     CU - Worm. He hesitates...looks at Stanley and says:

                    WORM
          I'm sorry to put all this on you, Stanley --

                    STANLEY
          I have money.

                    WORM
          ...what...?

                    STANLEY
          I have money to give you.

                    WORM
          No. No. I have to do this on my own.

                    STANLEY
          I can take you to get money. I don't
          need it...I don't <u>need</u> it -- listen to me:
          I can let you have my money so your father
          won't hit you ever again -- you'll have the
          money because I don't need it.

     CAMERA pushes in a little on Worm, he looks up. 30fps.   *

                    WORM
          Where do you have it?

     CAMERA holds 2-shot, looking out the window onto the street.
     We PUSH PAST THEM AND THROUGH THE WINDOW, picking up with
     a YELLOW CAB as it drives by, PAN with it....

                                        QUICK DISSOLVE TO:

301. <u>EXT. VENTURA BLVD. - THAT MOMENT</u>   301.

     CAMERA travels with the CAB for a moment or two...CAMERA goes
     inside the CAB....

                                        QUICK DISSOLVE TO:

302. <u>INT. CAB - MOVING - THAT MOMENT</u>   302.

     CAMERA is in the back with CLAUDIA. She slouches down. She's
     still crying...she snorts some coke off her hand....

                                        CUT TO:

303.   EXT. VENTURA BLVD. - THAT MOMENT   303.

CAMERA moves with the CAB a bit....it makes a right hand turn and
the CAMERA PANS and DOLLIES away, over towards a JAGUAR stopped
at the intersection.....it's making a left turn at the intersection,
going the same way as the CAB did....we push in close and land to
see ROSE behind the wheel....She's in tears.....

Light turns from RED to GREEN.

                                                              CUT TO:

304.   INT. JIMMY'S HOUSE - THAT MOMENT   304.

Jimmy, without a real trace of coordination walks from the
living room and into

THE KITCHEN

He moves to a drawer and removes a REVOLVER. His hand is shaking
and his hand/eye coordination makes it very hard to grasp
hold, but he finally does....he's shaking and tearing....

                                                              CUT TO:

305.   EXT. BILLINGSLEY'S PARKING LOT - THAT MOMENT   305.

CAMERA tracks with Jim Kurring to his car. He gets behind the wheel.

                                                              CUT TO:

306.   EXT. INTERSECTION - MOMENTS LATER   306.

CAMERA overhead as Jim Kurring's car drives past the Magnolia/Tujunga
intersection....

                                                              CUT TO:

307.   INT. JIM KURRING'S CAR - MOVING - THAT MOMENT   307.

CU - Jim Kurring driving. HOLD. He drives past Solomon and
Solomon Electronics.....

JIM'S POV - THAT MOMENT - MOVING
he sees the parked Buick Regal and Donnie (in shadow) get out
and head for the back door....

CU - Kurring. He registers what he saw.

                                                              CUT TO:

308.   EXT. SOLOMON AND SOLOMON/LOADING DOCK AREA - THAT MOMENT   308.

CAMERA moves with Donnie over to the back door...he reaches
down to his KEY CHAIN and sees:

The BROKEN KEY....it's snapped off the key chain....one half
remains....the other half is on the other side of the door in the
lock....

                         DONNIE
              Fuck.

                                                    CUT TO:

309.   INT. JIM KURRING'S CAR - THAT MOMENT   Sequence J   309.

Jim Kurring drives a few more feet....slows down...then starts
to make a u-turn to go back to the store....

JIM'S POV - MOVING - THROUGH THE WINDHSIELD.
The car starts to turn 180 degrees......as soon as it is headed
going back the opposite direction....

........CRACK........

From the sky, out of the blue, a large GREEN FROG lands on Jim Kurring's
windhsield.

CU - Jim Kurring. Scared shitless.

POV - Another GREEN FROG slams on the HOOD OF THE CAR.

CU - Brake. Jim's foot SLAMS ON THE BRAKE.

                                                    CUT TO:

310.   EXT. MAGNOLIA BLVD. - THAT MOMENT   310.

CAMERA holds a wide angle as Jim Kurring's CAR SLAMS AND SKIDS TO
A STOP IN THE MIDDLE OF THE EMPTY STREET.

CLOSER ANGLE, PUSH IN ON THE DRIVER'S SIDE WINDOW.
Jim is scared and sweating.....he looks up, out the driver's side
window....

JIM'S POV - LOOKING STRAIGHT UP.
It's dark and empty sky.....

....hold on him....he looks at the Frog that has landed on
the windshield....it's dead and splattered.....

SUDDENLY:

The SOUND of ANOTHER FROG FALLING FROM THE SKY AND SLAMMING
ON THE ROOF OF THE CAR.

Jim jumps.....looks up again....

....from straight out of the sky comes ANOTHER FROG falling
DIRECTLY INTO THE CAMERA....it SPLATS....

...then another and another and another....

WIDE ANGLE. THE STREET.

It starts to RAIN FROGS in the middle of Magnolia Blvd.

CUT TO:

311. INT. CLAUDIA'S APARTMENT   311.

CU - Claudia snorts a line of coke off her coffee table.

She comes up and INTO FRAME. Outside the window, behind her....

...a FROG FALLS straight past....

She hears the sound and turns around....sees nothing...

CU - Profile on Clauida....through the other window...another
FROG falls past, through the tree outside on it's way down....

She turns her head again....sees nothing....

BEAT.

Another FROG FALLS...she looks...she walks to the window....

.....A dozen FROGS FALL IN VERY QUICK SUCCESION.....

She jumps back from the window...stumbles a bit...knocks
over a lamp, which SMASHES to the floor.....her apartment
goes DARK....except for street light...more FROGS FALL and
we hear the sound and see them through the window in glimpses.....

CUT TO:

312. EXT. CLAUDIA'S APARTMENT/STREET - THAT MOMENT   312.

The FROGS are falling sort of heavy now....Rose's JAGUAR comes
through it....skids and SMASHES into a PARKED CAR....

CAMERA DOLLIES over to her....she looks up at them....they FALL
STRAIGHT INTO CAMERA AND ONTO THE HOOD, WINDSHIELD AND ROOF....

..Rose puts the Jaguar in reverse and tries to back away from the
smashed parked car.....the bumper's are stuck....

CUT TO:

313.   <u>INT. EARL'S HOUSE - THAT MOMENT</u>   313.

        CAMERA holds on Earl and Frank. Frank has his head buried
        in Earl's bed....holding his hand, crying....it's very quiet....

        CU - Phil. He's crying a bit standing off to the side.
        He looks out the window's and the glass doors and sees the FROGS
        come raining down. His mouth drops and he can't speak.

        Frank doesn't notice. The FROGS fall in the backyard and into THE POOL.

                            PHIL
                There are frogs falling from the sky.

                                                CUT TO:

314.   <u>EXT. WHITSETT/NORTH HOLLYWOOD MED. CENTER - THAT MOMENT</u>   314.

        The PARAMEDICS are driving real fast down the street.....

                                                CUT TO:

315.   <u>INT. AMBULANCE - MOVING - THAT MOMENT</u>   315.

        Linda is on life support stuff in the ambulance. Looking past her,
        we see the view of the road through the windshield -- the amubulance
        driver going real fast and just about to pull into the hospital
        emergency entrance....

        FROGS START PELTING THE WINDSHIELD.....THE DRIVER SWERVES...

                                                CUT TO:

316.   <u>EXT. STREET/AMBULANCE - THAT MOMENT</u>   316.

        A WIDE ANGLE where we see the FROGS falling onto the moving,
        swerving Ambulance....one FROG lands so hard on top of the
        red lights on the ambulance that it CRACKS....

        ...the FROGS in the middle of the road start to act as a
        lubricant on the already wet/damp street and the Ambulance
        starts to SKID SIDEWAYS....

        ...it FALLS ON IT'S SIDE.

                                                CUT TO:

317.   <u>INT. AMBULANCE - POV</u>   317.

        As it falls on it's side and skids a bit....over the Frogs...

                                                CUT TO:

318.   EXT. EMERGENCY ROOM ENTRANCE - THAT MOMENT   318.

        The Ambulance skids right up to the emergency room entrance.

                                                    CUT TO:

319.   INT. JIMMY'S HOUSE - KITCHEN - THAT MOMENT   319.

        Jimmy with the Revolver to his head...he cocks it back...

                                                    INTERCUT:

320.   EXT. SKY/INT. HOUSE - THAT MOMENT   320.

        CAMERA above Jimmy's house, looking straight down and MOVING
        towards a SKYLIGHT above the kitchen...a FROG enters FRAME,
        falling straight towards this skylight --

321.   ...Inside the house,   321.
        Jimmy about to pull the trigger...SOUND DROPS OUT.

        ...The falling FROG comes STRAIGHT THROUGH THE SKYLIGHT, SMASHING
        THROUGH....

        ...falls straight down onto Jimmy's head....the GUN GOES OFF
        WILDLY.....SMASHES the TELEVISION.......

        Jimmy falls to the ground....GLASS FALLS from the broken skylight....

        ...more FROGS continue to fall through it and into the kitchen
        and around Jimmy.....

        ...the BULLET into TELEVISION has sparked something and the SOCKET
        it's plugged into CATCHES FIRE.....

        CU - INSIDE THE WALL, NEAR THE SOCKET.
        Camera moves in and sees some SPARK and FLASH and FIRE started....

                                                    CUT TO:

322.   EXT. SOLOMON AND SOLOMON ELECTRONICS - THAT MOMENT   322.

        Donnie starts to climb up a ladder attached to the side
        of the building....near the loading dock area....

                                                    CUT TO:

323. **EXT. STREET NEARBY - THAT MOMENT**   323.

Jim Kurring is in the middle of the Frog Rain...he puts his
car into gear and drives down the street....

....about twenty yards later and he's out of it....

...he pulls into the parking lot behind Solomon and
Solomon.....it's not raining frogs here.....

Kurring's HEADLIGHTS catch a glimpse of Donnie starting to climb...

...Donnie gets scared and FREEZES....

...Kurring is oblivious to Donnie for the moment. He looks in
his REARVIEW MIRROR and sees the FROGS FALLING....

...Donnie looks past Kurring and now sees the FROGS FALLING
in a 50 x 50 area in the street....

...Donnie looks up...

....FROGS ARE FALLING STAIGHT AT HIM/CAMERA AND THEY KNOCK HIM DOWN
AND TO THE CEMENT.....he falls flat on his FACE...

...Jim Kurring turns his head and sees Donnie, fallen flat face
and bloody on the pavement....he gets out of his car and runs over
to Donnie, through the Frogs that rain down, and picks him/drags
him out of harm and under shelter in the LOADING DOCK AREA.

                                                          CUT TO:

324. **INT. CLAUDIA'S APARTMENT - THAT MOMENT**   324.

CAMERA (STEADICAM) follows ROSE as she runs up the stairs to
Claudia's place and frantically BANGS ON THE DOOR...

Inside the apartment, Claudia JUMPS and SCREAMS at the sound....

                          ROSE
             HONEY, HONEY, CLAUDIA. IT'S ME.
             IT'S MOM. MOM. OPEN THE DOOR.
             OPEN YOUR DOOR HONEY.

Claudia jumps up and goes to her door in the darkness and
opens it up -- Rose comes in quick, scared shitless...they fall down
and hold onto each other, sweatin/crying/shaking....

                                                          CUT TO:

325. INT. EARL'S HOUSE - THAT MOMENT   325.

Frank lifts his head and watches the FROGS FALL outside the house.
Earl looks to Frank....he musters something...Frank notices....

All SOUND DROPS OUT except for the breathing of Frank and Earl.

                              EARL
                    You are not what you think you are.

Frank breaks down.
                                                      CUT TO:

326. INT. LAMPLIGHTER - THAT MOMENT   326.

Stanley and Worm. CAMERA holds as all around...through the glass
windows...it RAINS FROGS....smashing to the ground.....hitting a couple
odd parked cars...they sit, watching, stunned...in a sort of daze.
Stanley seems almost happy. Worm shocked, scarred;

                         WORM
                    What is that?

                         STANLEY
                    It's frogs. It's raining frogs.

                         WORM
                    ...fuck you mean, it's raining frogs?

                         STANLEY
                    It's raining frogs from the sky.

                         WORM
                    ....what the fuck, what the fuck....

                         STANLEY
                    This happens....this is something that happens.

                         WORM
                    What the fuck is goin' on, WHAT THE
                    FUCK IS GOING ON?

CU - STANLEY. HOLD ON HIS FACE extremely tight.

In the reflection of his eye, we see the Frogs falling....
past the neon sign that reads "Fresh Coffee."

ANGLE, DIXON. He comes running into the Lamplighter and over to Worm
and Stanley....he's scarred shitless and frantic --

> DIXON
> DADDY! DAD! DAD WHAT THE HELL IS GOIN' ON?

> WORM
> Stay quiet...stay quiet, son --

> DIXON
> LET"S GO, LET'S GO, LET'S GET HIS MONEY
> AND GO -- DID YOU GET HIS MONEY? DID
> YOU GET IT? DID YOU GET HIS MONEY, DAD?

> WORM
> No, Son...be quiet...be quiet now...

> DIXON
> C'mon, Dad. We gotta just GET HIS
> MONEY AND GO, LET'S GO. Let's get the money --

> WORM
> We're not gonna do that now. We're
> not gonna do that now and that's over.

> DIXON
> BULLSHIT. BULLSHIT, DAD WE NEED
> TO GET HIS MONEY AND GO.

Dixon takes out a large POLICE ISSUED REVOLVER, AIMS at STANLEY'S FACE.

> DIXON
> GIVE US YOUR MONEY MAN.

> WORM
> Son, don't --

> DIXON
> BULLSHIT, BULLSHIT DAD WE GOTTA GET
> HIS MONEY --

> WORM
> -- no.

> DIXON
> (to Stanley)
> GIVE US YOUR MONEY.

> WORM
> Put the gun down, please, boy.

> DIXON
> GIVE US YOUR MONEY, KID.

                    WORM
          Son, please, now....

                    DIXON
          DAD --

                    WORM
          Please, boy, put it down and it's ok.

Dixon starts to get nervous and well with tears...he shakes a
little....

                    WORM
          It's ok --

                    DIXON
          We gotta get his money so we can get
          outta here -- we gotta --

                    WORM
          That idea is over now.
          We're not gonna do that now.

Dixon starts crying and shaking and backing away --

                    DIXON
          DADDY, FUCK, DADDY, DON'T GET MAD AT ME.
          DON'T GET MAD AT ME --
                    (to Stanley)
          JUST GIMME YOUR MONEY.

                    WORM
          I'm not mad, son, I will not be mad
          at you and it's ok and please put it
          down and I won't be mad and I won't --

                    DIXON
          DAD.

Dixon starts to lower the gun a bit, crying and shaking....He lowers
the gun and hands it over to his Father....Dixon is sort of
flinching....the possibility that his Father may strike him...

...Stanley is frozen...Dixon is hyperventilating....

                    DIXON
          I - just - thought - that - I - didn't
          want - I - didn't - I - didn't -

                    WORM
          It's ok, boy.

HOLD. Que. "Bein Green," by Kermit the Frog/Aimee

327.   <u>EXT. LAMPLIGHTER/VENTURA BLVD. - THAT MOMENT</u>   <u>Sequence K</u>   327.

CAMERA holds a wide angle on the Lamplighter Coffee Shop.
Frogs falling from sky onto and around the streets....

                                                    CUT TO:

328.   <u>EXT. THE SKY - THAT MOMENT</u>   328.

CAMERA up with the Falling Frogs....CAMERA is moving down with them...
it becomes almost musical....like Busby-Berkely-style coreography of
Frogs That Fall In The Sky...

                         MUSIC/KERMIT THE FROG
                  "It's not that easy bein' green...
                  Having to spend each day the color
                  of the leaves..."

                           CARRIES OVER CUT TO:

329.   <u>INT. JIMMY'S HOUSE - THAT MOMENT</u>   329.

It is on FIRE now....CU image of Jimmy on the floor of the kitchen
with shards of glass around him...and FROGS...a few of them
still alive and jumping around...the FIRE moving closer and closer...

                                          CUT TO:

330.   <u>EXT. SOLOMON AND SOLOMON/LOADING DOCK AREA - THAT MOMENT</u>   330.

Jim Kurring and Donnie underneath the shelter area. Donnie's
MOUTH IS FULL OF BLOOD and his TEETH ARE BROKEN...

                           DONNIE
                 My teeff...my teeef....

                        JIM KURRING
             YOU'RE OK...you're gonna be ok....

                                          CUT TO:

331.   <u>INT. CLAUDIA'S APARTMENT - THAT MOMENT</u>   331.

Claudia cries to her Mom. Rose holds her and they rock back
and forth.... Claudia cries loud and over and over --

"Mommy...mommy...mom."

Rose calming her and petting her head, "It's ok."

                                          CUT TO:

332.   INT. EMERGENCY ROOM - THAT MOMENT   332.

        CAMERA is with Linda and DOCTORS as they PUMP HER STOMACH.
        Follow the process and get to point where it's clear that
        she is going to make it, she will not die.

                                                    CUT TO:

333.   INT. EARL'S HOUSE - THAT MOMENT   333.

        CAMERA w/Frank and Earl and Phil. Earl's last couple
        of breaths are short and quick...short and quick...short and
        quick...and then he dies....his eyes are open.....

                                                    CUT TO:

334.   EXT. SKY - THAT MOMENT   334.

        CAMERA moves down straight towards the ground...towards the Magnolia
        intersection with a LARGE FROG....right before it hits the pavement --

        CUT TO BLACK.

        Title Card Reads: So Now Then

        - Replay Lumiere Footage from the opening of "Three Men Hung"
        Green, Berry and Hill.

        - Replay Delmer Darion in the tree and getting lifted out of the water.

        - Replay Sydney Barringer jumping from building

                            NARRATOR
                    And there is the account of the hanging
                    of three men....and a scuba diver and
                    a suicide.....

                                                    CUT TO:

335.   INT. EARL'S HOUSE - DAWN   335.

        The door is opened by Phil and two MORTUARY MEN in suits
        nod their heads. Phil lets them in.

                            NARRATOR
                    There are stories of coincidence and
                    chance and intersections and strange
                    things told and which is which and who only knows...

                                                    CUT TO:

336. <u>INT. EARL'S HOUSE - LIVING ROOM - THAT MOMENT</u>   336*

       Frank and Phil watch Earl get covered in a sheet and put on   *
       a stretcher. CAMERA moves around and finds the MORPHINE DOG   *
       placed on a stretcher, covered in a sheet.   *

       HOLD CU on PHIL and then Frank.   *

                              NARRATOR
                   ...and we generally say, "Well if that was
                   in movie I wouldn't believe it."

       ANGLE, IN THE KITCHEN, MOMENTS LATER
       Phil enters and answers the phone, "...hello...oh no...yes, yes..."
       Phil looks to Frank --

337. <u>INT. HOSPITAL - DAWN</u>   337*

       CAMERA looking down the long emergency room corridor as the doors
       open and Frank enters and moves to the reception desk, asks some
       information --

       CAMERA pans off him, and over to a room, looking through the door   *
       jam onto Linda in bed. Her eyes a bit open, respiratory equipment   *
       attached to her. A DOCTOR standing over her, calmly asking questions; *

                              DOCTOR
                   Are you with us? Linda? Is it Linda?

       She nods her head. Doctor continues talk, etc. Frank, from   *
       behind enters FRAME and stands off nearby. MATCH TO DIXON'S FACE   *
       OVER CUT TO: *

                              NARRATOR
                   Someone's so and so meet someone else's
                   so and so and so on --

338. <u>EXT. EMPTY PARKING LOT AREA - DAWN</u>   338.

       CU - Dixon as he gets into the old beat up car with Worm.
       Their call pulls away and drives off. Dixon looks at Linda's Mercedes
       which is still parked way across the lot -- they exit FRAME.

                                                              CUT TO:

338A <u>EXT. MAGNOLIA - DAWN</u>   338A*

       Worm's car drives down the street. LONG LENS. ANGLE, at the car,
       Dixon leans up and out the window a bit....he's got the gun wrapped
       in newspaper, taking the fingerprints from the gun....he throws
       the POLICE ISSUED WEAPON from the speeding car...

                                                              CUT TO:

339. <u>INT. LAMPLIGHTER - DAWN</u>   339*

Stanley sits in the back of a squad car....an OFFICER watching
him...probably supposed to be comforting him, but instead drinking
coffee, chating with other OFFICERS questioning the coffee shop   *
employees --   *

                         NARRATOR
              And it is in the humble opinion of this
              narrator that these strange things
              happen all the time....

Stanley gets out of the car and walks away, out of sight of all
the officer's and people around...he just walks down the street....

                                                        CUT TO:

340. <u>INT. SPECTOR HOUSE - RICK'S BEDROOM - DAWN</u>   340.

Stanley enters Rick's bedroom. Rick is asleep.

                         STANLEY
              Dad...Dad.

Rick opens his eyes, but doesn't move.

                         STANLEY
              You have to be nicer to me, Dad.

                         RICK
              Go to bed.

                         STANLEY
              I think that you have to be nicer to me.

                         RICK
              Go to bed.

Stanley exits.

                                                        CUT TO:

341. <u>EXT. JIMMY'S HOUSE - DAWN</u>   341.

CAMERA with Fire Trucks and County Coroner people. A body
bag and a stretcher carrying JIMMY'S BODY come out of the house.

                         NARRATOR
              ...and so it goes and so it goes and
              the book says, "We may be through with
              the past, but the past is not through with us."

                                                        CUT TO:

341A <u>INT. POLICE STATION - MARCIE</u>   341A*

Marcie looking down at the table in front of her, tape recorder
and microphone in front of her, (and all that goes along w/full
confession/etc.)

                         MARCIE
          I killed him. I killed my husband.
          He hit my son and he hit my grandson
          and I hit him. I hit him with the ashtray
          and he was knocked out and I killed him,
          I strangled him. I strangled my husband
          to protect my boys. I protected my boys.

                                              CUT TO:

342. <u>EXT. SOLOMON AND SOLOMON - DAWN</u>   342*

Jim Kurring and Donnie sitting together at the loading dock.
Donnie, mouth full of blood, holding a kleenex to it, crying a bit.
Kurring listens. HOLD.

                         DONNIE
          I know that I did a thtupid thing.
          Tho-thtupid...getting brathes...I thought...
          I thought that he would love me.
          ...getting brathes, for what...
          for thumthing I didn't even...i don't
          know where to put things, y'know?

Kurring holds his look, nods. Donnie really breaks tears, looks up;

                         DONNIE
          I really do hath love to give, I juth
          don't know where to put it --

CAMERA holds the 2-shot on them, BEAT, THEN: The Police Issued   *
Revolver FALLS FROM THE SKY AND LANDS ABOUT fifteen feet in front   *
of them. Jim Kurring and Donnie look. HOLD. CU - Jim Kurring.   *

                                              CUT TO:

343.   INT. SOLOMON AND SOLOMON ELECTRONICS - THAT MOMENT   343.

Donnie and Jim Kurring walking inside the store, towards the office --

                    JIM KURRING
          ...these security systems can be a real joke.
          I mean, a frog falls from the sky and lands
          on the x-4 box 'round back and opens all the doors?
          Triggers a siutation? You don't know who could
          be driving by at any moment, walk in and rob
          the place -- I was you I'd talk to your boss
          about a new security system --

                    DONNIE
          ....ohh-thur-I-thur-thill....

                    JIM KURRING
          You guys make alotta money, huh?

                                                  CUT TO:

344.   INT. SOLOMON AND SOLOMON - OFFICE - MOMENT LATER   344.

Donnie puts the money back in the floor safe. CU. DONNIE.

                    JIM KURRING (OC)
          I got a buddy a mine down at the
          med. center, he'd probably do quite
          a deal on a set of dentures, you're
          interested in that. He's in training,
          you know he's not a dentist yet, but
          he's real good at corrective oral
          surgery from what I understand...

LAND ECU. DONNIE. He smiles a little bit.

345. <u>EXT. SOLOMON AND SOLOMON - THAT MOMENT</u>   345.

Wide Angle, Donnie and Jim Kurring shake hands and part ways,
getting into their cars. A few words more about, "Call me up
for that guys number and he'll help you out with the teeth."

Donnie gets in his car. CAMERA stays with Jim Kurring who walks
over to his car and gets behind the wheel.

CAMERA HOLDS ON HIM. He does a little "Cops" talking to himself.

                    JIM KURRING
          ...alot of people think this is just
          a job that you go to....take a lunch
          hour, the jobs over, something like that.
          But...it's a 24 hour deal...no two ways
          about it....and what most people don't
          see: Just How Hard It Is To Do The Right Thing.
                    (beat)
          People think if I make a judgment call
          that it's a judgment on them...but
          that's not what I do and that's not
          what should be done...I have to take
          everything and play it as it lays.
          Sometimes people need a little help.
          Sometimes people need to be forgiven
          and sometimes they need to go to jail.
          And that's a very tricky thing on my
          part...making that call...the law is the
          law and heck if I'm gonna break it...but
          you can forgive someone....? Well, that's
          the tough part....What Do We Forgive?
          Tough part of the job....tough part of
          walking down the street...

CAMERA stays with him and HOLDS as he puts the car into gear
and drives away....HOLD with him as he drives...he starts to
cry a little bit to himself.

                                                   CUT TO:

346. <u>INT. CLAUDIA'S APARTMENT - THAT MOMENT</u>   346.

CAMERA holds on Claudia. She's sitting up in bed, covers around
her, staring into space....a SONG plays....for a very, very long
time....she doesn't move....until she looks up and sees someone
enter her bedroom....a FIGURE from the back enters FRAME and walks
in and sits on the edge of the bed....from the back it is clear
that it's Jim Kurring. She tears a bit and looks at him...HOLD....

She turns her eyes from him and looks INTO THE CAMERA and smiles.

                                                   CUT TO BLACK.

                              <u>END.</u>

interview with
Paul Thomas Anderson

Writer Chuck Stephens met with Paul Thomas Anderson on October 6, 1999, for the following interview.

Q: Where did *Boogie Nights* leave you, and what did it leave you feeling like you needed to do next?

My goal, really, in writing *Magnolia,* was to not think about that at all. To not let things that other people were saying about me, or going to say about me, affect my work. I didn't want a bunch of stuff like that rolling around in my head, and I didn't want to take a vacation and wait to start my next film. I wanted to do my job, which was to start writing. And my plan was, I'm gonna write something that's 90 pages long. I'd just been through this mammoth motherfucker, two and a half hours long, and based on that, I was thinking let's go do something quick and immediate and cheap to make, so that whatever was buzzing around in my head in terms of *Boogie Nights,* I could make sure it didn't affect me. And it didn't—because if it had, I never would have written this three-hour movie.

But what did happen was that, in my life, I was falling in love [with Fiona Apple] and writing a movie at the same time, and all that that implies.

I'm sure there was stuff from *Boogie Nights* that I wanted to tackle without the shackle of porno, or that I wanted to have done better than I did in *Boogie Nights,* but at the same time, I wanted to be very self-conscious about not repeating myself.

Q: The "shackle of porno"?

Well, mainly what that means is, I didn't want to come out of the gate every time being expected to be the guy who tackles "that" topic, or any other specific topic.

Q: Was there a "first thing" about *Magnolia* that you had in mind?
Absolutely. It was the situation between Claudia and Jimmy Gator. It was
Philip Baker Hall coming through the darkness, through the rain, and up the
stairs to Melora Walters's apartment, and he's knocking on her door, and she's
not answering.

That, coupled with the lyrics from this Aimee Mann song: "Now that I've met
you, would you object to never seeing me again?" It was just this notion that
I am so disastrously fucked up that you have no chance of loving me. Just the
whole notion of people feeling unlovable.

Q: Did the title come to you early along?
Yeah, but at the time, I couldn't say exactly why. Yes, Magnolia is the name of
a street in the Valley, and I knew something was going to happen at an intersection in the Valley, but it was still not totally clear why that was going to be
the title.

And it wasn't until the last two weeks of the writing that certain validations
for the title really started coming. One of them was the discovery of this
thing called the Magonia, which is this mythical place above the firmament
where shit goes and hangs out before it falls from the sky. I think I'd come to
it through Charles Fort, who wrote about strange phenomena like rains of
frogs and Greenberry Hill. The Magonia is this place where, when ships
disappear from the ocean, that's where they go, and only later on will an
anchor from it fall from the sky.

Another validation was, for me, a purely coincidental thing I did in naming
a number of the women in the movie after flowers: Rose, Lily . . .

**Q: You're often thought of and referred to as a quintessential product of
the San Fernando Valley—what does that mean?**
I grew up on the very far edge of the bleed where Hollywood stops and the
Valley begins. And there truly was a sense, living in the Valley, of "going over
the hill"—of there being something not as comfortable, not as safe, over there,
over the hills, on the Hollywood side. But there was also the very definite
sense, when you're an adolescent, of "Oh, you live in the Valley—what a
loser." A sense of alienation, and for me, as a wannabe filmmaker, a sense of
humiliation. No movies are made about the Valley; movies are made about

wars, movies are made about urban jungles—what have I got to add to the movies? Fortunately, at some point, a long time ago in his career, Steven Spielberg made it okay to make movies about suburbia.

Q: What was it that attracted you to the world of game shows?

I'd worked once as a P.A. on a game show called *Quiz Kids Challenge,* an update of an old radio show. Part of my job was to go through and edit together videotape of all the kids they'd interviewed across the country as potential contestants. Doing that really linked up with the J. D. Salinger short stories, with the Glass Family, and their involvement with a show like *Quiz Kids.* This idea of, hey, let us go through you and pick your brain and use it for entertainment. All that, coupled with wanting to see Philip Baker Hall do a new kind of role, and especially to see him do something like a game-show host.

But it also all touches on the idea of what it means to grow up in L.A., but not be part of the industry—or to only hold the most marginal relationship to it.

Q: For whatever dark undercurrents *Boogie Nights* contained, it was, for the most, a kick—a very pleasure-filled movie. Why go so far into despair and darkness this time?

The subject matter led me there: family problems, cancer. Without getting too personal, I'd been through a lot in the last two or three years, and especially a lot of cancer-related things—with everyone from people who I knew just a little bit to people who I knew very well and truly loved. And I came to recognize the way that, when cancer comes into people's lives, it seems to come in a wave. And I'd been there; I'd just gone through a really severe cancer spiral.

Q: *Magnolia* is filled, even crowded, with a number of fascinating characters. Could we go through and talk about them one by one? Let's start with Earl Partridge.

I know and have known many guys like that. Lovable, curmudgeonly older guys who are really, really strong, but at the same time, total softies. Guys who had been around, who were old enough to still speak in kind of jazz rhythms. And with Earl, for me as a cineast, wanting to write four-page monologues—especially in writing them with somebody like Jason Robards in mind for the role—it was like, okay, I get to do my Eugene O'Neill scenes now.

Q: Frank T. J. Mackey?
Long story short, I had been turned on to a cassette someone had surreptitiously made of two guys talking, and using expressions like, "Dude, what you've got to learn to do is to respect the cock and tame the cunt." It turned out that they were actually quoting another guy, named Ross Jeffries, who taught courses and gave seminars on how to seduce women. On, basically, how to destroy a woman.

And I'd already been fascinated by Don Dupree, who does infomercials, and has speech patterns and a demeanor which just really represented the Valley to me. He is exactly like somebody I had gone to high school with.

And around the time I had been thinking about all this, I got a chance to go to the set of *Eyes Wide Shut* and meet with Tom Cruise. You know, you never even consider getting Tom Cruise for one of your movies, in the same way you never even consider becoming president of the United States. But Tom Cruise called me, and suddenly, there I was. And I found myself in a position where, wow, oh my God, I really want to show off for Tom and to create a real gold mine for an actor to work with.

Q: Is there a way, other than the enormous rig he has in his pants, that Frank is related to Dirk Diggler?
Probably so, especially in the sense of his being—like Mark Wahlberg was in *Boogie Nights*—an outsider coming into the group, a bigger star joining an ensemble that was already familiar with each other. And as a character, there's this sense of a flamboyancy and a slight stupidity, and of being damaged by parents. And a peripheral, bad version of show business that's being acted out in both characters' lives.

Q: What about the boy genius, Stanley?
I've always thought that Spielberg did such a great thing with portrayals of kids in his earlier career. The kids in *Close Encounters* and in *E.T.*—they were like portraits of kids that only Salinger had done. And I remember seeing Anna Pacquin in *The Piano* and seeing how a kid could be so

fascinating and complex, that she could both hold on to her mother and betray her.

Add all that to the psychoanalysis inside me, writing about a kid character while *Boogie Nights* was coming out and there was all this pressure and observation on me. And feeling like, hey, I wanted this and I created it, but I'm far too young and I'm far too fucking juvenile to truly be in this position.

On top of that, I had recently met Fiona and she had told me this story about how, when she first started performing, there was a situation where she really wanted to go to the bathroom, but her managers or whoever made her go out on the stage. Here's this nineteen-year-old girl who was totally feisty and strong as a motherfucker, but also at times, as she would totally regret having to say now, Bambi-ish and beaten up. She wanted to go to the bathroom, but was being forced to "grow up," to be a fucking professional, to get out on that stage. And with Stanley, there's this thing where you really feel like, wow, I'm a genius, but I can barely tie my shoelaces.

And one other thing Stanley provided me with was the opportunity to write some really direct and very simple lines; lines like "Dad, you have to be nicer to me." It's "See spot run"—an expression of an emotion that was really clear and exact.

Q: Jimmy Gator?
Well, in one way, Jimmy Gator is an homage to Robert Ridgely [the late, great character actor who played The Colonel in *Boogie Nights*] and his character in Jonathan Demme's *Melvin and Howard*—the game-show host Wally "Mr. Love" Williams. I wanted to expand on that character, and to approach him in a more realistic way. To make him more Alex Trebek—harder, less fun and games.

I also wanted to do something new with Philip Baker Hall; to give him an opportunity to be stuttery, to shackle him with some stuff, because in my other two films, he's so eloquent and exact.

And it's funny, because while the character isn't exactly something new for me as a writer, it's the first time when I've been able, at the end of a film, to hate one of my characters. There is truly a sense of moral judgment at work with this character. I can't even let him kill himself at the end—he's got to burn. And that's what he deserves. I wanted it to be really clear that with this character, I'm saying "No." No to any kind of forgiveness for him.

Q: Donnie Smith?

It's the good old-fashioned study of a Gary Coleman, or Jackie Coogan, or potentially what might happen to Stanley. A "How did I get from there to here?" kind of character. His is a scandalous kind of "true Hollywood story," like the true genius who ends up becoming a crack addict.

Q: Phil Parma?

That one's simple—I wrote it for Phil [Philip Seymour Hoffman], and it is Phil.

When Phil played Scotty in *Boogie Nights,* that's an actor playing a part. But Phil's been called upon to play so many weird parts by now, I wanted to see what would happen if I just wrote Phil: the way he talks, the way he is. And I hadn't even seen him in *Happiness* when I wrote this part for him, but I'm really glad, in retrospect, that I decided to write Phil's part kind of against the roles he's been getting recently. And the emotions Phil Parma goes to—this nurse who cries way too much—that's just the way I could see Phil Hoffman reacting to those moments in real life.

Q: Jim Kurring?

That came out of a time in our lives, John C. Reilly's and mine, when we had made *Sydney,* and during the editing, it was being taken away from me. And as a way to get away from all that, we just took a video camera and went out driving around, improvising would-be scenes from a *Cops* episode. We'd come up with a beginning idea and just see where it went—John with mirror shades, driving his car, doing these monologues, talking to himself.

And I just loved that stuff. But where that stuff was really schticky and having-fun-in-the-summertime kind of goofing around, I wanted to take it as a basis for something a lot more real. So I put some meat on him: Now he's divorced, and he lives a lonely, truly lonely life. He's talking to himself in his car as if he's on *Cops,* and it's really sad.

At the same time, I wanted something that would allow John to be a romantic leading man. I've always seen him, even if no one else has, as a kind of Jimmy Stewart or a Joel McCrea figure.

Q: Claudia?

She's my love. My affection for her is just massive. And I worry that there may be a lack of connection, by audiences, with her because she's a drug addict. But I had a massive desire to write that character as truthfully as possible, because I have known that girl. I've known so many girls like her, and having seen representations of girls like that in cinema before, I wanted to get to a new level of nuance with her. To something that might have previously been lost on mass audiences. Getting to the level of nuance of, she's doing drugs and there's a knock on the door, and instead of throwing the drugs away in a panic, she hides them and saves them for later instead.

I wanted to deal with the whole situation of struggling with drugs and trying to figure out when not to do them. Like when Claudia goes on the date with Jim Kurring: It's like, I've been doing drugs all day, but this is something that might be important, this date, and I've got to get through without drugs. But I'm doing the drugs anyway because I can't get through it without drugs. Here was something I really wanted to do without drugs, and here I've just corrupted it by doing the drugs. And so that when Claudia kisses Jim Kurring, it becomes a curse. Did I just do drugs to get up the courage to kiss him, which I knew I could have done if I'd been sober? And then why did I need the drugs to do it?

And I also wrote the part specifically for Melora, whom I've known for so long. I just wanted to write something great and star-making for her. I wanted to be, in a way, her lover in the moviemaking way. And it turned out to be my personal favorite performance in the film.

Q: Do you think of yourself mainly as a writer, a director, or a filmmaker?
[Big pause.] This is the part of the interview where you'll be writing, in brackets, "Big pause."

Because my gut response is, well, I don't know, I've forgotten my gut response already. But now that I've taken too much time to think it over, I've got to say filmmaker. Because I think I direct in a way that's technical and show-off-y, and that's not something that's generally said about writers who direct. With those sorts of writers who direct, like David Mamet or Woody Allen, you don't usually think of them as applying a lot of cinema—in the Scorsese or Oliver Stone kind of way—to their movies. I can say to you right now, I'd never direct anything that somebody else wrote. But I would write something for somebody else to direct—and I am doing that right now.

Q: How did you decide to make Aimee Mann's songs a kind of character in the film?

Because she's so fucking cool, and I wanted to be able tell everybody that I think so.

Specifically, though, is was that line, from Aimee's song "Deathly": "Now that I met you, would you object to never seeing me again?" So much stemmed from that.

Aimee writes songs that are, underneath, basically songs about her torture in dealing with record companies, but much closer to the surface, they're love songs. Nothing is good enough for people like you; you have to have somebody to take the fall—that's her singing to a lover, that's a relationship song. But truly what it is, is Aimee singing to a record label, and I really wanted to deal with that kind of ability to make something function twice. This is a love song, but it's also the biggest "fuck you" around.

Aimee was the person who turned me on to the investigation of who you are and what your background means to you. And there's this theme that recurs in her music, and in Fiona's; this idea that being in love is the hardest fucking thing in the world, and you don't want to put yourself through the tragedy of trying to be in love with me.

And another thing is, instead of the thing you've already heard a million times—"This was influenced by the Bob Dylan record from 1960-whatever," etcetera, etcetera—this is a situation where Aimee and I have been friends so long that I've been able to watch the evolution of her songs. And not just that, it's that she's my friend and I can call her on the phone and get in touch with certain things that are going on in her songs that were created, at least in some ways, in relation to things that were going on in my life. And hearing things in your life re-created by another artist really gives you a greater awareness of the way things are going on around you. And a greater sense of how to put them into your own stuff.

Q: This must all be related to the scene where all the characters begin singing along with one of her songs.

"Wise Up" is the name of that song, and the line is, "It's not going to stop."

I can truly remember the moment I wrote that scene. Usually when you're going into writing a script, you sit down at the table and you know there are

204

all these things you want to get into the movie. It's like you're thinking, well, I want it to be sad and funny and have action set pieces in it. [Laughs.]

And sometimes they just happen, and sometimes you feel like you're wedging them in there, and it just doesn't work. Writing that scene, when Phil has just dropped morphine into Earl's mouth, I was crying myself as I was writing it; it was all coming from a true emotional place, and I suddenly realized, I've always wanted to do a musical number, how about right here?

And in production, everybody was really curious about, well, is it going to work? Can he pull this off? But every time we'd get to the point of shooting a character's "Wise Up" scene, it was kind of like, okay, ante up. Will it work as well with this person as it did with the one before . . . and it did, every time.

I also think—as a cineast and as a person—that it's the sort of thing that happens, no matter how gimmicky or clichéd, all the time. Characters, or people, who are going through some really tough emotional shit, suddenly find themselves singing along to something that's playing on the radio, and they just go with it. They just surrender to that moment, sink into it, and sit there and cry their eyes out.

Q: "It's something that happens"; "But it did happen"—these are both refrains throughout the film.
There it is, right there, the simplest possible expression of a truth. "It did happen."

I'm a film geek; I was raised on movies. And there come these times in life where you just get to a spot when you feel like movies are betraying you. Where you're right in the middle of true, painful life. Like, say, somebody could be sitting in a room somewhere, watching their father die of cancer, and all of a sudden it's like, no this isn't really happening, this is something I saw in *Terms of Endearment.* You're at this moment where movies are betraying you, and you resent movies for maybe taking away from the painful truth of what's happening to you—but that's exactly why those moments show up in movies. Those things "do happen."

And I also wanted to get those moments in life that don't get covered in movies. Like, you're going to a funeral and all the parts of it that you've seen in movies are there—the mournfulness, the sadness—but then there come those moments that are foreign to you because, in a way, they haven't been shown to you in a movie before. The part where, say, you're going to the funeral and you're faced with the little realities of things like, where am I going to park my car?

But the two things do intersect all the time. It's like that moment when Phil Parma's on the phone at Earl's house and says, "This is the scene in the movie where you help me out."

One thing that I learned as a writer, happened when I was writing *Boogie Nights,* in the scene where Rollergirl and Amber are doing drugs, and Rollergirl suddenly says to her, "Will you be my mom?" I'm still pretty far from being able to make stuff like that happen on all 190 pages of a script, but what it totally clued me in to was this: I looked at that scene right after I'd written it and realized I'd just written it almost as if it was an out-of-body thing. It was totally from my gut. And while I looked at it and said, well, something seems odd about that moment and the smart writer in me could go back and "fix it up." I could make the rhythm better, make the rhythm of the writing and the scene better, but I realized instead, wait a minute, I've just broken through a barrier here. There's something odd and wrong and embarrassing here, but if I just follow through on it, it'll become a scene where you'll go [inhalation of surprise], I've just seen a scene I've never seen in a movie before.

Those are moments that are golden, and it came from writing and writing and letting everything just pour out.

Q: Of all things, why frogs?
It truly came from a slightly gimmicky and exciting place. I'd read about rains of frogs in the works of Charles Fort, who was a turn-of-the-century writer who wrote mainly about odd phenomena. Michael Penn was the one who turned me on to Fort, and who, when I went to one of Michael's shows in New York once, made reference on stage to "rains of frogs." At that moment I just went, Wow! How cool and scary and fun to do that would be—and what does it mean?!

So I just started writing it into the script. It wasn't until after I got through with the writing that I began to discover what it might mean, which was this: You get to a point in your life, and shit is happening, and everything's out of your control, and suddenly, a rain of frogs just makes sense. You're staring at a doctor who's telling you something is wrong, and while we know what it is, we have no way of fixing it. And you just go, so what you're telling me, basically, is that it's raining frogs from the sky.

I'm not someone who's ever had a special fascination with UFOs or supernatural phenomena or anything, but I guess I just found myself at a point in my life where I was going through some shitty stuff and I was ready for some sort of weird religion experience, or as close as I could get to one.

So then I began to decipher things about frogs and history, things like this famous notion that, as far back as the Romans, people have been able to judge the health of a society by the health of its frogs. The health of a frog, the vibe of a frog, the texture of a frog, its looks, how much wetness is on it, everything. The frogs are a barometer for who we are as a people. We're polluting ourselves, we're killing ourselves, and the frogs are telling us so, because they're all getting sick and deformed. And I didn't even know it was in the Bible until Henry Gibson gave me a copy of the Bible, bookmarked to the appropriate frog passage.

Q: What made you decide to use the sequences dealing with episodes of weird historical coincidence as a framing device for the film?
In a way, it's a promise. A promise that, hey, look at these three stories which, to whatever extent they're true or not, are weird and fantastic and filled with amazing coincidence—and that, if you give me three hours, I will give you a story that is just as filled with weird and fantastic coincidence as they are, because "this stuff does happen."

Q: Is the end of the film, for you as a writer, cathartic, or unresolved? Is it a matter of, despite everything that has happened, there is some sort of hope at the end of the day? Or is it a matter of agreeing with what's come before, that all the sadness is just "not going to stop"?
For me the writer, Yes, it equals totally cathartic, and totally hopeful, and Yes! They are going to get together at the end!

But it's also completely gratifying to hear that question, because everything you've seen for the last three hours has been so fucked up, and so emotionally confusing, that the real reality is that, yes, they're going to get together and form a relationship, but in no way is it going to be easy or entirely possible. But it is a surrender to falling in love, no matter how much shit that's going to entail.

The problem is, in traditional movies, it's usually one way or the other. And for the people for whom that sort of resolution is important, then Claudia's smile in that last shot is about, yes, it's all going to work out, I am going to be happy. But for the people who are comfortable going a little deeper, hopefully what it's really saying is, yes, I do lean toward the side of happiness, but there's just too much in life to go straight to the point of okay, we're getting married and living happily ever after. It's not that simple.

And finally, my goal, at least at this point in my work, is that I want to always go to the place where I'm going to write the saddest happy ending I possibly can. That's just the way that feels good to me.

cast & crew

Written and Directed by ..... Paul Thomas Anderson
Produced by .... JoAnne Sellar
Co-Producer .... Daniel Lupi
Executive Producers ... Michael De Luca, Lynn Harris
Director of Photography .... Robert Elswit
Production Designers .. William Arnold, Mark Bridges
Editor .... Dylan Tichenor
Costume Designer .... Mark Bridges
Music by .... Jon Brion
Songs by .... Aimee Mann
Visual Effects Supervisor .... Joe Letteri
Casting by .... Cassandra Kulukundis

CAST

Stanley Spector .... Jeremy Blackman
Frank T. J. Mackey .... Tom Cruise
Rose Gator .... Melinda Dillon
Gwenovier .... April Grace
Luis Guzman .... Luis Guzman
Jimmy Gator .... Philip Baker Hall
Phil Parma .... Philip Seymour Hoffman
Burt Ramsey .... Ricky Jay
Donnie Smith .... William H. Macy
Solomon Solomon .... Alfred Molina
Linda Partridge .... Julianne Moore
Alan Kligman .... Michael Murphy
Jim Kurring .... John C. Reilly
Earl Partridge .... Jason Robards
Claudia .... Melora Walters
Rick Spector .... Michael Bowen
Thurston Howell .... Henry Gibson
Cynthia .... Felicity Huffman
Dixon .... Emmanuel L. Johnson
Dr. Landon .... Don McManus
Mary .... Eileen Ryan
Dick Jennings .... Danny Wells
Sir Edmund William Godfrey .... Pat Healy
Mrs. Godfrey .... Genevieve Zweig
Joseph Green .... Mark Flannagan
Stanley Berry .... Neil Flynn
Daniel Hill .... Rod McLachlan
Firefighter .... Allan Graf
Delmer Darion .... Patton Oswalt
Reno Security Guard ... Raymond "Big Guy" Gonzales
Craig Hansen .... Brad Hunt
Forensic Scientist .... Jim Meskimen
Sydney Barringer .... Chris O'Hara
Arthur Barringer .... Clement Blake
1958 Detective .... Frank Elmore
1958 Policeman .... John Kraft Seitz
Young Boy .... Cory Buck
Infomercial Guy .... Tim "Stuffy" Sorenen
Middle Aged Guy .... Jim Ortlieb
Young Jimmy Gator .... Thomas Jane
Jimmy's Showgirl .... Holly Houston
Little Donnie Smith .... Benjamin Niedens

Dentist Nurse #1 .... Veronica Hart
Dentist Nurse #2 .... Melissa Spell
Dr. Lee .... James Kiriyama-Lem
Pedestrian #1 .... Jake Cross
Pedestrian #2 .... Charlie Scott
Nurse Juan .... Juan Medrano
Police Captain .... John Pritchett
Marcie .... Cleo King
Captain Muffy .... Michael Shamus Wiles
Doc .... Jason Andrews
Cameraman .... John S. Davies
Geoff/Seminar Guy .... Kevin Breznahan
Avi Solomon .... Miguel Perez
Coroner Man .... David Masuda
Officer #1 .... Neil Pepe
Detective .... Lionel Mark Smith
Coroner Woman .... Annette Helde
Librarian .... Lynne Lerner
WDKK? Page #1 .... Scott Burkett
Richard's Dad .... Bob Brewer
Richard's Mom .... Julie Brewer
Julia's Mom .... Nancy Marston
Julia's Dad .... Maurey Marston
WDKK? PA .... Jamala Gaither
WDKK? Page #2 .... Amy Brown
Dr. Diane .... Meagan Fay
Mim .... Patricia Forte
Todd Geronimo .... Patrick Warren
Worm .... Orlando Jones
Pink Dot Girl .... Virginia Pereira
Brad the Bartender .... Craig Kvinsland
Cocktail Waitress .... Patricia Scanlon
Julia .... Natalie Marston
Richard .... Bobby Brewer
WDKK? Floor Director .... Clark Gregg
Young Pharmacy Kid .... Pat Healy
Old Pharmacist .... Art Frankel
Officer #2 .... Matt Gerald
Pink Dot Guy .... Guillermo Melgarejo
Chad (Seduce & Destroy) .... Paul F. Tompkins
Janet (Frank's Assistant) .... Mary Lynn Rajskub
Smiling Peanut Patron #1 .... Jim Beaver
Smiling Peanut Patron #2 .... Ezra Buzzington
Smiling Peanut Patron #3 .... Denise Woolfork
Harmonica Players ...... New World Harmonica Trio
WDKK? Show Director ...... Bob Downey, Sr. (a prince)
WDKK? Director's Assistant .... William Mapother
WDKK? Medic .... Larry Ballard
Mackey Disciple Twin #1 .... Brett Higgins
Mackey Disciple Twin #2 .... Brian Higgins
Mackey Disciple in Middle ... Michael "Jocco" Phillips
Donnie's Old Neighbor .... Lillian Adams
Paramedic #1 .... Steve Bush
Paramedic #2 .... Mike Massa
Paramedic #3 .... Dale Gibson
ER Doctor .... Scott Alan Smith

CREW

Unit Production Manager . . . . Daniel Lupi
First Assistant Director . . . . Adam Druxman
Second Assistant Director . . . . Tina Stauffer
Associate Producer . . . . Dylan Tichenor
Chief Lighting Technician . . . . James Plannette
Key Grip . . . . Ben Beaird
Sound Mixer . . . . John Pritchett
Stunt Coordinator . . . . Webster Whinery
Stunts . . . . Michael Adams, Richard Burden,
　　　　Jack Carpenter, Phil Culotta, Ousan Elam,
　　　　Debbie Evans, Ray Gabriel, Terry Jackson,
　　　　Ethan Jensen, John Moio, Hugh Aodh O'Brien,
　　Dan Plum, Jeff Podgurski, Dennis Scott, Rick Seaman,
　　Harry Wowchuk, Bob Yerkes, Mike Massa, Allan Graf
Executive in Charge of Production . . . . Carla Fry
Production Executive . . . . Leon Dudevoir
Executive in Charge of Post Production . . . Jody Levin
Post Production Supervisor . . . . Mark Graziano
Production Supervisor . . . . Craig Markey
Production Accountant . . . . Kelly A. Snyder
Production Coordinator . . . . Eileen Malyszko
Unit Supervisor . . . . Dan Collins
Production Associate . . . . Jennifer Barrons
Assistant Art Director . . . . Shepherd Frankel
Set Decorator . . . . Chris Spellman
Script Supervisor . . . . Valeria Migliassi Collins
Property Master . . . . Tim Wiles
Camera Operators . . . . Paul Babin
Steadicam Operators . . . . . Guy Bee, Elizabeth Ziegler
Camera First Assistant . . . . Michael Riba
Camera Second Assistants . . . . Steve Craft
　　　　　　　　　　　　　　　　　　Christos C. Bitsakos
Additional First Assistant Camera . . . . Mike Marquette
Still Photographer . . . . Peter Sorel
Best Boy Electrician . . . . Michael DeChellis
Electricians . . James Barrett, Nikola Ristic, Billy Craft,
　　　　　　　　　　　Justin Stroh, Raymond Gonzales
Rigging Gaffer . . . . Kenneth Schneider
Rigging Electricians . Paul E. Avery, Thomas S. Holmes
Best Boy Grips . . Glenn "Bear" Davis, Shawn M. Neary
Dolly Grip . . . . Jeff Kunkel
Grips . . . . John O'Grady, Nick Beaird, Chris Oliver
Rigging Key Grip . . . . Bob Babin
Rigging Best Boy Grip . . . . Craig Brown
Rigging Grip . . . . Jim Leidholdt
First Assistant Editors . . . . Monica Anderson
　　　　　　　　　　　　　　　　　　　　Ladd Lanford
Avid Assistant . . . . Chris Marino
Apprentice Editor . . . . Marie Gaerlan
Additional Apprentice Editors . . . . Gary Trentham
　　　　　　　　　　　　　　　　　　Lara Khachooni
Boom Operator . . . . David Roberts
Cable Person . . . . John Glaeser
Video Assist . . . . Alfred Ainsworth
Video Playback by . . . . . . Playback Technologies, Inc.
　　　　　　　　　　　　Steve Irwin and John Brosnan
Set Designer . . . . Conny Boettger-Marinos
Graphic Artist . . . . Kim Lincoln
Art Department Coordinator . . . . Darlene Salinas
Art Department Production Assistants . . . Egan Gauntt
　　　　　　　　　　　　　　　　　　　Fariba Benham
Assistant Props . . . . Chuck Askerneese

Second Assistant Props . . . . Scott Bailey
Additional Second Assistant Props . . . . Andrew Siegel
Leadman . . . . Mark Weissenfluh
Art Department Buyer . . . . Kristen Gassner
Set Dresser . . . . Martin Milligan
On Set Dressers . . . . Richard Anderson,
　　　Bryan Hurley Shupper, Matt Shepherd, Wes Long
Key Make-up Artist . . . . Tina K. Roesler
Make-up Artist . . . . Selina Jayne
Make-up Artist for Tom Cruise . . . . Lois Burwell
Make-up Artist for Julianne Moore . . . . . . Elaine Offers
Key Hairstylist . . . . Kelvin Trahan
Key Hair . . . . Rita Troy
Costume Supervisor . . . . Karla Stevens
Costumer . . . . Linda McCarthy
Set Costumers . . . . Tammy Williamson, Andrew Slyder
Additional Set Costumer . . . . Kelly Everett
Tailor . . . . Pablo Nantas
Costumer Production Assistants . Rebecca Cummings
　　　　　　　　　　　　　　　　　　　Lisa Campbell
Location Manager . . . . Timothy Hillman
Assistant Location Managers . .Justin Healy, Sam Glynn,
　　　　　　Chanel Salzer, Dave Evans, Larry Ring
Visual Effects Producer . . . . Joseph Grossberg
Executive in Charge of Visual Effects . . Lauren Ritchie

SPECIAL VISUAL EFFECTS & ANIMATION
by INDUSTRIAL LIGHT & MAGIC
A Division of Lucas Digital Ltd.
Marin County, California

ILM Visual Effects Producer . . . . Camille Geier
Animation Supervisor . . . . Paul Griffin
CG Supervisors . . . . Gregor Lakner, Greg Maloney
Lead Animator . . . . Marjoliane Tremblay
Modeling Supervisor . . . . .Tony Hudson
Frog Construction . . . . . .Aaron Pfau, Derek Gillingham
Production Coordinator . . . . Robin Saxen
Digital Artists . . . . Matt Bouchard, Julie Neary
　　　　John Helms, Barbara Townsend, Joshua Levine,
　　Andy Wang, Tia Marshall, Lindy Wilson, Steve Molin
Animators . . . . Colin Brady, John Zdankiewicz
Color Timing Supervisor . . . . Bruce Vecchitto
Lead Matchmover . . . . Luke Longin
Matchmovers . . . . . Danielle Morrow, Jeffrey Saltzman
Digital Paint & Roto . . . . . Beth D'Amato, Mike Van Eps
Art Director . . . . David Nakabayashi
Digital Matte Artist . . . . Brian Flora
Software R&D . . . . . . Florian Kainz, Zoran Kacic-Alesic
Visual Effects Production Assistant . . . . . Leslie Safley
Visual Effects Editor . . . . Michael Gleason
Visual Effects Assistant Editor . . . . Lorelei David
Production Engineering Software . . . . Josh Seims
Technical Support . . . . Jason Brown, Ian McCamey
　　　　　　　　　　　　　　　　　　　Michelle Motta
CG Operations . . . . .Vicki Beck, Tony Hurd
Negative Line-Up . . . . Andrea Biklian
Digital Plate Restoration . . . . Michelle Spina
　　　　　　　　　　　　　　　　　　Stephanie Tolbert
Scanning . . . . Mike Ellis, Todd Mitchell
Senior Staff . . . . Chrissie England, Patricia Blau,
　　　　　　　　　　　　　　　　　　　　　Jim Morris

Practical Frog Effects by Steve Johnson's XFX Group

FX Supervisor . . . . Dan Rebert
Lead Artist . . . . Bernie Eichholz
Sculptor . . . . Glenn Hanz
Lead Painter . . . . Vince Niebla
Painters . . . . David Monzingo, Don Rutherford
Lab Techs . . . . Bill Fesh, Bret Stern
Thermal Plastic Engineer . . . . Steve Shubin, Jr.
Animatronics . . . . Enrique Bilsland
Coordinators . . . . Bob Newton, Fernando Favila
Special Effects by . . . . F/X Concepts, Inc.
Special Effects Supervisor . . . . Lou Carlucci
Special Effects Administrator . . . . Diane Carlucci
Special Effects Team
      Rick Thompsen, John C. Carlucci, Ken Tarallo,
    Ethel Edwards, Michael Bisetti, Michael J. Clarke,
    William Dawson, Eric Dressor, Dan Edwards,
    James Girch, Tim B. Graham, Richard Hill,
   Eugene D. Hubbard, James La Croix, Louis Lindwall,
  Jeffrey C. Machit, Albert Marangoni, Wes Mattox,
    Barry McQueary, James Allen Ochoa,
  Ron Petruccione, Rick San Nicholas, Steve Sosner,
    Blumes Tracy, Tony Vandernecker,
    Mario Vernillo, Karl Walser
1st Assistant Accountant . . . . Steven Butensky
Payroll Accountant . . . . Cecilia Escobar
2nd Assistant Accountant . . . . Paul Real
Accounting Assistant . . . . Jennifer Clark
Construction Accountant . . . . Debbi M. Andrews
Post Production Accountant . . . . Jeff Behlendorf
Extras Casting by . . . . . Jerry Conca–Rainbow Casting
Casting Assistant . . . . Michele Short
Extras Casting Reno . . . . Nevada Casting
Second Second Assistant Director . . . . . Jorge L. Baron
Set Production Assistants . . . Michael "Jocco" Phillips,
   Jamala Gaither, James Moran, Kerry A. Fitzmaurice
Assistant Production Coordinator . . . . . . Nellie Adami
Production Secretary . . . . Aaron Tichenor
Special Projects Supervisor . . . . Will Weiske
Assistant to Paul Thomas Anderson . Jennifer Barrons
Assistant to JoAnne Sellar . . . . Kate Wilson
Production Associate to Tom Cruise . . Michael Doven
Production Assistant to Tom Cruise . . . . . Ken Daniells
Assistant Unit Supervisor . . . . Jonathan Krueger
Unit Production Assistant . . . . Greg Gately
Cast Unit Assistant . . . . Jennifer Duclos
Production Office Assistants . . . . Matt Bauer,
   Allison Harvey, Ivan Martin Del Campo, Hector Jumilla
Supervising Sound Editor/Sound Designer Richard King
ADR Supervisor . . . . Kimberly Harris
Dialogue Editors . . . . . Michael Haight, James Matheny,
                        Hugo Weng
Sound Effects Editor . . . . Hamilton Sterling
Foley Supervisor . . . . Christopher Flick
Foley Editor . . . . Ed Callahan
1st Assistant Sound Editor . . . . Linda Yeaney
Digital Assistant . . . . Andrew Bock
ADR Assistant . . . . Monique Salvato
Sound Effects Recordist . . . . Eric Potter
Voice Casting . . . . Barbara Harris
Rerecording Mixers . . . Robert J. Litt, Michael Herbick
          Michael Semanick, Steve Pederson
Recordists . . Marsha Sorce, Kevin Webb, Gary Ritchie
ADR Recorded at . . . . Walt Disney Studios

ADR Mixer . . . . Doc Kane
ADR Recordist . . . . Jeannette Browning
ADR Recorded at . . . . Warner Hollywood Studios
ADR Mixer . . . . Thomas J. O'Connell
ADR Recordist . . . . Rick Canelli
Foley Recorded at . . . . One Step Up
Foley Artists . . . . Dan O'Connell, John Cucci
Foley Mixer . . . . James Ashwill
Foley Recordist . . . . Linda Lew

Digital sound editing systems provided
by World Link Digital

Production Controller . . . . Paul Prokop
Production Resources . . . . Josh Ravetch
Supervising Production Coordinator . . . . Emily Glatter
Post Production Services . . . . Brent Kaviar
Unit Publicist . . . . Guy Adan
Project Documentarian . . . . Mark Rance
Construction Coordinator . . . . Robert J. Carlyle
General Foreman . . . . Ray Rarick
Propmaker Foreman . . . . Earl Betts
Propmakers . . Thomas Culberhouse, Timothy Gunther
      Roger G. Dudley, Jamie Litwak, Brent Dyer,
   Dikran Mahakian, Greg Elliot, Richard McConnell,
      Bill Fobert, Don Yaklin, Jeff Gross
Paint Foreman . . . . Gerald Gates
Painters . . . Jill Haber, Robert Hale, Danny Zingelewicz
Stand by Painter . . . . Mike Reiber
Labor Foreman . . . . Gary Stel
Labor Gang Boss . . . . Shaun S. Wiggins
Laborers . . . . Reynold Marotta, Tony Wright
Plasterer . . . . Tony Miller
Greensman Gang Boss . . . . Porfirio "Pilo" Silva
Greensman . . . . Juan Torres
Transportation Coordinator . . . . Geno Hart
Transportation Dispatcher . . . . Steve Larson
Transportation Captain . . . . Joseph Cosentino
Transportation Co-Captain . . . . Glenn Mathias
Drivers . . . . John Aliano, Chuck Alsobrook,
   Tony Barattin, Curtis Clark, Eric "Buck" Compton,
   Bob "Bullet" DeWitt, Angel DiSanti, Mark Forrest,
     David Garris, Jerry Glassman, Dash Hart,
   Paul "Huggie" Huggett, Benson Jones, Lou Mosto,
  Esteban Munoz, Bill Needham, James "Obie" Oberman,
    John "JP" Pellegrino, John Spaccarelli,
     David Wilson, Bob Young
Picture Vehicle Coordinator . . . . Hardy Ophuls
Aerial Coordinator . . . . Alan Purwin
Helicopter Pilot . . . . Dirk Vahle
Pilot . . . . Rick Shuster
Aerial Camera Operator . . . . Hans Bjerno
Underwater Camera Operator . . . . . . Cynthia Pusheck
Underwater 1st Assistant Camera . . . . . Maryan Zurek
Catering by . . . . Deluxe Catering, Inc.
Chef . . . . Lorin Flemming
Assistant Chef . . . . James Flemming
Additional Assistant Chef . . . . Linda Andersson
Assistant Caterers . . . . . . Gerry Hernandez, Juan Ruiz
Craft Service . . . . Charles Scott
Assistant Craft Service . . . . Clifford Scott
Production Medic . . . . Thomas Krueger
On Set Medics . . . . Larry Ballard, David Hayles
                     Dominic Jaramillo

Construction Medic .... Kenneth H. Clarke
L.A.P.D. Coordinator .... Martin E. Rose
Security .... Andrew Padilla - Dignitary Protection
International Agency
Studio Teachers ...... Judith Brown, Wesley Staples
Dogs Supplied by Steve Berens' Animals of Distinction

GAME SHOW UNIT
Gameshow Consultant .... Fred Witten
Gameshow Lighting Designer .... James Moody
Gameshow Gaffer .... Scott Moody
Gameshow Rigging Best Boy Electric .... Steve Galvin
Gameshow Score Keeping .... Ron Nugent, Billy Monk
Electronic Technician .... Chris Johnson
Motion Control .... Don Gray
Lighting Board Operator .... Tom Girskis

Opening Graphics .... Flip Your Lid - Steve Soffer
Police Technical Advisors .... Call The Cops

Executive in Charge of Music .... Toby Emmerich
Music Executive .... Dana Sano
Music Business Affairs Executive .... Lori Silfen
Music Clearance Executive .... Mark Kaufman
Music Coordinator .... Bob Bowen
Score Consultant & Conductor ..... Thomas Pasatieri
Music Recorded at .... TODD-AO SCORING
Music Preparation .... Julian Bratolyubov
Music Scoring Mixer .... Dennis Sands
Orchestra Contracted by .... The Music Team
Patti Zimmitti & Debbi Datz-Pyle
Music Editor .... Paul Rabjohns
Music Technical Consultant .... Jonathan Karp
Music Mixed at .... Signet Soundeluxe Studios
Assistant Engineer .... Tom Hardisty
SOUNDTRACK ALBUM AVAILABLE ON REPRISE RECORDS

SONGS

"One" Written by Harry Nilsson. Performed by Aimee Mann. Licensed from SuperEgo Records.

"Build That Wall" Written by Aimee Mann and Jon Brion. Performed by Aimee Mann. Licensed from SuperEgo Records.

"You Do" Written by Aimee Mann. Performed by Aimee Mann. Licensed from SuperEgo Records.

"Driving Sideways" Written by Aimee Mann and Michael Lockwood. Performed by Aimee Mann. Licensed from SuperEgo Records.

"Momentum" Written by Aimee Mann. Performed by Aimee Mann. Licensed from SuperEgo Records.

"Wise Up" Written by Aimee Mann. Performed by Aimee Mann. Courtesy of Geffen Records. Under license from Universal Music Special Markets as featured in the TriStar motion picture *Jerry Maguire*.

"Save Me" Written by Aimee Mann. Performed by Aimee Mann. Produced by Aimee Mann.

"Nothing Is Good Enough" Written by Aimee Mann. Performed by Aimee Mann. Licensed from SuperEgo Records.

Additional instruments and odd pieces of musical business by Jon Brion and Fiona Apple

ad-n-echo technology provided by .... tel-rey

Main Title Sequence Designed and Produced
by Balsmeyer & Everett, Inc.
Opticals by .... Pacifc Title
Negative Cutter .... Sunrise Films
Color Timer .... Phil Hetos
Titles by .... Brian King

Equipment by Cinelease, Inc., Camera Dollies by Chapman/Leonard Studio Equipment, Inc.

Camera by Panavision

Pathe Camera Provided by .... Carrie Williams
Pathe Technician .... Andre Martin

Rights & Clearances provided by Entertainment Clearances, Inc. Cassandra Barbour, Laura Sevier

Clearances by .... Marshall/Plumb Research

Risk Management .... Laurie Cartwright,
Jennifer Mount, Julianna Selfridge

Production Safety .... Jeff Egan and David Panzer

Insurance Provided by .. J&H Marsh & McLennan, Inc.
and AON/Albert G. Ruben
Completion Guaranty
provided by .... International Film Guarantors, Inc.

Production Attorney .... Erik Ellner
Contract Administrator .... Sonya Thompsen

Payroll by Cast and Crew Entertainment Services, Inc.
Extras Payroll by Sessions Payroll Management, Inc.

Travel by Travel Corps

Footage/Clips courtesy of: Bloomberg Television, Classic Images, KTLA, Mystique Films, Inc., National Film Board of Canada, NBC News Archives, PACE Motor Sports, Inc., a Company of SPX Entertainment, Inc., The Power Team, Spelling Television, Inc., Ronco Inventions, LLC., Turner Entertainment Co., Blooming magnolia stock footage provided by CINENET, Entertainment Tonight/Paramount Pictures Corporation, Domestic Television

Penthouse © 1998 General Media Pictures Communications, Inc.
Cover Photograph by Carl L. Wachter

Prints by Deluxe   Color by Deluxe

Claudia's Artwork by .... Fiona Apple, Melora Walters

magnolia
for fa and ea

photographs by Peter Sorel

Jim Kurring
(John C. Reilly)

Jimmy Gator
(Philip Baker Hall)

Linda Partridge
(Julianne Moore)

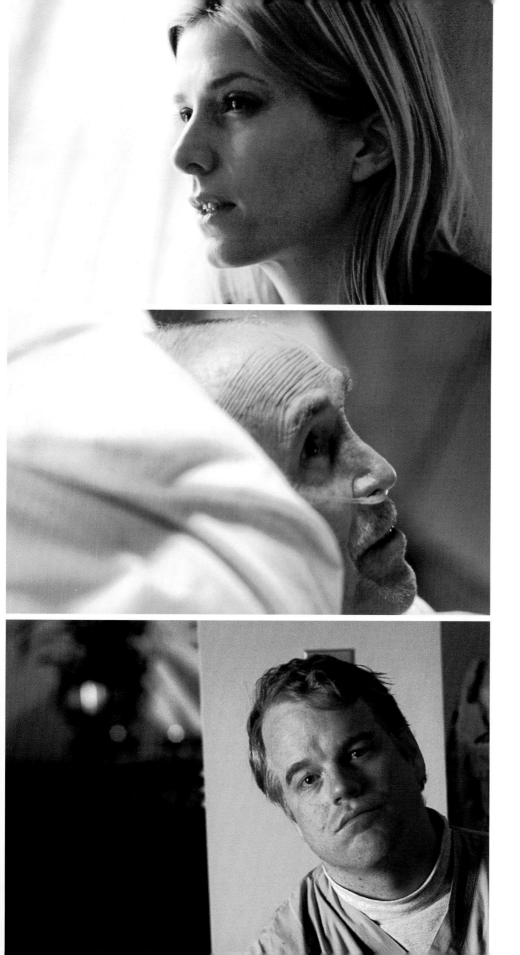

Claudia Wilson Gator
(Melora Walters)

Earl Partridge
(Jason Robards)

Phil Parma
(Philip Seymour Hoffman)

Frank T. J. Mackey
(Tom Cruise)

Stanley Spector
(Jeremy Blackman)

Thurston Howell
(Henry Gibson)

Donnie Smith
(William H. Macy)

Gwenovier
(April Grace)

Dixon
(Emmanuel Johnson)

Rose Gator and Jimmy Gator
(Melinda Dillon and
Philip Baker Hall)

Claudia Wilson Gator
(Melora Walters)

Jimmy Gator and Burt Ramsey
(Philip Baker Hall and
Ricky Jay)

Frank T. J. Mackey and
Gwenovier (Tom Cruise
and April Grace)

Jim Kurring and Donnie
Smith (John C. Reilly and
William H. Macy)

Jim Kurring
(John C. Reilly)

Above: The Greenberry Hill Pharmacy set on the Universal Studios back lot

Below: Behind the scenes of Claudia's Apartment, Melora Walters *(left)*, Paul Thomas Anderson and Mike Riba, first assistant camera *(right)*

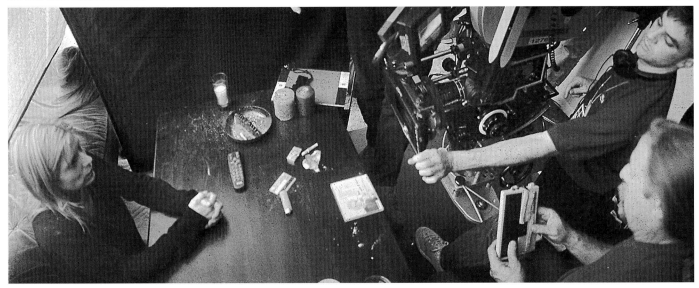

Below: Earl's House Location, Paul Thomas Anderson *(left)* with Philip Seymour Hoffman and Jason Robards *(right)*

Above: The Interview at the Holiday Inn, Tom Cruise *(left)* and April Grace, Paul Thomas Anderson *(right)*

Below: Smiling Peanut Location, Paul Thomas Anderson and Robert Elswit, director of photography *(left)* with Henry Gibson and William H. Macy *(right)*

Below: Emmanuel Johnson and Paul Thomas Anderson on location in Reseda, California

Above: Tom Cruise and Paul Thomas Anderson
on location in Burbank, California

Below: Philip Seymour Hoffman *(far left)* and Paul
Thomas Anderson *(far right)* at Earl's House

Below: Paul Thomas Anderson

Above: The Kiss at Billingley's, John C. Reilly and Melora Walters

Tom Cruise and Paul Thomas Anderson on location in Burbank, California

Sir Edmund William Godfrey's House on the Universal Studios Lot, Paul Thomas Anderson *(left);* Robert Elswit, director of photography, and Jeff Kunkel, dolly grip *(center);* John O'Grady, grip *(back right);* and Mike Riba, first assistant camera *(far right)*

Earl's House Location, Philip Seymour Hoffman, Tom Cruise, and Jason Robards

Earl's House Location,
Paul Thomas Anderson
and Julianne Moore

Claudia's Apartment,
Melora Walters

Smiling Peanut Location,
Paul Thomas Anderson
(left) and Valeria Migliassi
Collins, script supervisor

William H. Macy *(left);*
Jim Plannette, chief lighting
technician *(back left);* Paul
Thomas Anderson *(right);*
and Robert Elswit, director
of photography *(far right)* on
location in North Hollywood

Behind the scenes of WDKK?
Game Show Set, Daniel Lupi,
co-producer *(left);* JoAnne
Sellar, producer *(center);* Ricky
Jay *(right);* and Dan Collins,
unit manager *(far right)*

Behind the scenes at Earl's
House, Paul Thomas Anderson
(lower left), Tom Cruise, Philip
Seymour Hoffman, and Jason
Robards *(right)*

Behind the scenes of the WDKK? Game Show Set, Adam Druxman, first assistant director *(left);* Paul Thomas Anderson *(center);* and Valeria Migliassi Collins, script supervisor *(right)*

Behind the scenes of the WDKK? Game Show Set, Paul Thomas Anderson *(left),* Philip Baker Hall *(center),* and Ricky Jay

Paul Thomas Anderson on the Greenberry Hill set on the Universal Studios back lot

Above: In Interview at the Holiday Inn, Paul Thomas Anderson and Tom Cruise. *Below:* Tom Cruise on location in Valencia, California

Above: Robert Elswit, director of photography *(left)* and Paul Thomas Anderson *(right)* on location. *Below:* On location in Van Nuys, California, Paul Thomas Anderson *(left);* Adam Druxman, first assistant director *(right);* and Mike Riba, first assistant camera *(lower right)*